DREAMERS
AND THEIR SHADOWS

CONTINUITY / THE SECRET ANNALS

DOUGLAS J. PENICK

Mountain Treasury Press

LCCN: 2013939505
Mountain Treasury Press, Boulder, CO, USA

ISBN: 0974597449
ISBN-13: 9780974597447

TO YOU

TABLE OF CONTENTS:

I

V

DREAMERS AND THEIR SHADOWS

CONTINUITY / THE SECRET ANNALS

"In fact, the whole of Japan is pure invention. There is no such country, there are no such people.

Oscar Wilde- 'The Decay of Lying'

I. THE SECRET ANNALS: THE FIRST ANNAL

I. *CONTINUITY*

1)

    Edward leaves the meeting before it ends, filled with a feeling of profound release. He has accomplished what he set out to do. He asked a question and had a brief exchange. It is surprising, after so much anxiety, how easy it was. He feels liberated and outside the constraints of his habitual space and time.

    He makes his way down the steep dark stairs and out onto the sidewalk. He blinks. The brick buildings across the street are warm and vibrant in the sunset. Soft green pines on the mountainside beyond glow beneath the blue sky. The evening is suffused with a poignant inner quiet. It feels like the world is on the verge of some new possibility. Edward inhales. He does not want this ever to change.

    But there is now a faint unease, a constriction working at the edge, pulling him backwards. The moment of promise is close to being lost. Edward sits on a stone bench, takes a deep breath. He must make an effort. Recovering that moment, holding on to it, perhaps this will happen if he can remember exactly how it came to be.

    Edward feels suddenly unsure. Memories offer something solid. Chunks of the past, some he's imagined, some lived, some he's read, some inferred, return to the to surface. Holding them for a moment, it's comforting.

2)

    "In the evening stillness,
    The bells of the Gion temple
    Echo the sorrows of impermanence and loss."

    For Edward Bowman, these lines are where it all begins. He is 17, destined to run his family's struggling farm equipment dealership in Western Pennsylvania, trapped in a world that is drab, inflexible, solitary. A scholarship to the University of Pennsylvania sends him wandering on a whim into a class on Japanese literature. He hears the lecturer read these opening words from the Tale of the Heike: "In the evening stillness,

The bells..." A wordless yearning dawns. A world, remote but somehow familiar, opens. He takes every course they offer in Japanese language, culture, history. He excels. His life is transformed. "Japan? How come Japan?" his father shakes his head. "We fought a war to kill those bastards." Edward can't explain. His mind is in another world. His father can't imagine it.

3)

Edward shivers slightly. A cool breeze rises from the coming night. It's time to go back to his campus apartment. He wishes there were something to do, someone to visit. He decides not to take the bus. Walking will keep him warm. Near the city park, on the corner by the band-shell, some hippies in tie-dyed t-shirts, dirty jeans, long matted hair are passing a joint, trying to look blase. Edward nods in their direction, smiles, walks on.

So many disparate events and random conjunctions have brought him here beside the mountains, here walking by the park, here leaving an assembly hall where he has just spoken with someone he had 'til then only feared. Edward knows that before he was in college, things happened in Japan, events of very little importance, but they would shape his life. It makes him quiver, imagining how strangers blindly pursuing their own fates have unknowingly and decisively shaped the life he calls his.

Edward stops at the red light. People in cars are racing home, are going out on dates, driving to parties, to work. Who knows where anything leads?

4)

In May of 1952, nine years after firebombs leveled most of Tokyo, three laborers are clearing the last wreckage of an old house on a street adjoining the Yasukuni Shrine. All are former soldiers recruited from the horde of unemployed who wait daily at the labor exchange for any chance of work. They are digging away at the scorched brick, mud and ash. Suddenly, there is a hollow metallic clunk. They stare at each other, then quickly look around to make sure the supervisor has gone for lunch. They hurry to excavate their find.

The dull sheen of a large steel casing is visible through the dirt. They shovel faster. It is a smoke-stained safe. It is intact. Faces streaked with dust and sweat, the three men grin. They all need a stroke of luck. Each knows exactly what he would do if he had money. Each looks at the others. Can he trust them? As they hesitate, a passing police officer senses the conspiratorial atmosphere, comes over. He takes a quick look. He confiscates the safe.

5)

Next day at the police station, a senior officer from the Burglary and Theft Division identifies the safe as a 1905 American Diebold Fireproof Wall Safe with custom-made triple density chrome steel casing and polished, engine-turned door. It's not the first time a strongbox has been discovered, though this one is the most elaborate. If money, stock certificates or other papers are inside, they won't have much value now. But jewelry is always a possibility. In the Shibuya District, the police recovered a safe containing a bag of diamonds. Everyone in the station shared in the ten percent left after the government's share. For some, it was enough to buy a small house. It takes two days of careful drilling to open the safe.

The policemen crowd forward to look inside. There is a large black lacquer-ware case with shimmering, long s-curved riverine swirls of gold undulating across its smooth glossy surface. They remove and open it. On the interior of the lid, a single golden lotus in full bloom floats on a red lacquer sea. Inside the box, lustrous gold brocade is folded around what turn out to be two scrolls. These are objects from another world. Instinctively the men step back, awe mixed with disappointment. The faint smell of peony combined with a metallic scent of incense floats up into the air.

The captain calls the National Museum. Technicians come and take possession of the box and its contents.

6)

Experts first examine the lacquer box. It is not long before it is clear that this is a rare piece of 17th-century Rimpa School lacquer-ware of enormous value and historical significance. It may actually be the work of the school's founder, Sotetsu Tawaraya.

They cannot believe their luck. So many objects of beauty and historical importance have been lost in the war that the discovery of a formerly unknown treasure is greeted with elation. The box is designated a National Treasure and given a prominent place in the museum collection.

The fabric within the lacquer case is also beautiful and even more rare, but is of interest mainly to connoisseurs. It is a meter-long bolt of ancient, very heavy gold brocade with interlocking rows of stylized dragons. It dates from the Sui Dynasty and is most likely Mongolian. It too becomes part of the National Museum collection, where it may be seen by special permission from the curators.

7)

The precious container and the radiant brocade wrapping imply that what lies within is more valuable still. Beneath glaring spotlights in the conservation studio of the National Museum, within the lacquer box and brocade wrapping, *the curators find two large scrolls. The outer wrapping of each is deep purple silk with a damascene lotus pattern. Inscribed in fine clerical script on the outer ends are written: SECRET ANNALS I and SECRET ANNALS II. The scholars charged with the initial examination of the scrolls do not doubt they have found something extraordinary.*

8)

 The scrolls describe events that would have taken place beginning in about 1531 and cover a period of approximately 15 years thereafter. In fragmentary manner, they tell of a hitherto unknown spiritual teacher, the Prince of Ling, who, in that time of social and cultural chaos, set out to establish enlightened society in remotest Hokkaido. In the words of his followers, particularly those of a frivolous consort and a feckless relative, the documents describe his life, his teachings and the outrageous journey he shared with his students.

 Six of the most eminent scholars in the field of late medieval Japan are consulted. None know of any historical, municipal or monastic record that hints at the existence of such a Prince or the kind of social movement he is said to have inspired. This is perplexing, but in the Japan of the early 1950's, it does not cause the suspicion it might have otherwise. Indeed it elicits secret hope.

 Every Japanese man and woman has seen the nation subjected to the unthinkable. Their armies, air force and navies have been annihilated. Their homes have been bombed and destroyed, their families displaced. They have experienced squalor and starvation. All have endured the humiliation of the occupation. Many wonder secretly if this disaster is the result of adherence to long established traditions and beliefs.

 The possibility of a concealed spiritual path and an alternative history is deeply appealing. News of the discovery of the Secret Annals causes cautious excitement. Soon copies of the Secret Annals are being furtively circulated throughout the academic world.

 Even the most circumspect of readers find themselves prey to longings they have not wished to acknowledge.

9)

 The texts themselves are of differing ages and written in different calligraphic hands. Each looks to have been removed from a longer document and then glued into the scrolls.

 The First Annal consists of the reminiscences of a woman referred to as Lady M. It is written in the beautifully delicate running script of the late Heian though it describes events much later. Readers at this time find the effect entrancing, even romantic. The questions this anachronism might have raised do not get asked.

10)

    Edward pours boiling water into a Styrofoam cup of dried noodles. The salty steam burns on his face. Like all the other junior faculty apartments, his rooms are standardized: beige walls, tan shag carpeting, avocado counters, dark brown sofa and armchair, fake oak desk, dining table, chairs, book case. The goose-neck lamp gives a yellowish light. But for once, it's quiet. The stillness that earlier felt promising now carries a wave of desolation. He sits at his desk.

    Edward is sure his life really could change, but suddenly he is afraid. He longs for something tangible. He pulls out the manuscript of the Annals. The translation is finished, but he is reluctant to let it go. He opens to the beginning and starts to read though it again. The text, as much as anything that happened, has brought him to where he is now. It has been a cause of craziness and possibility. And not just for him.

THE SECRET ANNALS:
ANNAL I: Concerning Lady M. - Part 1

1)

> When did it become memory?
> Life veers on.
> At what exact point can we say:
> A memory began there?

2)

    "Tell me," people said when they heard I was once close to His Majesty, that I'd spent time with him, knew him when he was Prince of Ling. They'd look at me with avid half-smiles. "I've heard that he..." They'd heard gossip about his many lovers, his brilliance, his drinking, his elegance, his wildness. "Is it true that...?" Even monks and nuns asked me slyly over tea during retreats. I smiled, looked down. I did not answer.

3)

    I heard of the Prince by accident.
    Everything in the world around me was in suspension. A century of destruction had produced no successor to the throne. Only total exhaustion had caused warfare to wane. The nation lay in chaos: ancient fiefs dispersed, family businesses ruined, farms and towns abandoned. Cultural traditions, social conventions, established laws were no longer constraints or supports.
    Suddenly, anything was possible. My father was dead. I could not stay with my mother; I could do as I wished. No one really cared. I was wandering in a crowd of pilgrims through a landscape of ravaged splendor. Someone mentioned the Prince of Ling. My mind stopped. The small hairs on the nape of my neck rose.
    I traveled a long distance to meet the Prince. It was a journey not without risks. I soon became his lover, his student, his secretary. Then, before he had established his own kingdom, I left for other companions, other teachers. I returned when he was dying.

4)

    The past for me is often more seductive than the present. I remember how the light of a late summer evening deepened the dark green of pines and the bronze of fluttering maples. Lavender air, a faint yellow shimmer on the waves of the black pond, assertive fluorescence of the green rushes on the bank. And above, a sky vibrantly blue and so alive with towering pink clouds. The scent of cooling soil.

Altogether, a moment when I was suspended in something perfect. And in such stillness, it seemed nothing could ever change. But even with that thought, change began.

This memory binds me to the Prince of Ling. He was wearing a plain cotton robe, standing barefoot in the mud by the pond with his back to me, stooping as he examined a clump of watercress.

5)

I and many women like me used to spend our days reading Lady Murasaki, Sei Shonagon, Izumi Shikibu. We passed our nights gazing at moonlight as it filtered through wisteria blossoms. We dreamed of poetic love, at least until we would be married off to someone in the local gentry. Circumstances changed and cut us loose from that inevitability.

My father died of cholera. Then my mother had to go back to her family, a mother who could no longer care for her daughter. I was sent to my mother's brother; he'd renounced his samurai background and now sold second-hand swords and armor in Osaka. My mother gave me her last money for the trip. We stood by the doorway while a servant waited. It had been a cool sunny morning. Finches swooped and gathered twigs for their nests. I held my mother's hand and wept.

6)

I lived for a year in the country's largest port city. My uncle was a kind man. Though business was poor, he insisted on hiring a young artist to continue my calligraphy lessons. I began as his student, but soon became his companion and muse. Suddenly, merely helping in the shop was unbearable. To my uncle's shame, I moved in with the artist. The excitement of love succumbed to routine, then claustrophobia, and I left. I couldn't go back to my family. I felt embarrassed.

> "I that am severed
> Like a reed cut at the root,
> Should a stream entice
> Would go, I think."

Sotoba no Komachi's poem echoed in my heart. I wanted peace and felt drawn to the spiritual life. I became one of many seekers then. Despite the risk of bandits, I went on pilgrimages and stayed in secluded monasteries. There, whether governments rose or fell, within the ancient stone walls, the way of life did not change. This was a great solace. When I became restless, there were always pilgrimages to other temples.

7)

One morning, I sat beside the Prince in his bedroom. The air was cool and very still. Sunlight glowed on the open shoji screens, and we looked out at the silent surface of the pond. My mind was racing. I was tormented by the thought of losing him. I hated the way fears so often spoiled my happiness. If I lived in a convent, would such thoughts finally subside? Though I had not spoken, the Prince looked over at me as if I were a stranger. He shrugged.

"Abstinence is no path at all," he said.

8)

I see myself then swimming, searching amid fragments.

9)

By candlelight, I read the Duke of K's letter. His Majesty is dying. A momentary trick of mind allows me to think that 'His Majesty' is someone other than my former lover, the Prince of Ling. The illusion doesn't hold. A flood of longing and remorse rises on a wave of memories. I ache, wanting to see him. As if... As if I could do him some final service that would resolve the complexity of all that lay between us.

Thoughtful to a fault, the Duke has arranged everything. I am grateful, I wish I did not find his ability to anticipate my needs annoyingly intrusive.

10)

It is early spring. I am in a small boat rolling on choppy waves, making its way up the Sea of Japan, hugging the coast on the long journey from Tottori to Aomori. Raw salt winds cut to the bone. I pull my gray padded robe close around me. I feel wretched. I hate being cold. I can't help wishing I was still sitting by a brazier in my cell, hidden in the temple swathed in mountain cypress trees. I resent feeling sorry for myself. My moods rise and fall. Sorrow has worn me out.

As the boat moves towards the Prince's Kingdom, which he has named Shambhala, I know I must get used to using his more exalted title.

The grandiosity of it still bothers me. I am uncomfortable too with the noble titles conferred on his family, his functionaries, his lovers. Because the Duke of K is my regular correspondent, I'm used to thinking of him so. But I am apprehensive about the awkward pomp that he's described as pervading every social function. Despite his assurances, how will others, loyal to the Prince for so long, treat me? Will I be able to see His Majesty at all?

I sit tensely next to a shabby toothless old woman. I don't want to feel the old hag touching me. A thin sheet of salt water bubbles across the planks of the cabin floor. I recoil as the old woman bumps against me. "Oh, your ladyship, I ..."

In the midst of her apology, the old woman notices my clothes. A heavy gray cloak, the kind worn by nuns, has parted to reveal a most inappropriately beautiful green brocade kimono. The old woman's eyes narrow. Not a lady, I can see her thinking. The old woman closes her mouth without continuing. I try to remove myself, to meditate, but my mind drifts, taking refuge in memory.

II. CONTINUITY

1)

Edward hears the neighbor's door thud against the wall. He's an assistant in aeronautical engineering. Edward can tell he's been out drinking. At least he's alone. Edward sighs, goes to the refrigerator and gets a beer. He thinks he's done a good job. He has reason to be proud of his translation. He would feel a lot better, if there weren't so many questions about the Annals themselves.

All at once, he would like to show his work to the man whose lecture he just heard. He wonders what he'd think. He'd like to tell him about what happened next to the Annals themselves. What would he have to say about that?

2)

The Annals' fortunes suffer a great reversal just as scholarly interest seems justified and genuine excitement begins to catch fire. Then the experts charged with detailed scientific examination of the scrolls make a disturbing discovery. Spectrographic analysis of several shiny and anomalous spots of glue that fix part of the final narrative (scroll 2, text 2) to the silk backing reveals it is an American commercial glue, a product available in Japan only after World War II.

These dots of glue raise questions about how it is even possible that the scrolls were found wrapped in authentic ancient rare brocade and placed inside an authentic Rimpa lacquer box, locked in a genuine American safe, buried in a bomb site and uncovered nine years after the war. At the very least, the safe and its burial would have to have been faked. If so, the box and the brocade, incontestably genuine and extremely costly, must have been used as bait to place the authenticity of the scrolls beyond doubt. Obviously some kind of fraud has been perpetrated. But why or by whom is utterly unclear. Those involved in studying these objects find the whole situation unpleasantly redolent of stage magic.

3)

There is no word or symbol on or in the safe, the box or on the scrolls to identify the original owner. All property records were destroyed in the firebombing. Many of Tokyo's occupants were dispersed afterwards. It is impossible to determine who might have owned the house where the safe was found. There is no clue to who created the scrolls, who assembled and packed them or who could possibly benefit from their discovery now. The police are consulted. Aside from those of the curators, there are no clear fingerprints, but in the absence of either victim or beneficiary, the police decline to investigate further. There is no crime.

4)

Authorities who once studied the scrolls with secret hopes and furtive yearning now, like spurned lovers, turn away in embittered silence. No one has any further desire to unravel the riddles that surround the Annals. The scholars have been fooled. They are ashamed and angry. They want to forget the whole uncomfortable episode as quickly as possible. The scrolls are placed in cardboard tubes and stowed in a metal locker near a janitorial supply closet in the National Museum's basement.

5)

So things would have remained. Edward would not have known any of this. But twelve years later, in 1964, Yoshitaka Akiyama (1899-1968), an eminent scholar at the University of Tokyo, takes an interest in the Secret Annals. Professor Akiyama is highly respected, known to have a taste for the unusual. He reads some English but prefers French literature. He comes from a samurai family, is respected but not well liked. He is small and fussy. The oblique way he has of speaking makes people feel he does not take them seriously. His colleagues find him too aloof and too unpredictable, but his work is exemplary and beyond reproach. It is through him that Edward's life will become entwined with the Annals.

6)

When he receives a grant to study in Tokyo, his parents and sisters know they should be proud. His father wonders if Edward is a hippie. Ever since Kennedy was assassinated and then the riots, everything has been getting crazy. Edward is secretly relieved to be leaving. As he boards an airplane for the first time in his life, he hopes what he longs for will find a shape in Japan.

Soon he is struggling to find his way in the chaos of Tokyo, trying to obey the rules and regulations of the University, trying to observe the protocols his new colleagues require. There are demonstrations against the Vietnam War at the University. He tries not to be noticed. He has been assigned to Professor Akigami who is to be his tutor. He will serve as the Professor's assistant and as it turns out, his translator. The Professor puts him to work immediately. Occasionally he is invited to the Professor's house for an awkward dinner.

Edward secretly hopes that Professor Akigami and his family will treat him as a distant relative, but he is disappointed. The wife and daughters seem to dislike him on sight. The professor is always helpful, often friendly, sometimes even appreciative, but assigns so much work that Edward has time for little else. He is Edward's only anchor, and Edward makes every effort to please him.

7)

It is not generally known, but the professor's life is at an uncertain crossroads. A year earlier, his magnum opus, an exhaustive monograph on diaries of the Kamakura Period was published to universal acclaim. Since then he has been depressed. He reviews the English translation of the book that Edward has begun, but really he has nothing to do. Much to the annoyance of his wife and daughters, he stays home day after day. He sits in his study fumbling idly with his papers and smoking endless cigarettes. Even his colleagues are beginning to notice that the professor is more withdrawn. He knows this but does not care.

Slowly, as he familiarizes himself with the Professor's work habits, Edward begins to understand. Professor Akiyama is happiest when his mind is suddenly caught by the memory of an ancient tale or some long-ago intrigue. He drifts in the remoteness of distant times and vanished sensibilities. And the Professor has been lucky. His penchant for immersion in the obscure historical records has brought success. The Kamakura diaries show a subtle sensibility uncovering the then burgeoning samurai culture. They say he has made valuable contributions to the nation. The Professor is no longer so sure. His mind moves between past and present, and he finds nowhere to abide. Often he seems close to the edge of panic. He smokes continuously.

8)

Professor Akiyama begins to confide in Edward. He talks about his father; how, after he returned from the war, he sat rigidly upright in the corner of his room and stared blankly at the light shifting on the shoji screen. The Russians had released him after three years in a Siberian prison. He was a general, an intelligence officer assigned to help prop up the shaky Manchukuo regime. He never said a word about his captivity, but a fellow officer, also a prisoner, told the professor's mother. The Russians kept him chained in a latrine; he lived waist deep in feces for weeks on end. When he returned, he rarely spoke.

He'd been an advisor to the last Chinese Emperor. A picture of the Emperor, Pu Yi Aisin Gioro, in elaborate military uniform, wearing thick glasses, looking defensive and lost, is the only picture his father kept in the bedroom. He'd served the Emperor of Japan and the Emperor of China. All he had to show for it was a small yellow enamel box with the Chinese Emperor's seal in gold cloisonné. He'd survived three years of torture and somehow managed to keep this. He never explained. His son only knew that his isolation was impenetrable.

It's apparent to Edward that Professor Akiyama is being drawn to a deeper kinship with his father. He sees skyscrapers and apartment buildings replace the bombed out neighborhoods. Everyone tries to dress like an American. He does himself. There is no escaping it. People chew gum and smoke cigarettes on the street. They say: "OK." They no longer know who they are. The concerns that have held him in this world are loosening. But no, Professor Akiyama is not yet ready to let everything just fall apart. For better or worse, he can't sit there as his father did. He isn't ready for that. But, as Eward sees, he is afraid he doesn't know how to stop it.

9)

Someone in America, a colleague, sends the Professor a book on forged documents. On a whim, he begins to read. Soon Professor Akiyama is delving into the history of written fakes. It's intriguing. He sits in his office, books piling up everywhere. He chain smokes, cigarette held between yellowed ring and middle fingers. Thin clouds of smoke trail in the air. He doesn't notice the ashes overflowing in the ashtray. He pores through one book and then another. He finds history is littered with political forgeries, fake historical documents, false spiritual texts, fraudulent literary works. Usually one can determine their purpose, but not always.

Professor Akiyama is amazed to realize how fabrications, such as the Donation of Constantine, the Constitution of Chou, The Protocols of the Elders of Zion, the writings of Hermes Trismegistus often become even more active as cultural forces after they've been unmasked and stripped of authenticity. Discredited, their allure becomes stranger and more subtle. Identified as frauds, they are no longer part of an accepted logic. Their power no longer relies on conventional notions of truth and falsehood. True or not, they live on. How deeply, he wonders aloud to Edward, do counterfeits continue to leave their hidden mark in what we think and do?

One afternoon, Professor Akiyama is rummaging in some dusty boxes of files and comes across a faded copy of The Secret Annals. He recalls the enthusiasm of those who sent it. He was too busy at the time with the Kamakura diaries to pay much attention. He remembers later there was some sort of controversy, then silence. He reads quickly through the text, then begins again. It is unsettling but something in these texts have a deep resonance. He is sure that fate has brought the Annals to him. Edward sees that the Professor is somehow coming back to life.

10)

Once again Edward can see the dawning optimism in the Professor's face. He remembers that expression very well and wonders if the Professor was feeling something like the inner promise that has just opened in his own life. Maybe it has all come back so vividly because this began a great change in the Professor, a change, that in turn, certainly altered Edward's life.

Next day, Edward returns to the Annals and lets himself drift in the stream of the events that surround them. He may not want his life to continue as it is, but he wishes to postpone any change until he is ready. He wants to understand the effect the Secret Annals had on the Professor and the effect it may be having on him.

THE SECRET ANNALS:
ANNAL I: Concerning Lady M. - Part 2

1)

It was a bleak autumn morning long ago when I, tired from the jour-ney, full of misgivings about my impulsiveness, arrived for the first time at the Prince of Ling's encampment. It was not what I expected. I was, despite what I believed still quite inexperienced.

At that time, the Prince lived deep in the mountains hundreds of miles north of the capital. The land itself was no longer part of any lord's domain. Farmers and woodsmen had fled. The Prince had taken up resi-dence in an abandoned farmhouse surrounded by barns and outbuildings amid forests and rolling hills. Small tents had been set up nearby to house several hundred visitors. Three large tents served as a kitchen, a dining room and a meditation hall. It was obviously all improvised.

Men and women were bustling to make preparations for what turned out to be a month of teachings by the Prince. The first man I encountered just outside the compound tried to sell me a garish used kimono. "A bar-gain," he said with a salesman's practiced assurance. A gap-toothed girl shooed him away. She made me welcome as if I'd been expected, found me a small sleeping tent, a place to sit and wait in the dining tent before she ran off on some other errand.

As I sipped tea, I looked at the growing crowd with some suspicion. The Prince's followers were an assortment of seekers, uprooted from every class and background. All around me, young students, middle-aged schol-ars, young nobles, shopkeepers, artisans, common laborers, farmers, even some who looked like criminals, chatted amiably. Many women, mostly young, some beautiful and a few well dressed, mingled easily in the crowd. The atmosphere resembled the beginning of a festival more than a gather-ing of those seeking spiritual guidance. But all were seeking something, even if they themselves could not have quite said what it was.

2)

Three men and a stocky woman bustled to the front of the tent and made announcements. One gave the schedule for the coming month, another explained that everyone must volunteer for some kind of work; the woman gave firm instructions on the location and proper maintenance of the latrines, the bathhouse, the tents. Everyone listened politely if not very attentively. Announcements over, the steady hum of chattering and gossip resumed.

I concealed my dismay. There was no clear division between servants and those served. It was ridiculous to expect everyone to do menial labor. There was no proper order. I decided that after I'd heard the Prince speak, I'd leave.

"You're new?" a tall older woman with heavy features loomed over me. I recognized the type: one who attached herself to newcomers since those who know her better found her clinging disagreeable. I bowed slightly without encouragement. Oblivious, the woman plopped down and began confiding things she thought I should know: where the best seats in the shrine tent were, what food should be avoided, when the lavatories were least likely to be crowded, what kind of clothes one should wear.

Taking tolerance for acceptance, the woman began to make sure I understood all about the Prince. Yes it was true. He really was an Ainu Prince from the remote North. He'd been sent to the great temple at Mount Koya by village elders just before Japanese soldiers invaded, killed his family, his people, destroyed his homeland. As a child, he achieved extraordinary realization even as a student, traveled to China with his teacher, studied there with Tibetans and was recognized as an incarnation of some great lama whose name I couldn't understand.

Seeing that I was taking all this in, the woman moved closer. She began to whisper about the Prince's drinking, his many girlfriends, his wife who had yet to arrive. She continued, telling which long-time followers were in favor, which was not. Only the sound of a distant gong stopped her. The Prince was about to begin teaching.

The woman stood to rush and get the seat she preferred ("In front of a tent pole; you can lean back, you see."), but turned back and whispered. "Like I told you, sit at the front. I know he'll want to meet you. Bye-Bye." She winked, wiggled her fingers girlishly, and gave a roguish smile. My revulsion only steeled my determination to leave.

3)

For that first talk, I ended up in the crush at the back of the shrine tent and waited for a long time. For an hour, everyone sat quietly in meditation. Then there was whispering. People began to wander in and out of the tent, returning to sit quietly, then stirring around, then sitting again. In the late autumn sun, the tent grew warm.

I looked out as the tent flaps blew apart and watched the breezes rippling down the mountain trees. Eventually there was an expectant buzz. A group of nondescript young men and women bustled importantly onto the platform where the Prince would speak. They placed a vase of flowers, a carafe of what I later learned was rice wine on a small table to the right of a rather shabby brocade cushion and to its left a battered armrest.

Immediately the Prince walked in and sat down. His movements were slow and considered. He wore decent unostentatious robes. There was nothing exotic about him. I could barely hide my disappointment. His features were not noble or refined; his skin was quite dark and he looked almost Korean. But as he looked slowly at each member of the audience, his gaze was by turns indifferent, mischievous, intent and somehow a little menacing. Seated so far back, I doubted he really noticed me.

The Prince began to speak. His voice was high, a little strangled. The Prince made no effort to flatter or charm his listeners. He scratched his neck, drank from his cup, took long pauses, smiled, drank again, resumed talking. Each gesture was uncalculated but somehow completely conscious. I was mesmerized.

As if the around him space was fluid like water, the Prince's every movement unfolded and rippled in the air. When he lifted the cup, I could sense him feeling its shape, its weight; when he drank, he was aware of the temperature, the slipperiness, the taste of the sake, and when he swallowed, he followed its progress into his body. The way he put the cup down, lowering his arm slowly until the base of the cup touched the wood of the table, the small thud it made, the release of the cup's weight from his hand, made each of the gestures in this ordinary continuum magnetic. I felt I was in the presence of someone who was completely part of life. These things are still imprinted on me, as if he had been drawing a brush across my heart.

Later, only by making an effort could I recall some of what he'd said.

4)

"Gautama Buddha left his father's palace, left behind a life of luxury and power. He was committing himself to his deepest intuition, a kind of longing, a sense there was something more real, more true, more vast, more profound to life; something more real than running around in the face of our inescapable fate of getting old, getting sick, and dying. Yes?

"He was sure that he could uncover some unconditioned freedom at the heart of life. Somehow he was certain that simply by looking directly into his own mind, looking nakedly into his world, he'd discover all that was needed. So the Buddha took this journey without relying on a god or a philosophy or an example.

"And no one in history had ever done this before. It was a crazy thing really. Completely amazing. The Buddha had renounced his kingdom, his whole life, and there was nothing that confirmed him in what he was doing. Nothing. All he had was this longing, this intuition that he could discover something that no one before had discovered, and he could do it in this very simple way. We take it for granted: he was the Buddha. He was going to discover enlightenment. He was going to be the living face of enlightenment. But did he know that? No. He was completely alone. He was betting his life.

"Ever since then, the Buddha's way has passed directly from teacher to student, teacher to student, on and on. And even though Buddhism is obviously an established thing, each student is not relying on theories and promises, but is actually relying on an unexplored inner sense of possibility. And so no matter how great your teacher, how authoritative or powerful, no matter how profound or beautiful or eloquent the teachings, you walk that path, you find yourself alone on an untested, for you anyway, path. Completely alone. And actually without certainty. You are gambling with your life, and no matter what books and priests say, and how many temples are full of people practicing, you, you are alone. You're alone, betting your life.

"It is important to understand that these teachings have been passed down and come to you as an uninterrupted act of love. Every teacher, every student has to take this solitary journey in his or her heart. Because what the Buddha discovered is the vastness and profundity of heart. What the Buddha taught is his heart. He opened his heart completely to his followers. Nothing was held back. And so it continues to this day. Right now.

"So we could say, that we are gambling on true love."

A middle-aged woman asked: "Are you saying that the Buddhist path is about opening our hearts?"

A: "Yes… It's… reaching into your body with your own hands and pulling your heart open."

Q: "That sounds really…."

A: "Yes?" (laughter)

An earnest young man asked: "You said that the transmission of the teachings is like an act of love. But I've heard it said that the aim of a student's relationship with the teacher is the meeting of the minds."

A: "Heart. And actually I said the transmission IS an act of love."

Q: "So that's… what?"

A: "Yes, very what. (laughter) ... Like. you know, when you lie naked next to your lover and feel your lover's heart with your own heart? You've heard about that?"

Q: "Unh...Yes...?" (laughter)

A: "Well, you might cry. ... There might even be blood." (laughter)

A scholarly looking man asked: "And that would be transmission?"

A: "Maybe. ... Maybe not."

Q: "And that would lead to ...?"

A: "At the very least, a passionate relationship to chaos."

5)

My mind was ablaze. I felt that the Prince had been speaking to me directly. I left the tent determined to follow his teaching wholeheartedly.

I kept to myself until the gong rang for the next meditation. I meditated until dinner. I ate alone, fending off women, and more frequently men who tried to befriend me. I meditated long into the night, and was relieved when my assigned roommate spent the night elsewhere. I rose early and practiced throughout the next day. The Prince didn't give a talk that afternoon. The rest of the day and night felt flat, and at night, again alone, I felt gnawed by desolation. I recalled the Prince's words and this pushed me to endure my loneliness.

For the talk the following afternoon, I found a seat near the front of the tent. I dressed in my finest robes. I tried to catch the Prince's eye. He smiled at me. His talk, however, began in a very businesslike way.

6)

"As we've discussed, the essence of all Buddhist meditation, the essence of the Buddha's way of relating to mind, is not following thoughts. So the basic technique of meditation is to sit upright on the ground, square your shoulders; let your consciousness dissolve as you exhale. As thoughts arise, acknowledge them and let them go. Don't take up residence in your moods and thoughts and plans. Let them dissolve. Don't attack them. Let them go. OK. You've all learned that?"

"That's what the Buddha did. That's what we do." Then the Prince took a deep drink and paused for a long time.

"You might think this will be peaceful, smooth. That things might become clear and calm. More and more calm. More and more still. But the truth is, as you're sitting there, you're on fire.

"In some traditions they say: practice as if your hair is on fire. But actually, you are on fire. All of you. You are burning up. Everything in you is being consumed. You are being burned alive. Completely.

"Flames are licking, cutting through your skin, your outer defenses. Your fat is melting in the heat and roasting you. Your muscles spasm as they roast. Your bones are turning to charcoal. The world, as your eyeballs pop, is nothing but fire.

"You are naturally on fire. You may try to stop it. You may try to prevent it, but every instant, every bit of what you think you are is being consumed, eaten away, burned up, disappearing. Your body is changing. You are producing cramps, itches, sneezes, sweat, gas. Nothing you do can stop this.

"Your mind is on fire. You try to make things stable with your passion. 'If I can get something I want, then it'll be all better. Even it'll feel good. Maybe, or maybe your aggression can get rid of it, the pain, the fear. Maybe even if you just ignore it, it will go away.

"And definitely, you try all those things. Over and over. You feed the flames, even while you're burning up. You can't stop. No matter what you do, nothing stops. You are on fire. Your idea of yourself is on fire. You are sitting there and you are burning up.

"And you don't move. As the flames engulf you utterly, you don't move. You burn and burn and burn.

"We may call this meditation practice, but it's also the real thing." It was a long time before anyone asked a question. Finally, a well-dressed young man spoke up.

Q: "But is this really... mmm... a good thing?"

A: "It's the only thing."

A thin monk asked: "So are we burning up our karma?"

A: "And in the absence of your karma, what is there?"

Q: "Emptiness?"

A: "Somehow that doesn't sound very helpful."

After a long pause, the heavy-set woman who had made announcements asked: "Are you describing what I've heard called 'flames of wisdom'?"

A: "You certainly might want to hope so."

7)

I was trembling. I barely focused on the shy, slightly aristocratic looking young man in dark silk robes who came up to me and spoke discretely. With a jolt, I realized he was saying that the Prince had requested that I be his guest for dinner. I was terrified and wanted to say no, but followed as the young man escorted me through the crowd. I was too dazed even to be embarrassed by the knowing smiles of some I passed by.

8)

And so, on that marvelous late summer evening I never can forget, I stepped onto the dusty floorboards of the veranda surrounding the small, secluded farm cottage that the Prince used as an office and, I realized, a place of assignation. Though it was just a rough outbuilding with thatched roof and a narrow porch, it seemed, that afternoon, to have a special rustic elegance.

The soft light intensified the many subtle colors of trees and plants around the pond. The dark water shimmered beneath a deep blue sky and towering pink clouds. The Prince, his tan skin glowing gold against his plain gray robe, stood barefoot in the mud by the pond, turning, a clump of emerald green watercress dripping in his hand.

"You must be new." I bowed and nodded. "After all, you're on time." He had a high open laugh. "Most of my students have become much too casual." I bowed again, painfully aware of my awkwardness. My outer robes were dusty and inner robes worn.

We sat side by side as the sun set. He asked about my past and how I'd come to be here. He listened carefully. The long gaps in the conversation were not uncomfortable but seemed to open a deeper intimacy. The young man who'd led me here lit two lanterns, brought a simple meal of noodles and disappeared. The Prince poured sake for me and we drank together. It was deeply familiar and, at the same time, otherworldly as if I'd moved back into the time of Prince Genji. Every moment trembled and was fragile.

9)

I spent the night amid the chorus of crickets, the bright swaths of stars, the smell of cooling earth. As a lover, the Prince was more curious than furiously impassioned. Like someone exploring something new, odd even. He tasted my mouth, touched my neck, my breasts, and stroked between my legs. I could feel all his senses tuned to every movement, spasm, sigh.

Late at night, we wrote a poem together. First the Prince would write a verse, then, as he asked, I would describe its colors.

To draw out
To be drawn out:

As lovers glance
To clarify a secret
That remains:

                                    Mother of pearl.

As lovers whisper
To fill
An inexplicable silence:

                                    Silvery black.

As lovers touch
To open
What each holds apart:

                                    Pink and chrome yellow.

As lovers kiss
To expand
On the delicate edge of speaking:

                                    Violet and pale blue.

As lovers twine
To elicit
The essences of life in the body:

                                    Opalescent and blood red.

To draw
And be drawn out.
I was considering what color I would write next, but he stopped me.
"I think that's a good ending."
"Do you have to have the last word?" I teased.
"Yes," he said.

10)

    After that night, he asked me to stay with him for several months. I told him I couldn't pay and I didn't want to do chores like a common servant. He said that would be fine. That was the beginning.

III. CONTINUITY

1)

    "Seductive." Professor Akiyama says and gives Edward a thin smile. He then returns to watching curls of smoke ascending from his cigarette. Edward can still see it as easily as he sees his own face in the shaving mirror.

"Of course," the Professor says, *"Some texts are pastiches; the style, the philosophical outlook are well known, not hard to ape. But some passages evoke conventions much harder to place. The authors of the Annals inserted anachronisms and assumed habits of mind not common until much later. Whoever was responsible could easily have avoided such mistakes."*

Edward is not convinced, but Professor Akiyama has concluded that the seeming errors are not errors at all. Veracity, the Professor maintains, is not the point, and he confesses that an odd feeling has come to engulf him as he read the Annals. Past and present blur together in some third unknown and unreliable continuum, a continuum beyond orthodox history. Professor Akiyama shakes his head in wonder. He suspects this was the goal of those involved in writing, compiling and presenting The Secret Annals.

He takes Edward to the National Museum and talks with two men who helped in the early investigations of the Annals. His questions are precise, but it's hard to tell what he's looking for. His thick glasses make him seem vague and vulnerable, but he is very persistent. They tell him everything. They describe the safe, the removal of the lacquer container, the unrolling of the scrolls, examining the fabrics and papers and reading the texts. They tell of finding the glue, those fatal little dots of glue. They describe how all enthusiasm crashed and how betrayed they all felt. Safe, box, brocade and scrolls suddenly moved outside the bounds of reason and common sense. The professor tells Edward that they have experienced the same kind of queasy uncertainty that reading the texts induce in him.

Professor Akiyama spends two weeks examining the lacquer box and the gold fabric. The safe is lost and was probably sold for scrap. It takes the increasingly impatient staff a few days to find the scrolls. Their supervisors, the curators, become annoyed as the professor spends a month studying the discredited documents. No one wants scandal to be stirred up again. But Professor Akiyama has concluded that all of it, the safe, the lacquer box, the brocade, the fraudulent scrolls, are an ensemble carefully calculated to transmit a strange and unique sensibility. At this point, he has no doubts about the Annals' importance. He explains to the staff members who are helping him that their responsibility to the scrolls is a special one. Despite their impatience, the young men are somehow flattered. Then the Director of the National Museum catches wind of this and intervenes. He does not permit further study of the scrolls.

The professor is not concerned. He is moving in a new direction. As they leave the museum, he whispers to Edward conspiratorially, he is sure he can find evidence or echoes of evidence reflecting the intentions of those who assembled the Secret Annals.

2)

Professor Akiyama tells Edward: "It is a weakness of scholars to be so concerned with truth. As far as truth or falsehood is concerned, language has no bias. Errors and lies have just as much influence in the world. They say The Secret Annals are problematic. The thing is: the Annals exist. Their purpose exists."

Edward looks away, aware that he is flushing. He suddenly knows, painfully, that the professor values him because he is so isolated and so dependent. Colleagues barely speak to Edward. The professor's wife and his older daughter don't approve; his younger daughter flirts and torments him. Edward tries but is too awkward to fit in easily. There is no one else in Japan who would need to follow or would try to understand the Professor with such desperate intensity.

Professor Akiyama has decided that the Secret Annals cannot have been the work of just a few people. People with many different skills and resources were necessary. A large group devoted to a single cause. He is sure that these were people of subtlety, skill, determination and, obviously, wealth. The Annals are not the work of casual pranksters or forgers with limited means, run-of-the-mill skill and obvious philosophical or political aims. But who they are, how long have they existed, and where? He is sure they must somehow exist. And he knows where to begin looking. Professor Akiyama feels a huge alien longing emerging from the past. He decides to enter a shadowy and less certain world.

Edward, as he knows he must, follows.

THE SECRET ANNALS:
ANNAL I: Concerning Lady M. - Part 3

1)

    The sea becomes calm, and I sleep fitfully, then wake in the filtered half-light before dawn. Stepping carefully past the shadowed sleepers, I make my way to the deck. Large fluffy snowflakes are falling from the gray sky and float in the air, muffling the sounds of the creaking boat, the sailor's disgruntled muttering. I duck behind a crude bamboo blind and relieve myself. I watch as one white crystal after another hovers on the dark surface of the sea, dissolves. I return and try to sleep, but the cabin is dark, cold and smells of unwashed men and women.

2)

    It was also an early winter day long ago. I had been with the Prince for about two months. There was snow then too, and I snuggled luxuriously beneath the quilts. I was almost afraid to feel so lucky. I only recognized the pressures and fears that had filled my life as they lifted. Everything around me felt somehow lighter and more vivid. I was living in an enchanted world. Nothing was ordinary.

    People came in and out of the Prince's little farmhouse. I barely noticed them. He and I walked arm in arm as he went to give his talks. I sat next to the dais. I wanted only to watch his every movement, hear his every word and intonation. I wanted only to smell and touch him. The rest of the world was merely an unimportant backdrop. Only when he would smile at me or put out his hand was I connected to the pulse of life.

    For two weeks the Prince stayed up all night and slept all day. Night turned into daytime, and the world turned upside down. I did my best to cook for him, made breakfast at dusk and ordered dinners as the sun began to rise. He showed me how to pour boiling water over frozen meat, a dish he called 'bandit stew'. And with his devious grin, he did look like an outlaw. Other times, as he sat unmoving in the afternoon sun, he glowed like a Buddha.

    The Prince began giving his talks at midnight. The students struggled to stay awake, but I made a point of staying alert in the seat reserved for me at the front. After the talk, close followers and some new students came by to talk with him. I served tea, sake, snacks, but the guests were guarded with me. When they left, the Prince and I read aloud to each other, drank, wrote poems. One was called "Licking honey from the razor's edge."

Only the eye of the lover passes beyond sight.
Only the mind of the lover passes beyond mind.
O Bliss undispersed
Never co-separated
Never no
Never divided
Never unloved
O world of golden eyeball never blinked,
Such mind unwaked unslept.
Devotion spewed completely out
Heart lost love of laugh and cry.
There is never no ever no of you
Who for us delicately dances
And points a silver finger at this naked love.
Ah.

"Is that what being with me is like for you?" I was somehow unnerved.

"That's what everything is like," the Prince shrugged.

Of course, I was pleased he had written a poem to me, but my first instinct was to say no, to refuse it. The sheer scale of this passion frightened me. How could I accept such love? I had met someone who accepted me in his heart, more perhaps than I would ever accept myself. I had not expected to experience this. It was dissolving me, and I suddenly stiffened. I knew his love was too all encompassing, too intense to remain with a single person. I feared I would be abandoned, lost.

I could not consider leaving however. I loved the Prince. When the Prince slowly returned to a more normal schedule, we often took hikes to nearby villages and went for picnics in the cold. I set aside my fears. I bathed in a kind of happiness that, once I had seen something of the world, I had never allowed myself to believe in.

After a month, the Prince's talks ended. Most of the visitors departed. The Prince was exhausted and slept for a week, but then he became restless. When he was away from me, I began to suspect he was sleeping with other women. I tried to ignore their smell on his skin. I didn't dare confront him. I didn't want to lose him. He treated me as tenderly and passionately as ever, but I couldn't bear to think I might no longer be so special to him. I didn't want to return to a life where I was alone. I realized my manner was becoming forced, brittle, as I made ever greater efforts to please him. Though he never said anything, I felt clumsy and inept.

One morning when it was snowing, still half asleep, I reached out to touch him. He wasn't there. I awoke completely and rose to find him sitting by the fire. He nodded but was absorbed in thought. When I sat close to him he smiled, but seemed to pull slightly away.

"You know, people resent you," he said. I stroked his shoulder and shrugged. I tried to hide my panic. "After all, they work hard every day. They see you doing nothing."

"Should I care?"

"Doesn't it make you uncomfortable?"

"I'm here to please you, not them."

"But they're my students too. And if they are unhappy, it creates problems." Suddenly despite whatever fears plagued me, I resented being in this situation.

"You don't expect me to clean the latrine or wash dishes, do you?"

"No, but..."

"What?

"I thought maybe you'd like to be my private secretary."

"What would that mean?" I knew I was being eased into another role, and my only question was whether I would accept. I couldn't imagine myself apart from the Prince, so, without quite admitting it to myself, I knew I would.

"Oh, making my schedule, things like that."

"That doesn't sound too bad."

"No, and it would give other people a chance to get to know you." It was very painful to realize that now I would do anything to be near him. I forced myself to smile.

3)

From my first night with the Prince, I sensed he was not from our time. He had emerged somehow from a grander and more magical age. He still half-lived in that other world. And when I was with him, he brought me there. But I wondered at how, exiled from the world of his childhood, a traveler in alien lands, he had plunged into this painful and confused world with such abandon.

One morning I found the Prince sitting in the kitchen disheveled and unwashed, drinking heavily from a dirty cup.

"Are you depressed?" I asked. He glared at me. I felt his reply was a personal reproach.

"Yes."

"What do you do about it?"

"I get much more depressed."

For all his strength and swagger, I then felt how rare and how vulnerable was his presence amongst us. How continually painful. Was this love? Yes, and something more. Something I could not escape, even if I'd wanted to.

That afternoon, the Prince was in a different mood. "Many problems can be resolved by proper scheduling," he asserted. From that moment on, when anyone asked him for any but the most casual meeting, he insisted: "You must make an appointment with my secretary." I was thereafter his secretary. At first, the role felt artificial and embarrassing.

He began each day reviewing requests for meetings, arranging suitable times, and noting his activities for the coming day and week. He took all the details of his schedule very seriously, and though he never gave me any reason to believe otherwise, I couldn't help feeling it was a game for him. He took evident pleasure, nodding gravely when I announced the latest visitor, escorted him or her to and from the gate into his room. But soon I felt I was in a kind of naughty collusion with him, as if we were children conspiring to play a trick on grown-ups.

Of course the followers who had been with him for years greeted this new protocol with annoyance and exasperation. I took the brunt of it. The Prince told me not to worry. Within a few weeks, they had realized that this was a permanent change. Then, because appointments could only be made through me, they began to treat me almost obsequiously. But I wanted to know what they and the Prince said behind my back. I eavesdropped.

"I have not come here just to make a pleasant life for myself, to teach a few things, and die," he shouted at them one afternoon. And with that I began to realize the Prince was moving towards something larger than I had imagined. I heard some followers discuss the curriculum for future teaching, others plan building a larger shrine room and more cabins, others suggest where he might travel to find more students, while still others talked about raising money, political trends throughout the country and what might be done to keep the Prince's followers safe from harm. I didn't believe the Prince had any specific plan but rather a pattern emerged as he wove the possibilities presented to him.

At the same time, the Prince gave many individual interviews. Some particularly older students complained about each other, but most wanted advice both on spiritual matters and on every aspect of life. I was amazed by their trust in being so open with the Prince. The Prince always answered very directly.

A woman asked the Prince about how to deal with her son's violent rages.

"Never attack the obstacle," said the Prince.

A young painter asked about enlightenment. The Prince paused for a long time before answering. "The truth of the matter is that you do not attain enlightenment, you die." And also, "If you want to experience enlightenment, the most important thing is to clean your own kitchen sink."

A group of visitors asked the Prince to be their teacher. He told them: "Be careful. Following these teachings, there are no dark corners permitted. Not in yourself, nor in the world. Every deception must be uprooted and exposed before your very eyes. You will see yourself as a caricature. If you don't want this, stay away."

When they asked about the goal of this path. "No promises," the Prince said.

The Prince told a devoted young man about the great Tibetan yogi Milarepa. Milarepa's students praised their teacher as an incarnation of Manjusri, Boddhisattva of wisdom. Milarepa was enraged. "Whatever I have realized is from my own effort."

A man wept when telling of how his parents died. The Prince too wept and said: "Pain is the most real thing."

One of the Prince's older followers who had come to him for advice on a love affair that was going sour angrily accused him of manipulating both him and the girl. He had found out that, for some time, the Prince had been giving him one kind of advice while telling his lover exactly the opposite. The Prince remarked mildly: "You know, I don't manipulate at all. I merely observe and comment."

"You fucking liar," the student shouted, and left the Prince's house in a rage.

A new student, a very intense young man, told the Prince about the other teachers he had studied with. "They all were part of the path leading to you."

"No," the Prince replied sharply. Later I asked the Prince what he had meant.

"Sweetheart, you're supposed to pretend you're not listening." I was embarrassed.

4)

The Prince said that working with students was like cooking a stew. First you had to get them into the pot. Then you had to keep them in because each of the elements of the stew wanted to jump out of the pot before its own flavor was developed completely in a way that would harmonize with the others. He sometimes characterized each student as part of a dinner and dinner setting; as steak, as a knife, as a chandelier, as carrots, as broccoli, rice, potato, as black coffee, a coffee pot and so on.

"And what am I?" I asked.

"A crisp pink pear."

5)

I was constantly making mistakes, forgetting to write appointments down, putting them in the wrong order. I tried to maintain some equilibrium, meditating regularly. But practice was scarcely calming. The vividness of all my thoughts, schemes, fears, longing assaulted me unbearably, but the solitude provided some consolation.

I preferred the early morning group sitting, and it was there I became friends with the stocky woman I'd first seen making announcements on the day I arrived. The woman had met the Prince at Mount Koya years before he'd come to stay in his encampment. "I knew he was a genius from the first moment I met him," the woman began. "He was standing on a porch, wearing monk's robes. He was thinner then. He was by himself, looking down through the forest into the valley. Then he looked up into the sky and raised his hand slowly, palm up. It was so graceful. I couldn't take my eyes off him. I almost didn't dare to take a breath. But, I suddenly thought, he's the loneliest man I've ever seen."

From her, I learned of the Prince's haphazard wandering which led him to living for a while as the manager in a low-class brothel. "He was completely enthusiastic. He wanted me to get involved, but I didn't like that kind of thing. I didn't want to leave him, but I didn't want to be a prostitute or some kind of procuress. I had to get away, but I wanted to continue studying with him.

"So I made a plan. I came here, and I created something that he couldn't resist. I built a guru trap." This brazen manipulation astounded me.

"A guru trap. What's that?"

"The Prince is a teacher. The one thing he cannot resist is a student."

"And?"

"Yes, I found a place where students would come. I got a man to give us this land. I began to spread the word that pilgrims, all kinds of wanderers were welcome. I made sure people who came were well taken care of. I taught what I had learned. I told them about the Prince and they wanted to meet him. I wrote to the Prince and told him there were people who wanted to study with him."

"And so he came."

"Yes."

I believed what the woman had told me. I even admired the woman's determination, her intelligence, her cunning. But the story made me uncomfortable. I thought of the Prince trapped in the web of longing, ambition, desire woven by the students who loved him. I felt then his isolation all the more. I felt a sudden pang of guilt.

The next afternoon, in between appointments, I asked him if he felt imprisoned in the life that had formed around him.

"Caught is free. Free is caught," was his reply.

6)

Eventually the Prince called on others to share his bed, and sometimes with casual cruelty he asked me to escort them to the lakeside cottage. I crumpled the first time I was subjected to this humiliation. I tripped and fell as mutely I escorted the nervous young woman down the path. I felt more degraded with every step. Leaving her at the door, I wept. As I stumbled back to my cabin, I began imagining the Prince with this girl, this new lover. Would she now be receiving the same smiles, the same caresses, enjoying the same intimacies, the same little jokes as I had? Could I so easily be forgotten, become so completely non-existent to the Prince? Or, almost worse to imagine, would they share new kinds of lust and tenderness, ones that I had never known? Would they discover together an entirely different kind of intimacy? Such imaginings would not cease tormenting me. I did not sleep.

The next day brought a leaden mood of complete despair. I was as responsible for allowing myself to be trapped, as was the Prince for trapping me. I had been an utter fool to think I could retain some exclusive claim on such a being as he.

When told that the Prince had asked for me, I said I was sick. I stayed in my cabin. I couldn't bear to see him. But equally I couldn't bear to see the little smirks of those who would be pleased to see me humiliated. I knew that unless I accepted the situation, I would have to leave. But even if I departed, as I packed and left, there would be many all too pleased to see me go. I refused to let them dictate what I would do. I wouldn't give in. I decided I would brazen it out. I would find another kind of place in the Prince's life. I was not ready to leave him yet. So, the next time I was summoned, dressed in my finest, I walked proudly through the encampment, and smiled when I saw the Prince. I made his schedule and stayed for dinner. The new young woman sat at his left, and as he poured cups of sake for her, I tried not to show my feelings. But finally, when she left for a moment, I couldn't stand it any more. I was shocked at the intensity of my own anger.

"Why do you sleep with so many women?" I raged.

"It's a good way to get to know them, don't you think?" He replied in a tone of such absolute reasonableness that it stopped my mind. I felt that the Prince's love, his curiosity, his passions were truly devoid of any boundary. He was not a normal human.

And at that same moment, I felt imprisoned in the self-serving pettiness of my own desires and expectations. The Prince's impossible breadth only intensified my need to cling to the hopes and fears that had captured me. I did not know where to turn, what else to do. I burst into tears and ran from the room.

I ran to the nearby cabin he had given me, threw myself on the floor, but could not weep. Nothing made sense to me. And what I could not escape, what I could not avoid seeing in myself made me feel I was being flayed alive. I wanted to blame the Prince, but he hadn't deceived me. He never pretended to be something he wasn't. I tried to blame myself, but what else could I have done? I loved him. I tried to meditate to wash away my anguish. I tried to sleep. Late that night, some measure of peace came when, defiantly, I decided to take a lover of my own.

IV. CONTINUITY

1)

This is painful for Edward, and there's worse to follow. Professor Akiyama now firmly believes that The Secret Annals have been created to benefit an unknown cult. Japan's defeat and the American occupation have created yearnings not met by modern ways of thinking. New religious expressions, old millenarian sects and obscure quasi-Buddhist groups have sprung up everywhere. The professor is sure that exploring these marginal organizations will lead to discovering one that is preserving the Secret Annals as a hidden treasure. Edward is dubious. The professor says that they must leave the world of libraries, books and paper.

"We must search in the dreamland of manufactured culture where images are absorbing the past and transforming it. Our world is woven from lies and truths." To Edward, this sounds like a trip down the rabbit hole and into the looking glass. "You might even like it." The professor pats him on the arm. Edward is nervous.

2)

Edward knows it is an honor for an American, particularly one so young, to work with such a renowned Japanese scholar. Other faculty members and graduate students, even Edward's landlady often remind him of his good fortune. There are less than two hundred Americans who have been accepted into Japanese graduate programs, and he's the only one who has been accepted as a Professor's assistant. He's been in Tokyo for almost three years.

He still works hard to fit in, but pale, blond and skinny, he towers awkwardly amid swarms of small Asian men and women. He is tolerated more than understood. He knows that many subtleties elude him. He tries harder, but he is alone. He visits gardens, art exhibits, traditional theater, but what he loves in Japan is often hard to find.

His mother and sisters send monthly letters filled with hometown news. His father attaches his best wishes. The letters make him feel both homesick and homeless. The only one who writes real letters is his cousin Margaret, his mother's sister's daughter, a lawyer who works in New York. She is interested in what he's doing or at least is impressed.

Only in unexpected moments when he sees at the edge of the sky the cone of Mount Fuji hovering like a dream do the city, the crowds fade in his awareness. Then he is looking at something real.

Edward's nights are lonely. His apartment is shabby and he walks the streets. Occasionally he goes out for noodles with another American grad student.

"You've got it made in the shade, Eddie."

"You think so?"

"Put in your time. You can name your spot in any Asian studies program." Edward nods but looks doubtful.

"It's not like the senile coot I got assigned to. No one ever heard of him and no one ever will. Economic strategies in the mid-Tokugawa? Please. Your guy, Akiyama. He's a star."

Edward shrugs.

"You need cheering up, Eddie. Next time let's go somewhere more lively, hunh? Hit the hot spots, know what I mean?" Edward looks somehow unconvinced. "Pussy, Ed. That's what I'm talking about. Next time. Ok?"

Edward makes sure there isn't a next time.

3)

He knows that people at the university still smile at the sight of the gawky, pale young man stooping to listen to the small Japanese man in a dapper gray suit and goggle-like thick glasses as they walk down the halls. 'Crane and frog' they whisper. Edward doubts he will ever be at ease. He wishes he could be as indifferent to others' opinion as Professor Akiyama is.

Edward knows he has fallen under the professor's spell. Even amid his increasingly eccentric interests, there is something in the way that the old man can draw hidden meanings from ancient texts. He is like a diver finding unknown forms of life in the depths of the sea. The professor's wife and daughters call Edward "the devotee". Sometimes he wishes he could escape. He feels guilty not to be completely grateful. Of course, he has learned a great deal. Also, he is not insensitive to the Annals' odd fascination. He knows he must follow further if he is somehow to get free of the whole thing.

THE SECRET ANNALS:
ANNAL I: Concerning Lady M. - Part 4

1)

It was late winter. A bone-white moon, full and brilliant, flooded the empty sky. The snow banks sparkled all around me as I made my way through the pine forest to the baths. Men and women bobbed in the steaming tub. I recognized the voices of those invisible in the hot mist. I knew the secrets of so many. Two girls were whispering about a young man about to leave his year's retreat. They were recalling his good looks and speculating on what it would be like to make love with a man who'd been celibate for so long. I left the bath and hastened up the frozen trail to the retreat cabin.

The bearded young man opened the door when I knocked, stared goggle-eyed as I undressed and slipped into his bed. He was stunned as if some goddess suddenly offered herself to him. He had a strong animal scent, and his hunger for me was sudden. The ferocity of his lust made his awkward tenderness afterwards charming. I left when he fell asleep.

The Prince gave me a lewd wink the next day. I blushed, but afterwards I slept with whomever I wished, whenever the inclination struck me. It was strangely liberating, and strangely lonely. Sometimes one would become a regular partner for a while, a kind of love affair, but these did not last for I often visited the Prince as part of his inner circle of consorts, and he still often wanted me to spend the night.

I watched with some detachment as women flirted and competed to catch the Prince's attention, paraded through his bed. But even if I became somewhat accustomed to it, I still kept asking myself why he slept with all those women. I voiced this to a consort who had been with him longer than I. "What makes you think it's his idea," she laughed.

Now my relationship with the Prince was more companionable but had a deeper intimacy. I remained jealous of some consorts, despised others, but came to share closeness with those who somehow also felt the feeling of other-worldly enchantment that surrounded him. We pretended we were consorts of a great lord. Sometimes we all slept together. We gossiped. We shared an unspoken feeling that each of us, however painfully or ambivalently, had moved far beyond ourselves from long-held social norms. We shared a new kind of freedom and pride in that,

"Having sex with the Prince is really like being an insect examined by an extremely intelligent ten-year-old, don't you think?" said a young woman only recently admitted to our circle. At first there was shocked silence, but soon we are all rolling on the floor laughing.

One evening, I and two of the Prince's other favorites sat with him as he made calligraphies. I ground the ink, while the others held the paper taut. The Prince had received word that soon his wife would come to live with him. They had been separated for a year. Her family, wealthy landowners, had not approved of the secret marriage, had not let her go. Now their fortunes had changed. They were glad to send her to her husband. The Prince's calligraphies were verses of love to adorn her room. On a wide sheet of gold paper, he wrote:

Of many brilliant jewels,
You are the only diamond.
Of many brilliant jewels,
Only you reflect the true sun.

The easy camaraderie of the evening became strained as the Prince continually interrupted his work. He kept talking about how terribly he missed his wife. He sighed. He couldn't wait for her to arrive. He was consumed with anticipation. He didn't seem to notice how this irritated his companions. I exchanged glances with the others.

Finally, I asked: "Sir, what is it that makes your wife so special?"

"She is the only one who makes me feel real, " the Prince's replied matter-of-factly.

2)

The Princess arrived two weeks later to great fanfare. The Prince insisted that all his consorts dress in their finest robes. All his followers stood on either side of the road leading to the newly redecorated lakeside house. All bowed when finally she rode into the encampment. She was small, dark, surprisingly young. She was dressed in black silk brocade robes, and to everyone's astonishment, she wore the golden armor of a cavalry officer. She rode haughtily on a huge bay horse followed by her sister and a few attendants. She stared rigidly ahead as she rode by. When she dismounted, her movements were abrupt and awkward. She looked at no one other than her husband. This in contrast to her more hesitant, more feminine, more beautiful sister.

The Prince greeted her on the front steps and smiled happily. When the Princess finally looked at her husband's followers and his dwelling, she did not seem pleased. "Ah, don't worry. Soon I'll build you a palace. You'll have herds of horses, everything," the Prince assured her.

I thought that he was simply trying to placate this spoiled and imperious young woman. But, as we all found out, he would keep that promise.

3)

Soon, women flocked to befriend the Princess. I was disgusted as they fawned on the young girl simply as a way to get closer to the Prince. It was hard to tell whether the Princess was ignorant of her husband's many lovers, was indifferent, or had simply inured herself. At first, she accepted these offers of friendship with unconcealed eagerness. She said nothing when the women, having achieved their purposes or having realized that the Princess was of no use to them, disappeared. Her encounters with the Prince's male students were the same.

The Prince's students liked to spread rumors about the Princess's ineptitude. In one, she decided to clean house and tossed the dusty powder from a small golden casket, one of the only possessions the Prince cherished. "Ooops" he said, with a small smile and a shrug. "That was my father."

Soon she held herself apart from the Prince's followers. She was often insensitive, often condescending to them. I was probably the only one to realize that, aloof as she might present herself, the Princess had no guile. The Prince told me: "No one knows how much the things they say about her hurt me."

4)

With the Princess in residence, the Prince's assignations took place in an out-building he also used as an office. When I visited the lake-side house, the atmosphere was no longer the same. Horses grazed nearby. Saddles, bridles, horse brushes were scattered in the sitting room. In the lavatory, I once even found a pony munching hay. The Prince clearly enjoyed the new arrangements.

I felt sorry for the girl and often sat with her. I even took up riding. Eventually the Princess found it easy to confide in me.

"He married me in secret. I was only fourteen years old. My parents didn't approve. The morning after our wedding night, I woke when I heard him outside the tent, chatting to a passerby, someone I didn't know. He was saying how happy he was. How he was in love. How at last he was married. He couldn't stop telling the man about how beautiful, how intelligent I was, how courageous. What a great rider. Whoever he was talking to mumbled a question. The Prince pulled back the tent flapped and looked in at me.

'Sweetheart, what's your name?' he asked. The Princess burst out laughing. I, astonished, thought: truly, this was the only person who could have been the Prince's wife.

5)

I watch the snow fall ever more thickly. The boat barely moves. There is nothing to be done. I smile, let my mind drift. Memories become thick as the snowflakes outside.

V. CONTINUITY

1)

Edward trails in the Professor's wake. The professor wants to see the hidden teachings of these strange new cults. He wheedles information and introductions from colleagues, friends, acquaintances, even shopkeepers and restaurant waiters. Sometimes he simulates spiritual enthusiasms that are alien to everything else in his way of life. He insists that Edward join him on his forays into the wilder and often more desolate shores of Japanese religious practice. His family is not happy. But despite himself, Edward is fascinated to see the professor throw himself into the outer world with the same intensity he has up until now reserved for books. But the world into which he throws himself, the one into which he is dragging Edward, is appalling.

2)

After attending a few mass rallies and services held by the 'New Religions', the professor decides that the Annals would not be of use to those promulgating such emphatic certainties. Soon Edward and the professor are sitting stiffly on little gold chairs surrounded by fussy old men and anxious rich women in carpeted living rooms, straining to hear the whispers of female seers. These spiritual advisors, usually in elegant kimonos, usually in late middle age, are skilled at giving answers that seem specific but are both re-assuring and deeply non-specific. Not all the audience is satisfied. From the whispers of those wanting something more "authentic", they are guided to the séances of psychics, faith healers and trance mediums.

Here, where it is claimed and believed that the worlds of the living and the dead intersect, the atmosphere is more charged. The leaders' authority derives from their contacts beyond this world. The professor makes considerable effort to look like a spiritual seeker and wears shabbier clothes. He and Edward attend séances with a toothless peasant woman, a dapper advertising executive said to have been struck by lightning, a mute child, a gaunt middle-aged woman in flowing black robes who is instructed by her deceased father, a former General, a humble priest. Some go into violent trances; others merely blink and speak slightly differently. Some speak in a number of strange voices. But regardless of the trappings and theatrics, the spirits eventually explain: "No one has ever understood you. No one has ever understood how much love you have to offer." Tears and trembling sighs of relief follow. Edward is relieved when the professor wearies of these gatherings.

But within a week, he is following Professor Akiyama through crowded working class thoroughfares, plunging into back alleys, searching in shanty-towns, seeking the Dojo of some shifty wonder-worker or the improvised temple of an elderly shamaness.

Disguised in a frayed tweed jacket and rumpled shirt that make him look more frail, his gray hair unkempt, his thick glasses smudged, his jacket gray with cigarette ash, the professor is always intent. He simulates abject hopefulness. If the group they are visiting considers tobacco an abomination, he discards his cigarettes and sucks on a peppermint. If found out, he confesses his sincere desire to change. He is remarkably convincing and displays an easy guile of which Edward never thought him capable. He is particularly good at gaining the trust of somewhat younger women. He is quite flirtatious. He has a new verve. Edward is caught off guard.

3)

Edward and Professor Akiyama wait submissively among poor, despondent, lovelorn men and women lined up in ramshackle churches and damp basement assembly halls. They learn strange chants, wave their hands and shout, eat vegetarian food, lie on the floor and breathe deeply, jump into the air over and over. They listen to the insider gossip which lonely cultists are anxious to confide. They accept the condescension of the regulars. Edward endures the searching gazes, the tear-streaked blank stares, the hushed tones when referring to 'master', the ready assumption that he is a true believer (all the better for being American), the endless requests for donations (another and quite expensive aspect of this quest that does not please Mrs. Akiyama), and the unrelenting smiles of the saved.

More than the questionable teachers and strange practices, Edward is appalled by the huge number of people from all classes, people who, if you saw them on the street would seem completely normal, but who leave their jobs and search with desperate urgency for solace, love and some kind of transcendent embrace. Most are middle-aged and older. The young are busy learning American ways. There are more such people than he could have imagined, all struggling in a fever of anxiety and hope for which there is no cure in the normal world. He feels he is looking at dark and turbulent streams of anguish and longing that pulse beneath the surface of the world. He feels off balance. The professor's ardent displays of spiritual seeking are increasingly unnerving. He doubts he can stand these expeditions much longer. Often he imagines mocking laughter echoing just out of earshot, as if envious colleagues can see where his loyalty to the professor has led.

They are returning home late one evening after being blessed by an unshaven priest wearing a gold crown and a stained green satin robe. Edward is at the breaking point. He asks the professor if the Annals would be as interesting if they were undeniably authentic. The professor pretends he doesn't hear. Edward begins to suspect Professor Akiyama's motives for these expeditions may conceal some deeper yearning.

After eight months, it has become obvious even to Professor Akiyama that the confused doctrines of these pathetic sects bear no resemblance to what the Prince in the Annals teaches. The professor abandons their excursions. Edward is profoundly relieved. The professor's vain pursuit have already caused whispered doubts about his reputation and definite strains in his family life.

4)

Edward walks to Professor Akiyama's house through the rain. Western-style homes fill most of the bombed out vacant lots, but sometimes he still can smell burned timber. He's come to dread the twice-weekly visits. The professor's wife opens the door and looks disdainfully as water drips off his raincoat onto the foyer floor. Over her shoulder he can see the daughters waiting in silence for him to go into their father's study so they can resume gossiping. The elder daughter, Kimiko, bony and sallow like her mother, does not look at him. The younger, Harumi, flushed, plump, dressed in a short American style skirt and tight pale blue sweater, gives him a naughty wink and sticks out her tongue. It is wet and very pink. She wiggles it slightly. Edward feels himself blush and turns quickly away. While the mother and Kimiko hold themselves aloof, Harumi's flirting intensifies his awkwardness. She bursts out laughing. The mother shows him down the gloomy hallway in to the study. She makes no effort to conceal her disapproval. Edward doesn't know if she dislikes him because he's American, because of the Annals or both.

5)

Professor Akiyama remains certain that the Annals are connected to the aims of a hidden cult. He now concludes that the cult, though marked by Japanese traditions, could be centered in the U.S. The safe, the dots of glue are both American. The organization may now be based there. On this basis, he decides the Annals must be translated into English. Edward must make an English version of the Annals. "Someone will read it almost certainly. Someone in America, I think. Perhaps they will make themselves known then." He sees the translation as a kind of bait that will tempt this cult out of the depths where it hides. Edward simply cannot say no.

Edward is dismayed at how much Professor Akiyama longs for The Secret Annals to be true. He can barely believe he allowed himself to be cornered. He has actually promised the old man to translate the Annals. Professor Akiyama's emphysema is suddenly worse. Since he stopped exploring the cults, he is beginning to decline. Edward now finds him always in the shabby costume he wore on their earlier outings. He insists that over and over, they read the Annals together.

THE SECRET ANNALS
ANNAL I: Concerning Lady M. - Part 5

1)

The Prince began to travel, giving talks in the temples of small villages and in the reception halls of local magnates and a few remaining lords in the larger rural towns. I among a group of his older followers accompanied him.

2)

Once when the Prince taught in a large town, formerly renowned for its weaving, he said this:

"When we use the word 'compassion', it carries a slight tone of condescension. It has the idea of 'forbearance'. It brings the sense of one who is rich giving to one who is poor, or of a wise person speaking to a stupid one, or someone who is very composed enduring the tantrums of a child. So there's some kind of effort, some kind of fabrication. We have to decide to be compassionate. We have to exert ourselves.

"The real essence of compassion is putting others ahead of oneself. This is the natural, the intrinsic basis of compassion.

"It is not possible to have any kind of thought whatsoever which does not involve 'other'. All our needs, wants, longings, jealousies, satisfactions, hatreds, hopes, fears and so forth involve other. This is true for our pragmatic plans, for our spiritual intentions. Even thoughts about ourselves, from stomach pain, to worries over inner failing, one aspect of ourselves which we consider to be the real 'us' is looking at some other and less desirable aspect which we consider as 'other'. Even in meditation, whether as Shamatha which is developing the peaceful aspect of mind or Vipassana which is the refinement of clear awareness, this is so.

"Mind" as has been said, "is that which seeks an object." From this we may conclude that the basis of mental activity and the basis of compassion have the same nature. The point is to let go of the illusory I, and place the illusion of 'other' before it. That is to say, our practice is to be in the world. And, for that reason, it is not a practice, not something we do to be able to do the real thing later. This is the real thing on the spot.

"So, when it is said that the essence of Shamatha is to let mind rest in basic awareness, the basic nature, empty luminosity, the essence of Vipassana is compassion, our wholehearted, inescapable, and from the beginning selfless engagement in the world of phenomena. It is the essence of art."

At the end of his talks, the Prince answered questions, and after that people would stream up to speak with him personally. Later some would have dinner with him, and afterwards some would return to wherever he stayed. Some would stay the night, and in the morning, others would begin arriving at breakfast.

3)

I noticed the weather-beaten, hard-muscled man. He moved warily as he took a seat at the rear of the hall. His lynx-eyes scanned the crowd uneasily, obviously unsure if he belonged there, if he would be allowed to stay. The crude tattoo on his neck marked him as a former convict. I had never known anyone like that. I found myself drawn to this predatory creature. I watched as he listened. At some point, the man smiled and his face relaxed. I caught his eye and we lingered briefly, looking at each other across the crowd.

After the talk, I signaled the convict to come meet the Prince. The three of us then went out drinking and ended up in a bar patronized by herdsmen and butchers. Two herdsmen were playing dice. Every time one was about to throw the dice, the Prince would bump his elbow. I wanted to stop him, but the convict waited to see what would happen.

The herdsman soon became enraged, pushed the Prince outdoors, and pulled a knife. The Prince stepped suddenly forward. He grasped the herdsman's blade and pulled it up against his neck. "Sssssssssnip," he said, with a smile. The herdsman, frightened, fled. The convict, there and then, asked the Prince to be his teacher. That night, I took him to my bed.

From then on, many itinerant laborers and petty criminals became attracted to the Prince. The Prince treated them with the same affection as he did the more respectable followers. The two groups did not mix easily.

4)

One afternoon, a merchant brought a fine collection of ancient paintings on silk for the Prince to see. The paintings were portraits of the Buddha's original disciples, and as the merchant unrolled them, the other guests crowded around to hear the Prince's opinion.

"Master, what can you tell about the kind of practice these people did?"

The faces of the ascetics visibly moved the Prince. "Most importantly, what you see is that these are the faces of people who left their homes completely, " he said.

5)

I like being in new places, but I do not like travel. I remember those expeditions with the Prince as exhausting. The roads were often treacherous. There was the constant fear of bandits. The Prince however proceeded as if there were no problems and no risks. Then there were the difficulties of setting up house in a variety of dwellings, of making sure the halls where the Prince would teach were clean, setting up meetings with local worthies, setting up a schedule of interviews. People craving attention, wanting this and that, each thinking his or her problem was uniquely important. The Prince never seemed less than ready. He saw everyone. When tired, he slept, sometimes for days, regardless of whom he was supposed to meet with. It was up to me to explain.

"How do you stand it?" I asked the Prince.

"Oh, I just make it up as I go along," the Prince answered blithely. But for me it was becoming a nightmare. I tried to find places and times to meditate, but it did not help.

6)

Wherever he went, the Prince often became something of a local celebrity. Those interested in religion wished to find out secret spiritual methods for enlightenment. Local scholars wanted information. Merchants wanted to obtain magical blessings. Many simply wanted to claim acquaintanceship with this exotic newcomer or to present him to their other guests as a strange new social ornament.

Once in a large port town, the Prince was invited to the house of a wealthy merchant who had recently assembled a large collection of Buddhist statuary. The statues were displayed on pedestals all around the merchant's reception hall.

The merchant had arranged a large gathering of all those he thought might be most interested in and helpful to the Prince. All were eagerly awaiting his arrival. The Prince arrived quite late, strode past the merchant who was anxiously awaiting him, ignored all the guests, and slowly, made three full prostrations, flat out on the floor, to every statue in the room one by one.

This gross display of religiosity embarrassed host, guests, even the Prince's students. As the Prince said to the embarrassed merchant:

"You must understand: these statues may just be man-made objects, but they are the repository of great devotion from thousands and thousands of people."

7)

It was during our stay in the populous weaving center that after a talk, I looked across the room and saw a man and woman, young with a far more sophisticated air than the rest. City people. The woman, willowy, elegant was dressed in a beautiful lavender silk outer robe, then under-robes of pale blue and saffron. I felt dowdy just looking at her. Her friend, I could tell they were lovers, wore rakishly cut dark blue brocade, a red scarf. I wanted to know them. So I arranged for them to meet the Prince.

We four soon became intimate. The woman, Y was a dancer; the man, S an artist. Together we spent many days walking through the town, drinking. Throughout our haphazard peregrinations, the Prince and S talked about art, the possibility of applying basic Buddhist principles to design, of presenting the spiritual reality evident in basic forms, colors and arrangements. They drew designs for furniture, lamps, dishware, banners and all kinds of decor that would uplift the humblest environment and dignify the dwellings of the poorest without much cost.

They designed and printed banners in vibrant primary colors on huge swaths of the cheapest materials. Using ancient Buddhist symbols, seed syllables, tigers, lions, garudas and dragons in brilliant reds, blues, golds and black, these banners invoked the power of the elements and of the Prince's lineage. They provided an environment of great dignity and distinction, no matter how humble or bleak the surroundings. Y and S became a permanent part of the entourage. They were entertaining companions for me.

8)

One spring, the Prince was teaching on Buddha Nature, intrinsic enlightenment. During the question period, a woman said that she felt that deep within her was the seed of great insanity that she could not escape.

"But it's alive in you, darling. It is life force. It is love. It is you. Let it expand to embrace your fear. Please sweetheart, don't be afraid. Just do it."

9)

For many, the Prince's extravagant displays re-enforced his reputation as a powerful and persuasive teacher, as well as hinting at the wildness rumored to pervade the life around him. The halls were invariably filled with a wide assortment of characters: scholars in brocades, perfumed courtesans, herdsman in wet, steaming wool, army deserters, girls running from home, criminals, clean and proper students, and so on.

The Prince always began teaching late. The audience often became very irritated. "I can't start until they're settled, can I?" he said.

10)

In a barn in a small farm town, the Prince spoke to a small group of dispirited former lay practitioners whose temple had been burnt down.

"You cannot follow the Buddha's path by trying to make yourself try to fit into the words of the teachings. You must search for the teachings in yourself, as bones, nerves, skin, heart. On this path, we are looking for our heart.

"Enlightenment... the awakened state... whatever that might mean... is not a THING. It is never the same ... never quite the same in how it appears...is understood... is experienced. It is always fresh... new... bright... unexpected.

"As sudden fear, cosmic fear, falling in love, laughter, endless laughter. The essence, the fulfillment of our journey of awake is always new. Therefore, our practice IS always the renewed...renewing...ever new. Our practice is the encounter, the instantaneous embodiment of awake, momentary, alive. New because it is by its nature free from concepts of any kind... therefore free of expectations... not accessible by memory.

"I've heard some of you say that your practice was good... Does that mean it conformed to your expectation, your concept, your memory? If so, doesn't that mean your practice was bad? And if you say your practice was bad, doesn't that mean something happened that was not part of your expectation, your plan, your understanding? Then couldn't that mean your practice was good?

"The question you might want to ask yourself: at what moment do they switch?

"The best way to practice is to doubt everything. Believe nothing. Trust nothing."

At the end of the talk, a strange middle-aged man, dark and hairy, rose and began berating the Prince, calling him a charlatan, his teaching fraudulent, and his aims malign. The man went on for twenty minutes and through it all, the Prince sat impassively, only moving to take a sip of sake.

Finally the man began to run out of things to say. He paused for a while, then said: "I just want you to know that I feel really good I've been able to say all these things. I just wanted to get them off my chest." To which the Prince replied:

"For you, this may be the biggest day of your life, but for me, it's just another day's work."

It became common for someone in every place he spoke to attack the Prince. His ability to deal with such situations became well known, and people wanted to see him perform.

11)

Once the Prince met with a group of poets who were locally celebrated. One was particularly vociferous in calling into question the Prince's literary education, his understanding of current political events. The Prince's answers satisfied his questioner, if grudgingly. The poet changed the topic to the Prince's way of writing poetry. After a long time, the Prince smiled at the man almost shyly:

"You must understand. I do not prolong anything."

12)

A young woman from a wealthy family came to the Prince and asked to be his student. She told him she had been traveling across the mountains for months changing direction only according to dreams. If she dreamed of a blue bird, she followed a caravan in which a bale was wrapped in blue cloth. If she dreamt of something red, she went towards the red sunrise. Now she wanted to serve him.

The Prince advised her to become a waitress at a busy restaurant. Though puzzled, she did so. Some years later, she became accustomed to listening to instructions from real people outside her. Then the Prince gave her more formal teaching.

13)

The Prince was staying on the second floor of an inn. The staircase was long and steep, interrupted only by a small landing where the steps turned. Descending early one summer, the Prince whispered to the new follower who accompanied him:

"Let's not hold back. Let's do it." With that he threw himself bodily down the stairway. He went head over heels and collapsed flat on his back on the landing. The student, completely appalled, raced down after him, and helped him to stand and to brush off his clothes.

"I wish I could be free enough to do that," the student said.

"Why not?" the Prince replied, and threw himself in the same way down the remaining steps.

14)

    F, a tall, wiry, smiling smuggler, told the Prince, on their first meeting that he wanted to be his servant. "We'll see," said the Prince vaguely.

    Some weeks later, the Prince ran into F and asked for a ride in his cart. F had a large ox cart at the time. That afternoon as they rode through the village, F said: "Well, at last I've captured you."

    "And I you." the Prince replied with a smile.

15)

    The Prince accepted every invitation, but began to weary of the expectations that were projected on him. The invitation to visit an old Buddhist hermit in his forest retreat lifted his spirits. This old priest was known for his austerity, his erratic comings and goings, for the casual roughness with which he treated his students. As requested, the Prince made sure he arrived before dawn.

    As tea was served, the old priest confined the conversation to conventional formulas of excruciating decorum and length. He continued in this way for more than an hour. Finally he reached behind his back.

    "This is all very nice, but I think you'd prefer... this." He drew out a large bottle of rice wine. The two proceeded to drink in silence for the rest of the morning. That night, the Prince brought his followers and requested the hermit to teach. The students sat and waited. It was just before dawn before the hermit spoke.

    "Don't move. Just die. Over and over.

    "Don't anticipate. Nothing can save you now, because you have only this moment.

    "Not even enlightenment will help you now, because there are no other moments.

    "With no future, be true to yourself and express yourself fully.

    "Don't move.

    "Just die. Over and over."

16)

    Weeks later, one of the hermit's student asked the old man his opinion of the Prince.

    "The Prince is a rare being. For him rage, stupidity and passion are the energy of awakening. But in India, they say the peacock is the only creature that lives on poison.

17)

A retired scholar-diplomat came to visit the Prince in his quarters at the monastery. The Prince performed a divination ceremony in which a mirror was used to see into the future.

As if he were looking down from the back of a great bird, the Prince saw a kingdom resting atop a mountain range whose base was wreathed in swirling clouds. The air above it was filled with gold and lavender light. Breezes sounded like distant wind chimes, and carried the scent of subtle perfumes. At its center and highest point was the great capitol of Kalapa filled with green parks, sapphire lakes, shimmering temples and vast cinnabar palaces with roofs of gold and inset crystals that radiated white light.

There in august dignity, wearing a gold turban and a turquoise brocade robe, the Rigden King presided over his people and over the human realm in general. Around Kalapa and separated from it by an inner ring of mountains were eight principalities, each bounded by clear rivers. The people of Kalapa lived in these domains, farming, raising horses and plying many arts and trades. They studied and practiced the Buddhist path as lay people, and they were all warriors. They lived in broad stone houses. The entire kingdom was encircled by an impenetrable circular range of snow-mountains that rendered it invisible to ordinary sight.

The Prince recognized the legendary Kingdom of Shambhala. The old diplomat was impressed by the Prince's description of his vision. The two talked late into the night on how to navigate the social upheavals of the time.

18)

The Prince was once lecturing and extolling the virtues of the monastic path. At the end of his talk, a woman rose and said: "Well, if the monastic way is so good, why did you give it up?"

The Prince answered, but his answer did not satisfy the woman. She asked the question again, and again the Prince answered, but still the woman was not satisfied. When she asked the question a third time, the Prince answered gently: "Look, my mind is my own. And I took my mind and threw it in the fire."

VI CONTINUITY

1)

Each time Edward visits, Professor Akiyama is swathed in clouds of cigarette smoke, looks more lost and frail. The professor's eyes are huge behind thick glasses; his gray hair is wildly askew; his small pot-bellied body is crumpled in a large armchair. He needs more time to surface from whatever realms he now inhabits. Edward understands the professor doesn't really care if the Annals are authentic or not. The old man just wants to dissolve into a world of his own choosing.

Edward sympathizes. He is finding the anti-American snubs and slurs at the university more difficult. There are worse things than being drawn down into undercurrents within the professor's mind.

Edward wishes he could get out of translating the Annals; it can only damage his career. The old man smokes slowly, lifting his cigarette between his two middle fingers, sucking gently at the tobacco, watching the ember blaze, exhaling. He loses himself in the curlicues of smoke. He takes his time. Through the window behind the professor's chair, the gray sky blends with the dirty glass revealing only the blurred outline of a sodden maple tree. Edward sighs and waits.

3)

The professor searches among a pile of papers on his desk, then stares meaningfully at Edward. He wants to talk about Octavio Paz. Paz says everything ever written is a kind of translation. All writing has been lifted from the forgotten continuum of wordless, solitary experience and framed in the shared medium of language. The professor raises his finger heavenward: "Translation is the core of communal human experience. It is utopian activity. It fulfills the yearning of language."

Edward senses the professor is trying to urge him on. The professor hopes that by translating The Secret Annals, Edward will realize why this text is so important. He wants his protégé to understand. Edward is slightly embarrassed that though, of course, he has read the Annals, he has not really paid attention.

Edward is trying to keep some distance. He is simultaneously fascinated and claustrophobic. Sitting silently with the professor, their haphazard interchanges and now the process of translating form a whirlpool. In spite of himself, he is being sucked in. He is entering a world that is perhaps richer, but all the more unnerving for being, perhaps, pointless.

4)

As he is leaving, Harumi comes to the foyer and holds out his raincoat. He has never before been alone with her. He smells a heavy flowery perfume. She helps him on with his coat, and her breast brushes the back of his hand. He begins to pull away but she pushes forward, staring at him. Her smile is not entirely mocking. "I want to see you," she whispers. He feels her hot breath and smells the peanuts she has been eating. They hear her mother's footsteps in the hall and she pushes him out the door.

A new intensity suddenly consumes him. He wants to think Harumi might be attracted to him. It could be that she has been hiding her interest in him behind her sarcasm. It could also be that she is playing a more daring and more painful joke. Hope and fear bring new anxiety into his relationship with Professor Akiyama. Everything he senses and feels is now more acute. The text of the Annals is the only escape.

THE SECRET ANNALS
ANNAL 1:   Concerning Lady M - Part 6

1)

The Prince was invited to lecture at a monastery famed for producing many great scholars. He was very drunk and arrived very late. Though irritated, the abbot and monks waited respectfully as he took his seat. The Prince smiled warmly at them all and began his talk.

For twenty minutes, he moved his lips, paused, nodded to accentuate a phrase, gestured, shook with laughter as if sharing a joke but he emitted no sound whatsoever.

When they were leaving, the abbot pulled me aside. "Don't stay with him," said the hard faced old man. "He's a great man, but those who follow him will lose themselves in his energy."

2)

The Prince by this time had cut his dark lustrous hair and had begun to put on weight. He was almost burly and he rocked slightly from side to side as he walked, giving the impression of combative physical power. His skin was golden, and he was clean-shaven. He dressed in brocades and fine dark wool, in the manner of a merchant, not yet entirely prosperous, but with flamboyant ambitions. His smile was avid and sardonic.

I watched while my lover was carried off as by a spring torrent. "Yes", he would say:

"Come. Come to our encampment. Let's work together." "Come, I have a place that's very rough and you can help build it." "Come, we could start a printing company, a dress shop, a vegetable stall." "Come, you can live in my house." "Come for a little while. Then come back here and start a center. I'll send you some people to help." "Come, some friends of mine are starting something you would like." "Come, come with me. Let's step into the future." Those who joined his entourage tried to emulate his manner, though some were more inclined to knowing looks, others were flirtatious, and others grimly determined.

But he was not, I thought, leading them. He was steering his way on the forces that carried him. And sometimes, as I watched him amid people pressing around after a talk, I was afraid. He was so naked, so alone. At the same time, I knew how it aroused him. The Prince's passion radiated all around him. Almost without me noticing, my own passions had expanded out from the Prince to this world that was seething all around me. I was in love with a feeling of all the possibilities the world presented moment by moment. Within that, there was an idealism that suddenly, just possibly, the world might bend to all this passion and form itself in a new way.

The Prince became engaged in the lives of so many people. But I didn't feel he loved me less. I was simply part of a vaster passion, a larger world, a greater love. Our intimacies then were more likely to occur in moments stolen almost comically in the back of carriages, in a pile of maple leaves, in the study of a stranger's house. I did not find this degrading. The risk stimulated me. These haphazard couplings conveyed a deeper trust, all the more so for being slightly comic.

3)

But I did not like it when one of the Prince's new favorites sought me out.

"The Prince told me that I should model myself on you." Afterwards, I often spotted the girl watching my every move.

"I can't stand her. Her stupid cow-eyed stares," I hissed to my former lover and friend, the Duke, as the girl gazed at me from across the room.

Another time, I stood by the Duke as another new favorite passed by. "I saw her in the bath," I whispered. "She's covered with little knife cuts. What do you think it means?" Neither dared imagine.

4)

The Prince was given many introductions to people who could be his patrons. If he felt their interests were somehow self-serving, he would simply get drunk. He would flirt and dance, much to the disgust of those worthies whom he was ignoring. It became evident that he was not interested in financial saviors. In fact, he actively disliked the idea of any kind of financial security.

Nonetheless, the Prince would occasionally make a genuine effort to cultivate a patron if the project involved was particularly important to him. One such patron was a woman who was a wealthy merchant. She was a large hard woman, had traveled thousands of miles, been in innumerable lands, and was well known for her ruthless dealing. She was infatuated by the Prince, and he invited her to dinner. As the evening progressed, the woman's overtures became more and more overt.

"Tell me, tell me your highness.... tell me all about the love," she whispered.

The Prince, who had been holding on to the end of the table in an effort to maintain his composure, smiled, but suddenly like a crack of thunder the end of the table broke apart under the force of the Prince's grip.

5)

R was bold, but, at the same time, shy. He had studied yoga for many years, but when he heard of the Prince he had no other wish than to follow him. When the Prince met R he was overjoyed. Before anyone had told him of R.'s arrival, he told his attendants: "Today, I'm going to meet someone very special." And when R gazed at him with his soft brown eyes and prostrated, the Prince knew he had found his dearest heart-son, the person who could carry on his work after his death. Until that moment, he had not been sure that such a thing would ever happen.

At their first meeting the Prince tested his devotion in a very ancient and traditional way although he made it seem so casual. He offered R a big cup of rice wine and a plate of broiled meat. R, though, he had been a vegetarian and abstained from alcohol, drank and ate without hesitation. The two talked late into the night.

Afterwards, without saying anything to anyone, the Prince gave R ever-increasing positions of responsibility. He taught him how to teach and how to rule.

R was gifted with a great intuitive grasp, great loyalty, great outrageousness, great humor and great all-embracing passion. He trusted his passions completely. These qualities made him a worthy successor. He was also vain, lazy, self-indulgent, sometimes vicious, and fearful of humiliation. As all but the Prince would live to learn, these qualities also bore their unfortunate fruit. But R and I became close friends from the first time we met.

6)

"The purpose of Buddha dharma altogether is to enable us to be true lovers to this world.

"Oh, you say, but this world is an illusion, it is endless, cyclical suffering. Our emotional attachments and aversions keep us bound to endless pain and confusion. Isn't that what the Buddha said?

"Yes, that is what the Buddha said. Of course. But why did he say that? So that we could escape? So that we could train our minds to inhabit some invulnerable realm, or become as transparent as space?

"But my dears, we already are transparent as space. Frighteningly so. Hopelessly so. And filled with love as the sky is filled with light or darkness, for that matter. And the world, this illusion, these phenomena that are all around and within. To say they are unreal, what good does that do? They're here. Or not here. Beautiful or terrifying, charming or dull. Like bubbles. Here. Not here.

"Moment to moment, the world and we arise. Pop. Pop. Pop. Each time slightly different. Slightly the same. Always new. Always.

"How can we not love this? Loving it, how can we not strive to love each moment clearly, perfectly, thoroughly? Without bound or limit. Loving this world truly, how can we not strive towards eliminating from our mind-stream the many kinds of pollution that makes love small, timid, scheming, grasping, that makes it own-able, stable, controllable? That makes it, in short, our love.

"You see, people usually think the problem is how they should or can love. But the far greater problem is how to accept the love that is given to us. The love that another gives us, that the world gives us, that each moment gives us.

"Because, when you accept that love, open to it, you dissolve. Would the true lover then disappear into love? Obviously so. Why not? Would that fix anything? Who can say?"

For once, the large crowd had no questions. I was glad. I wanted to go back to my room and sleep.

7)

I had been in the ceaseless ferment of the Prince's world for several years. Headaches and stomach problems came to afflict me frequently. A doctor told me that my life was too exhausting, and I needed rest if my health was not to suffer permanently. The intensity of all this passion was wearing me out. But the whirlwind around the Prince went on and on. New faces, old faces blurred. I no longer cared. The Prince became ever more energetic, but I felt ever more detached. I was tired and sick. I kept to myself as much as possible. It was a relief when our caravan, now much larger, finally returned home.

8)

In our time away, the encampment had changed. Hundreds more men and women had arrived. New tents and lean-tos were scattered in the trees along the hillsides. Scavenged timber from ruined barns and houses had been used to construct a shrine room, a new house for the Prince, stables for the Princess' horses and a rough pavilion of offices. The students whom the Prince had sent ahead had overseen everything. Proudly, they stood in line at his return. At their head stood the Princess, their new first-born son in her arms.

The Prince lifted up the infant who stared back gravely. He proclaimed in a loud voice: "Because my son is so beautiful and strong, now I have no doubts that the teachings will flourish."

9)

For two weeks, I was sick and didn't leave my bed. When I recovered, I had no job. Several young women whom I knew only slightly had replaced me. I tried to speak to the Prince, but was told he was busy. When finally I ran into him on a path, he asked: "Where have you been?" I asked for my old job back. The Prince invited me to share his bed that night.

In the morning I reminded him that I needed something to do.

"Don't worry darling. Something will come along."

10)

I then spent most of my time meditating. It was the one quiet place in the encampment. Everywhere else, young men bustled importantly making plans, building things. I did not care for this new atmosphere of ambition. I overheard discussions that made no sense to me. Guard brigades were being formed. Scholars were talking like bureaucrats. There were rivalries between those in charge of education and those who worked on construction projects. The intimate circle of friends and lovers who had surrounded the Prince was being supplanted by ambitious people, almost all men. They were, without doubt, devoted to the Prince, were in awe of him, were even afraid of him, but they were motivated by the desire to 'get' what he had, to understand and master whatever it was that allowed him to have power over them. Of course, it was they themselves who had given him that power, if it existed at all. So really they were trying to master themselves as they strategized how to learn what they could from the Prince. They would endure whatever difficulties and disorientations to achieve this. They tried to outdo themselves in displays of devoted service.

But there were casualties. An old follower, who had spent all his money paying to build an office building for the Prince, suddenly left. At a public meeting everyone expected the Prince to comment on the lack of devotion that had led to this defection. The Prince said:

"He wasn't stupid, you know. None of you liked him and he got the message."

So it was a very different atmosphere. The teachings that had drawn me were being swept up into something devoid of poetry. It was about politics. Now, when men flirted with me, I sensed that my former closeness to the Prince was as much what interested them as anything about myself.

I began spending time with the still secret Successor, R. At first I did so simply to hear the news of the Prince's daily life. He was constantly by the Prince's side. And R was equally aware of the changes that were happening. He tried to explain to me that for the Prince's teachings to expand, the passionate and domestic atmospheres I had enjoyed must inevitably fade. "Just don't forget how lucky you've been," he said. R went out of his way to be affectionate, but, as I knew, he preferred young men as lovers. And many, sensing his future eminence, though not similarly inclined, did share his bed.

Even though the Prince spent the night with me once or twice, I began to sense I had no real place there. The Prince's teaching still inspired me, but I thought I must leave. I did not know what to do. R advised patience; I tried.

11)

The Prince gathered his followers and proclaimed:

"There is a lot of energy here, and all around us, a lot of different energies of all kinds. We don't want to compromise that. But at the same time, we don't want this energy to disperse every which-way. We must find a way to gather all this energy in a way that will respect the integrity and the originality and even the wildness of each aspect. But we don't have to invent the wheel.

"We only have to think of a mirror in which everything will be accommodated. Everything in the mirror will shine out more brightly by being gathered there. Fringe and center are all held within this mirror.

"This will be our organization, our mandala, our chaos. We shall call it: Melong Karme, the Mirror of Action." Then he read this poem:

"Let our appetites be the Dakinis
"Set to guard the mandala
"Of the Co-Emergent Mother's blatant secret world.
"Dancing on this protected ground,
"Samsara and Nirvana blaze and burn."

I, no longer seated in the front, slipped out before the talk was ended. There would be, I was sure now, no future place for me. I was distressed that, even with all their devotion, none of these new followers had any feeling for the Prince as a human being. For them he was an icon, an oracle, a sage, a saint even. They tried to care for him meticulously, to fulfill his every wish. But even as they were feeding him, they were feeding off him. I feared for the Prince as he plunged deeper and deeper into the world of his followers. But he was, of course, fully aware of what he was doing.

I recall a talk where he spoke of students pursuing the teacher as if he were a musk deer. The deer's musk had a beautiful scent, had healing properties, was of great value but only obtainable by killing the deer. The student coveted this precious substance so he could become admired, strong and wealthy. The student's weapons in this pursuit were his willingness to submit, to mortify himself, to undergo any hardship to accomplish his goal. But such willingness was hypocritical, even if unconsciously so. When the student obtained the musk of the teachings, he would abandon the teacher. There had never been real devotion to what was beyond self-interest. That was killing the deer.

And surrounded as he might be by hunting dogs and jackals, the Prince was unafraid. But his assurance made my fears worse. In the questions following the talk, it was clear to me that no one thought the Prince's words might characterize his or her own motives.

12)
A caravan of merchants from the environs of Mount Koya arrived for a brief stay. They were accompanied by armed guards. Bandit gangs had begun to attack unwary travelers. I decided I'd join when they left and began packing. On the evening of my departure, the Prince sent a message. "I need your help."

Over dinner he explained: "The Supreme Abbot of the monastery at Mount Koya has consented to visit. It would be helpful to have his blessings for what we are doing. Could you carry my invitation to him?"

From long before, from my time of pilgrimage, I had wanted to meet the Supreme Abbot. I accepted, but later wondered if the Prince had not now contrived for me to separate from him. I should have been pleased to be leaving a situation that had become so painful; instead I was inconsolable.

Before I left, I went to say farewell to the Prince. It was a late cloudy morning with a touch of rawness in the air. He was sitting on the side of his bed, dictating a letter to his secretary as a young woman whom I didn't know knelt and cut his toe nails. While still occupied, he signaled me to sit beside him. I sat and I waited. I noticed that a long yellowish curved nail clipping lay just in front of me on the floor. It seemed to me at that instant, that this was every bit as sacred and valuable as the relics of the Buddha around which over the ages so many great stupas had been built. I picked it up and slid it into my sleeve. Suddenly an elbow jabbed me hard.

"Fuck you, sweetie," the Prince said sweetly but very clearly, "Give it back." His thick golden palm was outstretched. I blushed and gave him the nail paring, which he promptly threw in the trash.

"I can't stand all the politics any more," I said quietly. I felt suddenly overwhelmed with sadness.

"But it's better than religion if you want to know about reality." The Prince smiled softly.

Suddenly he grabbed my arm and smiled fiercely:

"Don't forget, my dear Lady M, to become a Buddhist is NOT the purpose of the Buddha's teachings."

The next day as we drove off, much to the astonishment and eventual annoyance of the merchants whom I had pressed into taking me with them, I wept for three days until finally I had no more tears.

VII. CONTINUITY

1)

Three times a week, Edward comes to Professor Akiyama's house. He hopes Harumi will answer the door but she does so only twice. She is friendly, flirtatious even, but makes no further mention of seeing him. He tries to put her out of his mind as he sits beside Professor Akiyama. Often, the old man asks him to read the text, section by section. Occasionally he signals Edward to repeat something. Edward understands that his teacher is declining. Sometimes he dozes; sometimes he speaks about this text or sometimes comments on a topic tangentially related.

The First Annal: Concerning Lady M. is clearly the professor's favorite part of the text. He often asks Edward to read aloud. As he listens, he smiles wistfully and quotes lines from memory. At such times, quite unconsciously, Professor Akiyama often looks around to see if his wife is near.

It seems Lady M reminds the professor of someone he knew or maybe knew of long ago. "More courtesan than nun really. But in which role is her love greater?" he muses. As he considers Lady M's life, the old man makes a slight, appreciative hissing sound. "Oh, such an unsettled creature. Nothing satisfied her long." And he shakes his head in fond exasperation.

Edward does not press. He leaves voids in the conversation, tempting the old man to fill them with more specific recollections. The professor does not rise to the bait.

In an effort to focus the old man's concentration, he asks the professor about the confusing sequence of reminiscences at the beginning of the text. Professor Akiyama smiles and quotes Michel de Certeau: "An absence of meaning opens a gap in time." This serves well as Professor Akiyama's approach to The Secret Annals. He tells Edward as if giving directions to a bus route: "You know, when the logic of one world becomes frayed, the door to another world opens."

Edward is reading aloud to the professor from the first Annals. The old man seems to be daydreaming but suddenly bursts in: "Does Lady M. remind you of my daughter?" Edward doesn't know what to say. Professor Akiyama misunderstands his hesitation: "No. no. Not Kimiko. ... Harumi. I mean Harumi." Edward finds the suggestion disturbing. He smiles vaguely rather than reply.

2)

Harumi calls his apartment one morning while he is out. She leaves a message that Edward is not to come for the next week. When he returns, he is surprised as the professor's wife, without comment, leads him into the small solarium at the back of the house. Professor Akiyama's bed has been moved there. He lies surrounded by oxygen tanks and bottles of strange dark elixirs. Edward is stunned at the professor's sudden collapse. He looks to Mrs. Akiyama for an explanation but she turns away and walks down the hall.

He sits beside the professor, listening to him breathe. He is uncomfortably aware of the faint smell of urine. Sometimes the professor's features relax and become smooth. He resembles the student in the sepia photograph by the bed. It is a formal portrait, and the young man sits stiffly in his dark student uniform. He doesn't wear glasses. His features are refined, and he looks out at the viewer, cautious, but quietly confident in his own intelligence. Edward suddenly finds it heartbreaking that the young man who once found the world so full of promise, has now become a broken, bad smelling gasping invalid. Edward asks questions, even detailed ones, as he tries to rouse his teacher and draw him back from this squalid realm of silence.

Edward is pained to be excluded from wherever the professor's mind now drifts. He is frustrated by the old man's indifferent gaze as his mind moves into shadowy depths. He continues to read aloud and ask questions. Edward feels like a fisherman trying to entice an ancient silver fish up from the shadowed depths of a deep pond. The Annals serve as bait, hook and line. Sometimes Professor Akiyama breathes through his mouth, his cheeks puffing out and in and looks like a carp struggling for breath. When not asking questions, Edward reads the text loudly, over and over.

One afternoon, when Edward again begins reading the following section, Professor Akiyama raises his index finger skyward and in a pedantic voice, says: "As Walter Benjamin remarked so interestingly: 'Imminent awakening is poised, like the wooden horse of ancient Greeks in the Troy of dreams.'"

Outside the professor's sick room, Edward can tell that the atmosphere in the house is strained. Mrs. Akiyama can barely stand to look at him when he arrives. Harumi, the one time he sees her in the hall, has obviously been crying. Once far off in the house, Edward hears a girl, Harumi almost certainly, burst out laughing uncontrollably. He hears her stifle her giggles and can imagine her pressing her hands to her mouth.

3)

Edward's apartment building is an already moldy post-war building, so he thinks it's the just wind rattling. Harumi is standing there cold and wet when he finally opens the door. He doesn't have a chance to react. She reaches up, and pulls his face down to her. Her tongue pushes between his lips and is in his mouth. It is a little bit cold. She pushes her whole body against him and her hand reaches down the front of his pants and rubs his cock. Their clothes are gone, and they are on his hard narrow bed. He moves awkwardly but she guides him into her. He comes instantly with a little cry. He is aware of her smell. She rubs against him and tries to continue. She exhales and lies back against the wall. His head is swimming.

"Have you ever done this before?" she asks. It takes him a while to answer.

"...Yes." He is embarrassed.

"Hmm." She lights a cigarette and stares as he hurries naked across the cold floor to the kitchenette to get a saucer.

"You know...my father is going to die."

"I... Yes." She bursts into tears and buries herself, rocking in his arms, sobbing. He holds her and strokes her hair. He no longer feels ill at ease. They rock slowly together.

He has never felt such tenderness. He begins to get hard and moves to touch her breast.

Suddenly she grabs his hand and is glaring into his face with an expression of outrage and betrayal. She is out of the bed getting dressed.

"Please... I just..." She gives him a look of contempt and is gone.

Many things run through his mind, but they all settle on the urgent hope that she doesn't tell her family.

Without any explanation, Harumi begins coming to his apartment every ten days or so. Edward never knows when she will appear. She knocks at the door, pushes him into bed. Makes love with disconcerting fury, smokes a cigarette, leaves. Sometimes she cries. When Edward asks what she is feeling, she turns away. She refuses to go out with him. She doesn't want them to be seen together. It's not what Edward wants, but it's more than he expected. He sometimes fantasizes that they get married. He becomes Professor Akigami's son-in-law, his intellectual and cultural heir. Now when he walks through the city, passes by men and women arm and arm, makes his way through hordes of office workers, sees couples eating together in restaurants, he feels a warmth of kinship. It is a new feeling.

4)

Several days later, Edward finds the professor Akiyama surprisingly more animated than he's been in months. He's excited about an article a Japanese friend living in Los Angeles has sent. He doesn't notice Edward's nervousness. The article describes an eccentric museum recently opened and tells in considerable detail of a singular exhibit. It seems that in the African rain forest there is a very large termite called Megalopona foetens, the stink termite; it is the only insect that can make cries audible to the human ear. This termite forages on the jungle floor and, occasionally by mischance, inhales a fungus spore that soon enters its brain. The insect begins to behave strangely, wanders erratically, leaves its accustomed habitat and climbs high up onto trailing vines. There, as the fungus consumes the brain, it fixes itself to the vine with its clamped jaws and dies. The fungus however continues living and consumes all the termite's soft tissue. Two weeks after it has died, a chrome yellow spike erupts from the center of its head and grows a further 3 centimeters. From this spike, spores again shower down to infect other termites that chance to pass below.

Professor Akiyama tells Edward about this rather horrifying phenomenon with unconcealed glee. He cackles: "See! See!"

Edward is puzzled and slightly disgusted. He asks how this relates to anything in the Annals. The old man shakes his head, disappointed at his student's failure to understand.

THE SECRET ANNALS
ANNAL I: Concerning Lady M. - Part 7

1)

Many years later, I re-joined His Majesty on the last ten months of his arduous tour of the kingdom and of all the lands and places where he had followers. I had heard he was near the temple I was visiting and could not stay away. I had not seen him for ten years, and the change was horrifying. The elaborate decorations in the shrine hall, the brocade uniforms, His Majesty's own black and silver robes, the gold throne could not conceal that he had aged unnaturally. He was an old man, and I could see he would not live long.

"Oh, I think they have not taken such good care of you, My Lord," I wept. He looked at me and shrugged.

"People come. People go. Who am I to complain?" I blushed. "Perhaps you would consider accompanying me once again?"

I understood that the main purpose of the tour was to provide public receptions in which His Majesty could meet with new students and see old ones once again. I was not alone in understanding he was bidding us farewell. When I was invited to join him, I did not hesitate.

He no longer resembled the Prince I had so loved. He was no longer able to walk, and was often subject to strange dreams and unearthly inspirations, and he spoke only in the most cryptic utterances.

Everywhere he went, people sensed that his end was not far off, and waited in long lines just to touch his hand and pay their respects. Many who came were old followers, but almost as many were those who had only heard of him and wanted to meet him, if only once. As before, I confess that I eavesdropped, and when occasionally His Majesty caught me, he winked with the same conspiratorial glee.

And as before, many people came to ask for his advice. Now he often repeated the same thing. With great ferocity he would hiss:

"Just do it."

Alternatively, when consulted about problems of the state he would say:

"Couldn't care less."

Otherwise His Majesty had lost interest in speaking. He insisted that those around him keep silent in his presence.

Once he insisted that I eject one of his new consorts. Asked why, he said: "She talks too much."

"But sir," the attendant remonstrated, "She is completely silent when she is with you."

"Yes, but she never stops thinking," he said, as if it were so obvious.

2)

On the few times in this period when His Majesty gave formal teachings to his followers, he would say:

"I know each and every one of you personally. I love all of you. You make me so proud, and you have prolonged my life. Please join us in the good, life-is-worth-living Shambhala. Life is worth living. Shambhala."

3)

In one of his Western cities, his ambassador, sensing that many changes would soon occur, asked His Majesty how he should conduct himself in the future.

"Preserve the autonomy of what you have," His Majesty whispered.

4)

During the same journey, an old student of His Majesty's asked him what he thought the future would bring.

"There will be no more golden age, " he told her.

5)

His Majesty blessed the marriage of two old friends who came to visit him on the veranda of his summer pavilion. Over their heads, he slowly raised a vajra, as he spoke, pronouncing each word with greatest care. "This is Padmasambhava's Dorje made of meteoric iron. It symbolizes ....
.... whatever."

And with that he touched their foreheads.

6)

Late one night as I sat by his bed, I asked if he was disappointed in any of his followers.

"No," His Majesty said.

7)

Still, old students sometimes insisted, as in the old days, on asking him questions about their domestic problems. One came to His Majesty to complain that one of His Majesty's attendants was having an affair with his wife.

"I know. He's having an affair with mine too." his Majesty replied.

8)

His Majesty rode in his carriage homeward through Kalapa. He was troubled by illness and in a bad mood. I was attending him

"This world is so fucking stupid." he snarled. I was shocked.

"But haven't you always taught us that it is basically good and workable?"

"You'll make someone a very good wife, sweetheart," said His Majesty with a thin smile.

9)

His Majesty gave a final talk at one of the towns he had visited frequently. The shrine hall was full, and His Majesty, speaking very slowly, urged people to uphold the Shambhala teachings in all their lives. He said, towards the talk's conclusion, that with these teachings, one could overcome the basic duality of human life.

A young woman shyly asked what was the basic duality of human life.

"Oh, you know," His Majesty smiled, "Cheerful and strange."

VIII. CONTINUITY

1)

Edward's visits to the professor now make him acutely apprehensive. He never knows if Harumi will answer the door, act indifferent or try to draw him into a fast furtive sexual encounter. He is terrified that Harumi's mother will attack him if she has discovered what's going on. He worries that the professor will somehow learn of the affair and dismiss him.

Edward finds safety in the professor's room. It is a relief to follow the meandering of the old man's mind. It is several weeks before Edward realizes the professor is moving steadily to an inevitable and absolute end. Edward is paralyzed. He can't really conceive of a world where Professor Akiyama is no longer living. He is ashamed that his first thought at this realization, is how the professor's death will affect his future.

2)

    Professor Akiyama frequently becomes agitated, erupting from his lethargy and speaking with a garbled urgency difficult to comprehend. He tries to describe a terrifying uncertainty he senses seething within the most banal and serene moments. "There is nothing that justifies it," he says. Edward takes this to mean the professor senses his impending death ever more clearly. The old man seems to read Edward's mind.

    "No, it's not death," the professor shouts, spittle flying, "...It's everything. Nothing stops..." With these words, he seems to find some peace and soon thereafter asks Edward to continue reading the Annals to him. For a while, he resumes commenting in a manner that is almost serene.

    "I believe Lady M. is one of those people who overcome the pain of inner unreality by telling the same stories about themselves over and over. You know people like that? Life may change us beyond recognition, but we can tell the story. No. I think Lady M writes her memoirs to make herself real."

3)

    Professor Akiyama's insight about Lady M. would be completely reasonable if the text were genuine. Edward wonders if the text hasn't become a surrogate for memories the professor would have preferred, a substitute world he would rather have inhabited.

4)

    As Edward sits with the professor, he feels he is sitting with him beneath a cloudy sky in a small forest clearing beside a dark, sluggish stream. A pine-covered mountain looms far off in the sunset. He has no idea whether this landscape is passing through the old man's mind, but the sensation is very strong. Professor Akiyama's occasional utterances neither confirm nor deny this impression. Edward sometimes thinks he hears a kind of high inhuman laughter.

5)

    "Ineffable beauty comes at the perilous peak," the professor says slowly. Edward recognizes the line as part of a poem by Mao Tse Tung. He knows from earlier conversations that the Chinese ruler is no favorite of the professor's. He once told Edward:

    "Mao, Stalin, Hitler, Tojo, all the other gangsters make the present extend backwards from their utopian future. They shape the present, suppressing history, editing texts beyond recognition, denying individual memories. Barren, violent, inhuman, this is the 'ineffable beauty at the perilous peak.' It is the present turned into absolute abstraction."

Speaking now as if the Prince of Ling truly exists, the professor insists: "He is entirely different. There is no conceptual framework. He does not hide in the future. He has no plan."

6)

Professor Akiyama listens as Edward again reads aloud the section about the Prince's travels to establish himself as a teacher on a wider scale. He sits up in bed and folds his hands as if he is present in the room listening to the talk and is himself one of the Prince's followers. The atmosphere surrounding the dying man is unsettling.

7)

One afternoon, Edward finds Professor Akiyama sitting up, bright and lucid.
"Edward. I have a question." Edward is apprehensive. He sits on the bed next to the professor in response to his gesture. He sits close to the edge.
"When I die, " The old man's eyes sparkle. "Do you think I will know?" Edward is flustered.
"Say that I die. And I will, you know. Then there's the funeral. My wife takes charge. You go back to the US. My wife maybe she gets re-married. My daughters maybe they get married ... Why not? Life goes on. You all live on without me.
"But what happens if when you see me die, some part of me thinks I'm suddenly getting well. I get out of bed and get dressed. I feel new life. Something different. It feels completely real.
"Perhaps this version of reality where I die is then not the only one. Why shouldn't there be hundreds upon hundreds of different realities where I have different lives. Where you have many different lives. Hundreds, thousands, all branching off each other at different moments. Each containing slightly different versions of me, of you, my wife, my daughters. Millions of moments filled with millions of versions of each of us going in slightly different directions, moving at slightly different speeds. But our multiple realities are weaving together invisibly. Our many lives are intersecting simultaneously in different versions at different points. We can almost sense it. It's dizzying, our pasts and futures weaving and falling apart, a vast swirling filling all of space." Professor Akiyama looks at Edward searchingly.
"There is a reality where I will live, but my wife will get sick and die. There is a reality where I live but my daughters die, or you die. There are realities where we all die suddenly. They are all happening right now or will happen or have happened. There's a world where my daughter Kimiko has become my wife. A reality where I found a cult. I go to America. A reality where I adopt you, Edward." The professor gives Edward a sly look. "One where you and Harumi are secret lovers?

Hmmm." He sees Edward blush violently. *All at once, a huge chasm opens in the air between them. It lasts a long time.*

"You...No," Professor Akiyama finally whispers and shakes his head. *Edward wants to disappear.*

"It was just ..." he stammers.

"You didn't..."

"I..." Edward looks like a little boy about to cry. He wants to say it's all an accident, a terrible accident.*

"Edward," Professor Akiyama looks at his protégé. *"Oh, Edward."*

Professor Akiyama turns away. He never mentions the matter again. Whether he forgets what makes him unhappy or is being discrete, Edward can't know.

8)

Professor Akiyama presses Edward to finish the first section. Edward is relieved that they are not discussing Harumi. When the professor talks, Edward takes notes.

Up to this point, 'The Secret Annals I: Concerning Lady M' has followed a fairly close chronological sequence. The following begins after a hiatus in Lady M's story.

During this time, the Prince establishes his northern kingdom of Shambhala, which he rules from its capital, Kalapa. Here, in the first 9 episodes, it seems Lady M attends the Prince, by then His Majesty, as he makes a final tour in anticipation of his death.

When he is silent, Edward sits, listens to his breathing and tries to match his own in and out breath with those of his teacher. He is pulled along in the professor's journey. He sometimes feels he can sense directly what the professor is thinking. The air is filled with the fertile green fragrance of cut grass. He hears two workers grumbling amiably nearby. He is not sure whether he is imagining this or the professor is or both of them are or neither.

Edward is not able to disagree with Professor Akiyama's surmise that Lady M leaves the Prince's encampment and stays for a very long time at Mount Koya. It is consistent with earlier parts of the text to believe she continues to go on pilgrimage, and occasionally, perhaps even frequently, lives as a layperson and takes lovers. There is no reason to think she has children or she ever abandons her practices.

9)

In the two final sections of Lady M's tale, she has completed the journey with which the Annals began. She enters the shrine hall where her former teacher and lover is dying.

Professor Akiyama's skin has turned yellow; his cheeks are covered with gray stubble. He is unaware that he drools. His eyes are wide open. Sometimes he seems on the verge of utter panic. He has stopped talking almost completely. Edward can no longer bear to look at him. He sits and waits and tries to imagine being anywhere else. A human being he relies on is slowly turning into something not human. A strange and horrifying mystery is taking place. The sour smell of dying, the strange gurgles, sniffs, farts and sudden gasps that the professor emits increase his feeling of claustrophobia. Edward cannot leave. He escapes by imagining himself completely in the world of the text. He is unnerved to find that he makes the translation of this section with far greater assurance than earlier.

10)

The professor is lying on his side. He opens one eye and stares at Edward for a long time.

"Edward, when I die, do you think I will know?" He closes his eyes. "Maybe I died." He sighs, then goes back to sleep. Edward is afraid he'll repeat the conversation, but he doesn't.

11)

Professor Akiyama whispers. Edward leans close. The dry acidic smell of a decaying body is strong. "Here." The professor opens his palm, revealing a small bright yellow enamel box with a seal in cloisonné. "My father's," he wheezes. The box is about one by three inches. "Chinese Emperor's seal." the professor breathes, pointing at the gold cloisonné. He presses it into Edwards's hand and signals him to open it. Inside is folded a brittle clipping from a Chinese newspaper which announced the execution of a woman spy named Jin Bihui. There is also rolled up, a small faded photograph of a woman in a man's cavalry uniform with the name Eastern Jewel written on the back.

Professor Akiyama pulls himself up. He looks Edward in the eye. "This is for you. It's a secret between us." He smiles and presses the box into Edward's hand. It feels very cold. "Another little mystery for you. Don't tell anyone." He signals Edward to leave. Edward looks back from the door. The professor is seated in an erect almost military posture staring into space.

THE SECRET ANNALS
ANNAL I : Concerning Lady M. - Part 8

1)
   SARVA DAKINIE MANDALA SVABHAVA MANGALAM
SVAHA

Droning voices of the monks repeated mantras over and over. Bells
rang, hand drums rattled, cymbals clashed, reeds whined. The din was deaf-
ening, and the air thick with clouds of metallic smelling incense. Candles
glowed on the shrine near the dais on which, surrounded by attendants, His
Majesty lay under a red brocade cover. The covers rose slightly and fell with
his breathing, and for a moment, there was a shallow liquid cough. I tried
to catch a better glimpse, but someone pushed me.
   I had been in the vast throne room before, but now it had been
changed. At the far end, a gauze curtain veiled the chanting priests. His
Majesty lay on a low platform in the midst of his court. In rows to the right
sat Her Majesty and the women of the court, all dressed in dark mulberry
robes; to the left was the Heir, the Prime Minister, the ministers and courtiers in steel gray raw silk and officers in black. Without calling attention
to myself, I found a place at the back in the crowd of His Majesty's servants
and subjects. I was glad that no one noticed me. My robes were still damp
from the sea, and the hems were stained. Without time to put on makeup,
I must have looked drained and haggard.
   The monks stopped, and I recognized the steely imposing voice of the
High Priest of Mount Koya as he chanted alternating verses:
   "Great Dakini, Queen of Wisdom Space,
   Flickering amid glowing tongues
   In the heat of dancing fire,
   Radiant, devouring, untouchable,
   You are the vibrant essence that does not cease."
   Then the monks chanted mantras. Despite the demands of decorum,
wrenching sobs and soft waves of weeping swept through the hall. Nor was
I was able to contain my sorrow, when the High Priest resumed.
   "Wisdom Being, Spontaneous Light
   Rising in the ground of emptiness,
   Your crackling vermilion flames burn and rise.
   You are the quickness at the heart of life,
   Sustaining, intoxicating, consuming it completely.

"Restless, purposeless, vivid,
You ever ascend in ravenous fiery swirls of love.
You are the Queen of unappeasable yearning."

But I recognized this liturgy. It was 'Reversing the Call of the Dakinis'; its purpose is to turn the flow of consciousness back from returning to its origin and to reverse the dispersion of the body's four great elements. During my long stay at a sub-temple of Koyasan, we'd performed it once when one of the most revered priests had suddenly been stricken. I couldn't remember whether it had helped keep him in this world. Four young girls, wearing the elaborate gold crowns and shimmering multi-colored silks of deities, emerged from behind the curtain carrying silver offering bowls. They danced in measured steps as they circumambulated His Majesty's bed, and I knew that the ceremony was about to conclude.

"Queen of Queens,
Twining the blazing of the burning sun
And the cool nectar of the moon,
You are the vibrant wisdom body,
The pulsing melodious and eternal life of all.
Please, as space itself, accept our prayers."

SARVA DAKINIE MANDALA SVABHAVA MANGALAM SVAHA

In the roar of horns and thunder of drums, the girls dressed as deities passed near me carrying the offerings outside. They were so solemn, so obviously distraught, so intent on not making a mistake, so innocent that I felt utterly heartbroken. The rear doors opened to let them out, and overcome by exhaustion and grief, I slipped behind them out into the night.

2)

In the days that followed, I returned frequently to the throne room. I made a habit of coming just before dawn. Few courtiers were up at that hour. Thus, undisturbed by the two attendants who had sat with him through the night or by the priests behind the curtains whose chanting never ceased, I could sit beside my former love and teacher, and stroke his shrunken hand.

In the pool of light from the oil lamps at the head of the dais, I could now see him clearly. Had I not known who it was, I doubt I would have recognized him. He had aged forty years in ten. His skin was pale and drawn tight against his jutting cheekbones; his long moustaches and wispy beard made him look like an ancient Chinese strategist. His body was now small, and, most shocking, by some contraction of the muscles in his legs, his feet did not point upward, but extended straight without making a rise in the brocade covers. Under the clouds of cedar incense, I could make out a smell of organic decay somewhat like that of moldering leaves. I did not let myself think of how he was when we shared his bed.

Once, he opened his eyes, stared at me, and gripped my hand. He grimaced before emitting a strangled growl. He closed his eyes, and resumed his constricted breathless rasp. I don't know whether he knew me any more.

"He's more alert today. He's getting better, don't you think?" the woman sitting across from me said. And what could I reply? I nodded and made myself smile. I could only pray that it was so.

I left when the first courtiers returned and I wandered the streets of the capital that His Majesty had built and named Kalapa. The air was cold and foggy. I drifted in a daze past imposing government buildings, wide parks and stone-walled compounds. Then I found I was walking past an orderly array of food stalls and markets. Tea-shops were just opening. Grocers were putting out trays of cabbage and root vegetables, fishmongers were setting out tubs of ice; women swept the sidewalks, men of all ages walked slowly to work. All seemed slow and ghostly, half-floating in the mist. Nothing felt quite real. All our hearts trembled, linked to His Majesty as he hovered between life and death.

Why, just as a butcher lifted a squawking chicken from a cage, did I think of a priest, who was leading a retreat I once attended, a man who had known the Prince for a long time, laugh as he said: "Prince of Ling, Prince of Ling - Master of Illusion."

Then I thought: How quickly reality becomes our dream.

*

END OF ANNAL I

IX. CONTINUITY

1)

Several days later, Edward brings the professor new pages of his translation. He rings the bell and waits in the close humid air for almost twenty minutes. Finally Kimiko slides the door open a crack and stares out at him. Thin, disheveled, flushed, she's been crying. She glares at him with cold fury and hisses: "He's gone. You're not welcome any more. Don't you think you've done enough?" She slams the door in his face.

Edward turns away. There is nothing to say. His mind shuts down.

2)

    It takes a tram and a bus to reach Professor Akiyama's house. Back and forth, after three years, Edward makes the trip by instinct, but now he is deeply unsettled. He makes himself notice every detail. He notices there have been subtle shifts. He sees the bus stop signs have been repainted. He examines the itinerary. He doubts his own judgment and decides to make his transfer at a different station. He jumps off at an unfamiliar locale. Feeling at a loss, he waits in the hot early summer air for a tram that does not arrive. After ten minutes he realizes he has gotten off at the wrong stop. Reading the bus schedule somehow undermined his instincts. He wonders if this has become generally true. He is waiting for the next tram when he hears someone, a young man, burst out laughing. Edward doesn't turn. He thinks the man may be laughing at him.

3)

    He wants to cry, but cannot. His chest feels like it's made of thin brittle metal. He drinks some sake but it has no effect. He can't read. The light from his desk lamp is hard. He turns off the light and tries to sleep. Just as he is about to drift off, two women in the street below his window begin screaming at each other in the street. They're drunk. One shrieks that she's been a good friend and doesn't deserve to be treated this way. The other shouts back that she's not going to lend any more money. A chorus of angry neighbors begins shouting: "Shut up." The women shout back: "Fuck you." Windows slam, car tires squeal. Edward lies rigid in the bed and imagines that the sounds are passing through him. Eventually he falls asleep.

4)

    Edward wakes late the next day. It is overcast and he does not know the time. He makes himself remember that Professor Akiyama is dead. He knows it's true but it doesn't seem real.

5)

    Edward phones the professor's house. A stranger, a middle-aged sounding man answers the phone. Edward asks to speak to Harumi. The stranger asks who is calling and Edward answers. There is a long silence. He hears the man walk to and from the phone. The man tells Edward that Miss Harumi is not available. Edward says he will call back later. The man says that this will not be necessary. Edward does not know what to do. He is lost. He sits down to translate the Second Annal. At least, he knows the professor wants that done. It's a way to continue their life together.

6)

Edward once read a study in the newspapers, or perhaps the professor told him, those long-term prisoners who suddenly find their cell doors unlocked do not leave. At first they are simply afraid of the world outside. Secondly, they simply cannot believe that they are suddenly in a world where they could be free. As he sets out to translate this section, Edward thinks of this. Despite feeling enervated and depressed by the professor's death, he cannot conceive of stopping.

This document, purporting to be the report from a spy sent by a nearby lord, is a negative view of the Prince of Ling's followers and organization. The calligraphy is unrefined but efficient. It is not obvious why it is included in The Secret Annals, much less given a place of prominence. Professor Akiyama believes that the most likely reason is that the document seems to validate the existence of the Prince and achieves this purpose with sly effectiveness by being so dismissive.

This section is easy to translate. Nonetheless Edward finds his mind drifting. He feels the professor hovering nearby. It is not an entirely pleasant sensation. He wonders, after spending so much time with his teacher, if he has not inadvertently come to share something of the dead man's mind. He thinks about Harumi. Is she too upset to talk or is their affair at an end? He doesn't know how to sort it out. Edward finds the author's business-like reporting in what follows and his astringent cynicism bracing in this context.

7)

Edward calls and again tries to speak to Harumi. This time, though someone picks up the phone, no one speaks. He can hear faint breathing. Edward is sure it is Harumi. "Harumi," he says as gently as he can, "Harumi, I know it's you. I..." but before he can continue, she hangs up.

II. THE SECRET ANNALS: THE SECOND ANNAL

A SECRET REPORT

"The real gods are those that one serves instinctively, compulsively, day and night, without having the power to transgress their laws, and without even any need to worship them or believe in them."

(*Marguerite Yourcenar, Souvenirs Pieux, translated as Dear Departed - Farrar, Strauss Giroux, 1991)*

II THE SECRET ANNALS
THE SECOND ANNAL: A Secret Report

1)

My Lord H, in accord with your orders, for the last seven months, I have secretly observed the cult developing around the person known as the Prince of Ling. I have, as you know, performed several similar investigations and am grateful that you have been kind enough to entrust me with this mission. I hope the results justify your faith.

Before setting out, information had been received about the growing number of followers attracted to this Prince of Ling. Accordingly, it was your wish to know if any immediate action should be taken to curb their activities. In your instructions, you indicated that you were not contemplating direct intervention now, but sought information as to whether this cult could pose any kind of threat to future territorial aims in the central northern provinces.

Based on what I have seen with my own eyes and been told by people in the cult itself (They confided in me, ignorant of the fact I did not share their convictions.), it can safely be concluded that this group will present little cause for concern in the foreseeable future.

The founder has great brilliance, charisma, power and, it may be admitted, a uniquely inspired approach in what he teaches. However, his considerable strengths and the sheer range of his genius will, in my view, create the conditions of future failure.

Efforts to confirm or deny his status as an Ainu prince met with fail-ure. His credentials as a Buddhist priest who has visited China and Tibet do however seem to be true. That he regularly drinks to excess and sleeps with a very large number of women, though this may ultimately undermine his health, does not compromise his reputation or impair his ability to attract followers. Quite the contrary.

In several important ways, this 'Prince' does not conform to the methods of the more familiar kind of cult founder. He appears indifferent to money. He does like fine clothing, furnishings and horses for his wife, but purchases them himself. Someone on the inside of his administration told me that for more than five years, the organization had been supported almost completely by the Prince himself through fees and gifts he receives for lecturing. Another man, the Prince's secretary, told of looking in his bureau and finding all kinds of gold bars, silver ingots, gems, tossed there casually and forgotten.

Similarly, he takes no interest in holding power over people. True, he often makes great efforts to cultivate some of his followers, but sooner of later, he leaves them to their own devices. He encourages active skepticism and goes out of his way to make no promises or claims for the practices he teaches. He does not provide simple explanations. He takes pains to know what his followers are doing, but he does not provide an atmosphere to help or support them. He fosters an ambience in which all his followers feel isolated and on their own. Though he never abandons anyone, he does not encourage a sense of security. He neither conceals nor justifies his own behavior. As he says: "I want to make tough gentle people."

He tells his followers: "Things are worse than you think. You don't want anyone to know the secret hells you create in your own minds. And you don't want to know the kinds of hells you inflict on others." When he says things like this, he often laughs.

Despite such remarks, the Prince has attracted followers from all levels of society. The core of his adherents come from relatively wealthy backgrounds and are well educated. Few however have abandoned success-ful occupations or established positions of power to join him. Rather, the followers are people of intelligence who have been unable to find their place working in secular society and are, at the same time, averse to engaging the austerities of traditional spiritual institutions on anything other than an occasional basis. Thus the Prince's blend of spiritual and secular practice is perfect for them. It accounts for the growth of his following. Whether they could flourish in any other setting is not clear.

Despite the Prince's efforts to create an organization in which his adherents work together, it seems he has been unable to attract followers adequate to his inspiration or induce them to work together harmoniously. From what I have seen, many who work for the organization are sincere and hard working, but the higher echelons tend to use their positions to indulge in personal idiosyncrasies and desires. Extravagant sexual behavior, insistence on being treated in a special way, cultivating cronies, making displays of their 'insider' status, accepting gifts for favors and giving preferential treatment to those who become their lackeys are as common as in all other corrupt organizations.

I have seen almost all the principal functionaries of this cult behave this way. For instance, the man who is the director of education told me that he did not like to be "in any situation where I am not acknowledged to be the foremost". Another important functionary said that the Prince's words could be interpreted in any way useful because "he says different things all the time". Another said that he was "in constant contact with the Prince through mind alone". One man, charged with religious instructions gained a personal following by complicating his teachings so that he alone could explain them. Another, charged with a similar task, was reluctant to endorse the Prince's work publicly "as a personal matter of policy". One charged with legal affairs treated his near equals with disdain: "You don't really belong here," he often told them. "She isn't ready," said one representative declining a woman's request for instruction, where in reality she had refused to sleep with him. Each seems to feel that he, or in some cases she, alone truly understands the Prince. In this climate, the functionaries disparage each other and squabble continuously. As one young woman told me: "The one thing all the Prince's older followers have in common is that none of them agree on anything."

It must be said that the Prince's own methods are often at fault. He does not appoint people to positions based on their talents and skills. Rather, he seems guided in his choices by more poetic notions. I heard of one incident in which he requested one man be made head of his personal guards; his administrators thought he meant a very different man with the same name and installed him. The error was viewed as something other than chance; the wrong man remained in this position. On several occasions, the Prince appointed artists to take charge of finances, merchants to supervise educational endeavors, warriors to superintend the elderly. "Don't spend too much time on any one thing," he told his treasurer. "Don't let lawyers determine anything," he said to an administrator. He asked just about anyone without such ability to cook. Here I myself experienced the unfortunate results of this mode of selection.

This is clearly part of the Prince's teaching method. All followers I spoke with had occasionally been asked to undertake unfamiliar tasks such as running hotels, designing bows and arrows, sewing elaborate costumes, teaching, gilding, pottery making, financial management, putting on art exhibits, managing a jewelry company. This has fostered confidence about engaging the phenomenal world and a fair amount of humor if not true expertise.

Such daring might provide a source of strength were the followers capable of humility and harmonious behavior. A young man told me that, on returning from a long speaking tour, the Prince was utterly shocked that his higher functionaries had not come together either for a social occasion or to meet for any other reason. Thus, based on my detailed observation, it appears that the Prince must devote much of his time to keeping peace within his organization rather than making the kind of efforts he might like in order to expand dramatically. He does not resent this.

The Prince has innumerable passions and interests and is able to encourage a great diversity of activities. Naturally enough, each one so encouraged feels that he or she is bearer of the Prince's most essential concern and has scant regard for what the Prince has encouraged in others. So, rather than respect each other as bearers of other parts of the Prince's genius, they compete endlessly. Puzzlingly, the Prince appears to encourage constant rivalries and factions.

The rumors are correct that this Prince has formed a corps of guards in an attempt to stabilize his territory and to protect himself and his followers from the increased hordes of armed gangs, bandits and samurai who have lost their masters. It should also be noted that the Prince is often attacked verbally in his public appearances and even his own students occasionally treat him with disrespect. His troupes might be a matter of concern if the Prince were not more eager to use martial arts, drills and so forth as a method of training than he is to create a serious military force.

Strangely enough, my lord, he also seems anxious to use his military training as a way to inculcate reverence for traditional political rulers, such as yourself. When your cousin was recently assassinated, the Prince held a lavish funeral at which, his face streaked with tears, he spoke at length of your kinsman's valor. It was impossible to doubt his sincerity.

Perhaps an organization could bring the multiplicity of the Prince's aims to fruition in the world, but it seems that the followers cannot abandon their self-interest in order to do so. Perhaps also, they do not have the simple confidence. They are, it should be pointed out, no more egoistic or cowardly than other people who, I doubt, could do much better. More crippling in the long run is the followers' absorption with the minutiae of the cult's inner politics. The result is an inward looking organization with little interest in engaging the world on any but its own terms.

Thus it is unlikely that the organization will survive the Prince's death. As noted above, the Prince's health may not withstand the rigors of his way of life for very long. Then the older adherents, incapable of deferring to each other in anything, will go their own ways. The organization may, at best, then remain as a kind of nostalgic cult. All in all, the Prince's single-minded wish to create enlightened society seems at variance with what people in this world can bring themselves to accomplish.

I should make clear that while this task has been somewhat morally compromising, it was never dangerous. Aside from the tedium of pretending to meditate, simulating spiritual enthusiasm and eating poorly prepared food, I did not find my stay amongst the Prince's cult unpleasant. There was no lack of alcoholic beverages, dancing parties and complaisant, even eager, women bed partners. The cultists were amusing, some even very intelligent. All gossiped freely about the misdeeds of others so that my task, except in the matter of spiritual imposture, was quite enjoyable. I hope that your lordship finds my labors have been fruitful.

X. CONTINUITY

1)

The day after Edward finishes translating the Second Annal, it's gray and muggy. Edward takes the familiar tram and bus ride to Professor Akiyama's house. He hasn't slept well. Professor Akiyama' death has not yet penetrated his habitual routine. Professor would want to see the new translation and the momentum of his wishes has not yet dissipated. Also, Edward wants to see Harumi. He knows he's being unreasonable, but he can't resist.

2)

From a block away, Edward sees a long line of cars parked behind three black limousines, a hearse and a flower car. Men in black suits, women in dark dresses and a few women in kimonos go in and out of the professor's house. Solemn men in morning coats and grey gloves shepherd the guests to their cars. Edward recognizes many people from the University, people with whom he has associated for the last three years.

With a sudden ache, Edward feels hurt that he hasn't been invited. He was as close to Professor Akiyama as anyone. He should be allowed to pay his respects. He'd walk in right now but he's wearing khakis, a sweater and a battered raincoat. There's no question: he can't go. He leans beside a tree and watches.

There is a sudden hush. The casket, black lacquer with shiny silver handles, emerges from the front door. The door is narrow, and the pallbearers awkwardly switch positions to carry the casket from the ends. Mrs. Akiyama and her daughter, Kimiko no doubt, arm in arm, both dressed in black and heavily veiled follow the casket and make their way carefully down the front steps. It takes a few minutes for the undertakers to put the body in the hearse. This is what everyone except Edward is watching.

He is staring at the front door waiting for Harumi. Finally she emerges. She is adjusting her hat and straightening her veil. She looks up and sees him. She is slightly flushed but she grimaces. Quickly she turns away and joins her mother and sister. A tall, slender Japanese man in his 40's, quite handsome, comes out of the front door, moves quickly down the steps and fades into the crowd. He is wiping his mouth with a handkerchief. Edward doesn't recognize him.

Edward feels a huge emptiness in his chest. He spends the night walking the city streets.

2)

Edward sleeps feverishly. He dreams he is lying on a cot in a log cabin, drifting in and out of a sweaty sleep. Then he is walking through the dark of a narrow wood corridor.

Then he is standing in a doorway. The room before him is lined with rough timber and lit by a single candle. A woman wearing a heavily embroidered red kimono is bent over with her back to him. The kimono is pulled down to her mid-back, and a long stream of black heavy hair falls down across her naked bright pink skin. She is stooped over a small wooden table, washing her face carefully in a blue and white porcelain bowl. A round bronze mirror is propped in a red lacquer stand beside the bowl. The scene is delicately erotic and reminds Edward of a Japanese wood block print.

Very slowly, the woman begins to turn, looking back over her shoulder towards Edward. He sees that all her skin is an absolutely even flamingo pink and it shines in an unnatural way. As slowly she turns her head further, he sees she has only a large single, profoundly inquisitive eye in the center of her forehead. Her nose is even and elegant. She stares shyly at him and begins a smile. Edward sees that there is only a single sharp-pointed tooth, dazzling white in the front of her wide mouth.

She turns further, and in a delicate gesture poised between seduction and offering, she opens the red kimono which rests between her shoulders at mid-back. She shows him the single breast at the center of her chest, small and perfect with a tiny rose-pink nipple. Her gaze is steady, shy, almost modest.

Edward feels an inner struggle as he is staring before him at a being he may have read about but cannot really imagine. He knows with absolute certainty that were she to speak she would say: "You see, this is just how I am."

4)

Pounding on the door jolts Edward from a groggy sleep.

"Mr. Bowman, Mr. Edward Bowman. Open, please sir. Police." Surprised more than frightened, Edward pulls on a yukata and opens the door. Two small men in short haircuts and dark suits look up, surprised at his height.

"You are Edward Bowman?" one begins in hesitant English. Edward responds in Japanese. They bow. Edward does likewise, invites them in and offers to make tea. The atmosphere relaxes.

After a preliminary examination of his passport and complements on his linguistic ability, the police hesitate. They are embarrassed to explain that they've been sent on a request from the widow of the late Professor Akiyama. It seems, or she believes, that Mr. Bowman has taken a family heirloom.

"What?" Edward is outraged. The police are not anxious to press charges against a US citizen, but, as they explain, the professor was widely admired and his wife's family is influential. It seems that small yellow enamel box with a cloisonné seal is missing.

"It's not missing. Professor Akiyama gave it to me." The policemen look at each other. The senior officer takes a deep breath. He says: yes, when someone dies, there are often such misunderstandings. Edward is about to protest, but the officer continues that perhaps if Mr. Bowman will relinquish the object, all the difficulties involved in a formal accusation, arrest, attorneys, visa questions and so forth, all of that can be avoided.

Edward looks at the two men. They respond with a neutral stare and a shrug. It's up to him. He goes to the bedroom and retrieves the box from his bureau. Before he surrenders it, he takes the photo and the clipping and stuffs them in his wallet. He knows he has to give it up, but he doesn't want to abandon everything.

"I think you will find you have made a wise decision, Mr. Bowman. Thank you." They bow and leave. Edward realizes his position in Japan has become precarious much sooner than he would have thought.

5)

In the afternoon two days later, Edward comes home to find a battered carton of papers on the doorstep of his apartment. It contains all of Professor Akiyama's notes on The Secret Annals. They've obviously been thrown into the box hastily and without regard for order. There is no note. He calls to thank Harumi or Mrs. Akiyama. A woman he doesn't recognize answers but hangs up when she hears his voice

6)

Edward thinks he sees Harumi walking by herself in a crowd of students near the library. He hurries to catch up, but loses her when she turns a corner far ahead. He wonders what he would have said or if he would have had the courage to speak to her at all.

7)

A few days later, Edward is denied access to his office of the university. "We're very sorry. This was the professor's office of course, and now..." An embarrassed bursar tells him. He calls former colleagues for help. All find one reason or another to avoid him. His library pass is unaccountably withdrawn. He has become some kind of pariah.

8)

Edward thinks he sees Professor Akiyama moving briskly across a park at sunset.

9)

Finally Edward persuades a young librarian who has always been helpful to be his guest at an expensive dinner. The restaurant is lavish, and the librarian can't refuse. Edward plies him with sake. Eventually the truth comes out. Mrs. Akiyama and her daughters have told all the professor's friends and fellow academics that Edward, for his own purposes, forced Professor Akiyama to maintain an interest in a text he judged a fraud. Edward has ruthlessly taken advantage of the professor's age, has tried to make him convert to some unknown religious cult, and, in his dotage, has purposely alienated him from his family. He has even tried to molest the younger daughter and asked to marry her.

"These are lies. It's absolute slander." As Edward tries to explain, the librarian eyes him with detachment. Finally, as if looking at an utter stranger, the librarian says slowly: "But who will believe you, Edward? Why should these respectable people lie? You know what we lived through here. No one will even want to believe

you. No one will say it, but no one has forgotten the bombings. Everyone sees what is happening in Vietnam. People know that underneath the smiles, Americans are capable of anything." Edward is suddenly afraid.

10)

At night Edward thinks of Harumi, recalls holding her the time she cried, imagines them making love again, thinks of them living together. He knows he's not being realistic, but can't help feeling the loss of things that could have been.

He is sure he sees her in a tea-shop drinking with two other woman. She looks sad. He walks away before she sees him.

11)

Edward's grant to study in Japan still has four months to run, but he has nothing to do. He feels waves of resentment towards his former teacher. He begins drinking more. It is early fall and school is beginning. He sees young men hurrying to work. In a noodle shop he frequents, he sees a young couple touching hands shyly. Returning half drunk from a cheap bar in a trashy part of the city, he looks down a dark alley and sees an American soldier, pants around his knees, humping a Japanese prostitute. He's holding her up against a cement wall. Her skirt is up around her waist and bare legs wrapped around the soldier. She is writhing and moaning as the man grunts. As Edward passes by, he looks for a second. She meets his glance with eyes that are black and fathomless. He hurries away, but hears a woman laughing bitterly.

12)

Edward is hollowed out. He fills his days wandering the city, avoiding the occasional crowds of protestors, reading in the public library. The foundation that gave him his grant has contacted him. No one says anything. Everyone is very polite. But Edward can tell that everyone thinks something has gone wrong. They are ordering his ticket home. Edward has no idea what to do while he is still in Japan. He cannot imagine America, or Pennsylvania or where he grew up. He has no idea about anything that is called 'home'.

13)

Edward thinks he sees Harumi on the opposite platform of the subway. He begins to wonder if he isn't making it all up.

What is it Edward asks himself? Why is he tormenting himself? He knows that Harumi would never love him. Deep down, he knows he is not the lover she is looking for, whoever that might be. What he really longs for is the world in which they would be the lovers each is seeking.

14)

He feels almost seasick, but more aware than ever of the undoubtedly fraudulent nature of the text, he throws himself almost defiantly into polishing his translation of the third of the Secret Annals.

The Third Annal was the professor's first enthusiasm. "Poems like this show that a world can, if only for a fraction of a second, find harmony in unappeasable longing." It is, as titled, a series of songs. They are the most familiar kind of literature in the collection and possibly by a single author. They would seem to date from the period around the beginning of Annal I. The calligraphy resembles seal script, dignified and somehow fervent. Their diction, syntax and literary style have no clear Japanese antecedents.

They might be attributed to the Prince of Ling, but Professor Akiyama thought otherwise. He believed the poems were written to suggest a follower who, intentionally or not, imitated the Prince.

Of course, since the entire text is a forgery, the question then is again: why did the creator go to such pains? Professor Akiyama maintained these poems demonstrate a higher level of understanding and experience of the Prince's teachings than the preceding Annal would imply. Thus the three Annals together, with the second undermining the values of the first (while making the protagonist appear to be more real) and the third coming back to reassert those values, represent a dizzying level of guile.

At the beginning of this project, when these irresolvable considerations began to proliferate, Edward found that working on the songs brought a feeling of unambiguous exhilaration. Even if their context and meaning were not entirely clear, there was something direct in their conviction.

15)

Now, late in a sleepless night, as he rereads them in the dim and stuffy bedroom of his apartment, Edward is pleased that these translations once met with the professor's approval. He remembers the old man's smile. He is happy to recall the professor's happiness when the project was just a whimsical eccentricity; this before the professor delved into the world of cults and more obscure enthusiasms emerged.

Edward returns to the poems and their devotional atmosphere. He thinks that if he has to cling to something in a world that now seems utterly treacherous, why not this? However, the poems make him uncomfortable. They speak to him, then slip away. He might wish he could feel such conviction and passion, but fears some inner lack will make it impossible.

III. THE SECRET ANNALS: THE THIRD ANNAL

THE SECRET ANNALS: THE THIRD ANNAL
EARLY SONGS

1)

BLINDED WITH LIGHT

E Ma Ho
The army drops its weapons

He He
The merchants throw their money away

Ha
He is melted into a droplet,
Dissolves in her heart, disappears:
Emerging again as a letter in a dancing flame.

She is the rolling yellow-pink fire
That ends impoverishment.
She is the rising vermilion fire
That ends fear.
She is the continuous blue fire
That ends false distinctions.

They move together twined.

Joy, like a lightning storm at sunset,
Becomes the fourth moment.

2)

DOT

Dot

From plus of minus
Skandhas rise

Dot

Through a gap in space
We enter the non-thought realm

Dot

When I see your face,
My flesh melts.
My body turns to water.

Dot

When I see your face
This and That dissolve
Into the brilliant sun.

3)

CONSTANCY

Entered
Through the Gate of Passion

To the Place of the Heart,

No one has survived
Such shadowless brightness

Illuminating the spinning wheel
Of pleasure and pain.
With fear or fearlessness,
No one can be saved or parted
From this inconsolable love
Always born
From a fragment of itself.

Beginningless.

4)

Love from A to Z
The gentle dispersion of atoms
Of a body alone:

This autumn moment of complete perfect sadness
Radiating in the heart
Bringing to the eye
The world seen instantly entire:

Oh so lovely circling
Brave sun gilded orb
Provocative and sad
Containing all

A moment, a dot
To be loved utterly

So the huge restless roar of a torrential wind
Brings suddenly, fancifully,
Waves of soft snow.

5)

THE LAST POEM

When all the atoms
Have dissolved,

When the dots

Have returned
To the primordial state,
There will
Still and always
Be

This love we share

This lotus flame,
This love
This love

6)

AFTER COMPLETION

The flames of passion
Consume and liberate the unhesitant lover
Into the elemental realm of uncaptured joy.

HRIH
Lightning flashes, dark mountains,
Gold skies, rainbow palaces
Roll off your great red tongue,
Declaiming the syllables of existence
To those caught in memory-grasping grief;
And showing in your devastating smile,
The unquenchable love that liberates the lover
Into the sky of mind itself.
Dissolved there
Beyond yes and no,
There or here,
Inseparable.

Thus may a warrior
Dwell in sadness
Without a moment of regret,
And dance like a spark of light
On the sharp points
Of your gnashing teeth.

7)

A GLIMPSE OF TILOPA

Like the outward view
From the edge of a high cliff,
Like dawn above an abyss,
The desert is immense,
Probing, delicate, silent, alive.

On the still cool air,
Soon to be an ocean of heat,
The stirring of a grain of sand
Suggests the impossible beast,
The equivocal monster,
Vivid and ceaselessly stalking,
Which you may become.

In the roaring of the fire,
Your skin, your fur,
Your stripes and claws
Assume the fabulous wings
Of the desert's word.

8)

I, who by my inadvertent life and being
Have given life to all being;

By the vast space
Which, laughing and crying,
Enters the small,

May the golden face of the only teacher,
With his smiling mouth and three impassive eyes

Shine always on the wanderer who does not dwell.

May we ever enjoy the tantalizing Mahamudra kiss
As the rain of kindness pours down
And soaks us through the skin.

So the world consumes us
All.

XI. CONTINUITY

1)

 Edward decides he may as well discover what he can about the clipping and photograph in the enamel box. The professor wanted him to have them as well as their container. He has nothing else to do, and can't quite steel himself to continue translating. It will be easier to satisfy his curiosity while still in Japan. He is now barred from the university library, so he turns to the national public library. The reading rooms are filled with furtive, shame-faced men of all ages in shabby suits. They are, Edward guesses, unemployed. The atmosphere of dejection is pervasive.

 Research goes easily and more quickly than Edward had really wanted. Most of the sources are in Chinese, but Edward soon finds enough in Japanese to determine that the woman in the photo and the spy who was shot were one person, Yoshiko Kawashima. She was a Manchu Princess, raised in Japan by a high official in the security services said to have raped her. "Oh," he reads in an interview," no one liked her. She was the only girl who rode a horse to school. What did she expect?" She returned to China and spied for the Japanese. She had lovers, both men and women who amused her and advanced her aims. In all her convoluted intrigues, her one goal seems to have been to establish Manchuria as an independent kingdom. She persuaded the deposed Chinese Emperor, the last of the ruling Manchu Ching dynasty, to assume the throne there. She created her own army of 3,000 riders, most formerly bandits. That this Manchu kingdom was merely a Japanese puppet state, was, Edward guesses, simply momentary necessity as far as Kawashima was concerned. It was merely a step on the path leading to the greater goal.

 She was a strangely alluring creature, glamorous both in her officer's uniforms and her gowns. She wrote sad, longing pop songs in Japanese and Manchurian and recorded them. When Japan fell, so did Manchuria. She hid in Beijing where Chiang Kai-Shek's counter intelligence officers found her and shot her as a traitor.

 Edward realizes Professor Akiyama's father must have been one of Kawashima's lovers. Whatever kind of affair she had with him would have been part of her stratagem to bring a Manchurian kingdom into being. And he would have been part of its strange hybrid court. He would have known how she was using him. Perhaps he wouldn't have cared. Certainly, in all the time he was in the prison camp, he would have thought about her. And afterwards, as he sat silent in his bedroom?

 Edward imagines the atmosphere in the house as Professor Akiyama grew up. Perhaps it's not so strange that the professor also became fascinated with another fanciful kingdom, even if it only existed in a questionable text. Edward wonders where he fits into all this.

2)

Edward feels that his relationship with Harumi has changed him. He feels less naive, less hopeful, both more adult and more lost. He knows that to call whatever happened between him and Harumi a relationship is ridiculous. How, he wonders, can one be changed by an illusion?

3)

Edward passes a small demonstration outside the main administration building. He hears someone shout: "Yankee go home."

4)

The six weeks remaining of his stay in Japan spread out before him like a flat empty sea.

Edward begins to work on the Fourth Annal. He needs the routine as a distraction from the expanse of uncertainty and disappointment around him. He finds it soothing to immerse himself re-telling the story of K., a person making his way in alien circumstances.

5)

The Fourth is longest of the Annals. Edward finds this section the most piercing. So many uncertainties and weaknesses are mixed with an unimaginable intensity of inspiration in this account of how a religious movement becomes a social organization with territory and boundaries. And this is intertwined with the life of the Prince of Ling as he transforms from religious leader to ruler and king; his followers evolve with him from a group of spiritual cultists into a government and court. Like the first annal, it is inscribed in late Heian style running script. And again, the paper dates from the 15th-century, well before the period described.

Aside from its inevitable focus on the Prince of Ling and his principal followers, this part of the Annals also presents the partial biography of a minor figure, a young man of some education and intelligence who manages to become the Prince's brother-in-law, but who is otherwise of no real importance. While he believes the Prince to be a genuine and revolutionary leader, this young man is constantly subject to doubts and misgivings about the overall enterprise. Perhaps he would leave if he had the courage or imagination to create his own life. He does not however, and so displays the mentality of a person perpetually engaged in the willful suspension of disbelief.

IV. THE SECRET ANNALS: THE FOURTH ANNAL

"Implicit in the imprisonment of language is the promise of freedom. Partial, it is true, but sparing us the worst. Thus we exchange the wordless imprisonment of solitude, silence, disembodiment, for suggestions of music, dance, transformation, promise."

"I beautified my life with days I never lived"

—Pascal Quignard: Albucius.

THE SECRET ANNALS: ANNAL IV - Concerning K - part 1

1)   Song From The Red Garuda's Flight. Part 1

Now is the dark time when hearts grow weak
And inspiration fades like a dream on waking.
In the world one daily looks upon,
The earth is being torn apart;
Mountains old as earth are leveled for temporary gain;
Rivers are turned into smoking sewers;
Forests are shredded, and fields laid waste.
The creatures of land and sea are killed off,
And those that live no longer have a home.
Clouds of fatal illness circle on the wind.

Nations shatter from within.
Ancient human cultures collapse into internecine slaughter,
Families kill one another for imagined slights or minute advantage.
Children are shot, tortured, prostituted, enslaved, made murderers.
Corpses fill the streams and lakes,
And all roads are choked with homeless wanderers.
Menace and fear shadow every thought.
The glories of the past are blindly bartered off
For a despairing future with no vision save brute survival.

In this very time, there is no longer any hope of an external savior
Now is the time when the only path must be recovered from within.
Now is the time when the only path must be found in what is,
In the innermost essence of air, fire, water and earth,
In the vast expanse of pure space and in perception itself,
In the unceasing pulse of the human heart.

On this great wind of sorrow and longing
We rise up.
On this great wind of love and longing,
The all-seeing Red Garuda spontaneously takes form
And carries us aloft.
SO
In the free radiance of space itself,
In the light of ceaseless love,
Our seeing takes shape.
SO

2)

K was the Prince's student and later, by way of marriage, his relative for almost twenty years. Though the Prince elevated him with the title of Duke, K was a disappointment, and knew it.

One cold evening when the Prince had come for dinner, K commented: "The problem is, I've never really been comfortable with your people." The Prince smiled thinly and took a long drink of rice wine.

"Neither have I," was his calm reply. K felt ashamed for failing to grasp the unbridgeable loneliness of the Prince's life.

3)

K was the second son of an established merchant. The father, atypically, did not wish his son to follow him in the family business, but hoped he would train as a scholar and enter government service. Unfortunately, K had an artistic nature and was prey to inarticulate yearnings and often lost in waves of uncertainty. It was, of course, an unstable time. Traditional spiritual, cultural, and social institutions no longer served as anchors. Things changed too fast. No one could live the ways his or her grandparents lived, nor believe what they believed. Amid the chaos, there was a sense of new possibilities. K was adrift. He was haunted by nostalgia for traditional forms and conventions.

Early one autumn, K went to hear the Prince, who was speaking in the large town where K's father had his business. He was not a spiritual seeker. He went on a whim. The large hall was covered with bright banners and filled with self-assured, even pompous young men, confident young women. Some were dressed opulently, others like vagabonds. The Prince, who wore conservative unostentatious black robes, was smaller and more burly than he had expected. His expression was mischievous. He spoke slowly in a high clear voice.

"Perhaps you think that by abandoning attachments to home, to the past, to opinions, even to desire altogether, you will discover something wonderful. You will find a clear, unchanging terrain, unmarked by temporary pain and passing confusions. Perhaps you think the Buddhist teachings promise this. You may believe that you will uncover a completely permanent, stable and pure space that underlies everything. You will make this your perfect and only refuge. You will try to discipline your mind so that you merge with this.

"This is an idea of enlightenment or nirvana maybe that is born from the chaos and seeks to escape it. This idea of enlightenment is the projection of a confused and pained self. It is the bedtime story of a suffering being.

"If we must say something about enlightenment, something about how enlightenment actually manifests in this world, perhaps it is closer to say that the awakened state is the same as life force itself: all-powerful, ever-changing, all-embracing, swirling, tumbling, rolling unceasingly through life and death and death and life appearing in every form and moment.

"It is not consoling, confirming, or restful. The awakened state, enlightenment, is not a state or a thing. It is a continual process that never stops. It is continually alive and moving. It is never confined to any definition or form of being. It is alive.

"I didn't make this up, you know."

The words burned painfully in K's brain, and he was afraid. The Prince was more in touch with the energy of living than anyone he'd seen before. K was drawn to something he couldn't understand or describe and decided not to return.

A year later a young woman he'd just met insisted he accompany her to the Prince's retreat. He was attracted to the woman and went. It was a dry winter, and the journey lasted three days and four nights. He felt ill with unaccountable terror. The unfamiliar spectral luminescence of the aurora borealis that blazed in the black sky made him feel he was entering a strange and magical terrain.

K's first face-to-face encounter with the Prince took place by accident the first morning he arrived. He was entering the lavatory as the Prince emerged, tying up his waistband.

"How are you?" asked the Prince politely.

"Just fine, thank you." K replied and bowed as he covered panic with showy courtesy. Later, he realized he'd begun his relationship with the Prince with a lie.

4)

A sparkling afternoon in winter. A cloudless sky the color of a corn-flower. Young men and women suddenly ablaze with an inspiration that eluded limits. Gossip and flirtation. People buzzing with anticipation. A dozen strangers taking a bath together, laughing. He had stepped into a world where a tidal wave of unspecified possibilities released the hold of the past on everyone.

Late one night, a woman came into K's tent, slid between the blan-kets, and made love urgently. She smelled strongly. K did not believe he satisfied her and she left quickly. He never knew who she was, and as he looked through the crowds of followers he often tried to determine who, by some glance or smile, it might have been.

5)

The talks were given in a tent. K sat to the side where he could listen without calling attention to himself. After a delay of several hours, the Prince entered, cleared his throat and began talking in his high clear voice.

"When you begin to sit, you discover that you have many, many thoughts. Your mind is a boiling sea of unending hopes, fears, plans, regrets, jealousies, schemes, lusts. Some are pet projects. Some are deeply held secrets. Some make you gloat. Some make you cringe. And you may realize that all your life you have thought that what you are is this amazing collection of thoughts.

"But as you continue, you may begin to realize that you have never chosen a single one of your thoughts. You have not invented their contents.

"You do not control their tempo or their momentum. You can some-times choose to prolong one or shorten another. But why are you making that choice? To find something pleasurable? Avoid a certain pain? And who determined that? Why is one thing pleasurable and another not? And why must pleasure and pain be the basic logic by which we think and choose and live?

"Our thoughts ride through empty space on an ancient wind. Their seeming contents are ancient cultural accumulations. They are not personal. If we do not try to make ourselves out of them, they return to the space from which they arose. And they find their own freedom apart from us. This means that we do not pollute our vast pristine space by trying to make it into a little desperate space.

"Therefore, our practice is to let things arise and let them dissolve. This is what's called mixing your mind with space. We do not leave any residue. This continued arising and letting go is our constant clean-up activity. As Buddhists, you see, we are cosmic garbage men."

An old man in rags asked: "How do you begin to meditate?"

"You fake it."

"What?"

"You just fake it. Maybe you fake it forever. Maybe you never feel your practice is genuine."

"But does that do any good?'

"We'll just have to find out, won't we?"

The next night the Prince resumed.

"Awake is real. Awake is not subject to conditions. Awareness radiates through everything that is perceived and not perceived. It is the life of all. Thus, when you let your mind, your being, relax into this, it doesn't matter whether you think your practice is good or bad, effective or not. From the point of view of the awakened mind, that's just irrelevant."

K waited in the lavender light of the waning afternoon outside the tent until the Prince emerged. He told him how moving he found the talk and thanked him. The Prince stared at him strangely and made a gesture of dismissal. K understood that the Prince had no interest whatsoever in any such gestures.

6)

K began to meditate, but found most of his time was taken up watching others, wondering about women, dodging his own fears, trying to amplify some notion of clarity or peace. K doubted this was meditation, but persisted and came to follow the Prince. He watched and listened, gossiped, remembered and finally took notes. He was sometimes in the center of things, but never part of that center. Writing brought no particular clarity, nor understanding nor sense of finally having done something worthwhile.

He was like that small indistinct traveler in the lower part of a Chinese painting, moving on the twisting path upward through an unfolding landscape of looming mountains and pines swathed in wisps of cloud, a landscape that he could never see entirely or comprehend. And despite the pain, occasional delirium and the general tedium of a journey that often seemed pointless, he could not turn back.

7)

People were aware of stepping into a whole new way of living. People couldn't wait to display their own place in this new world by indicating who was in charge of what, who was becoming close to the Prince and who was on the way out. Thus K came to recognize from afar the Prince's wife, his sister-in-law, his Successor, his secretary and many others. They all appeared possessed of a kind of assurance, moving in accord with rules and aims he did not know. He did not have to study the Prince's confidantes for long to see that the atmosphere around the Prince was intensely competitive.

In the Prince's presence, people found themselves confronted by an unrestricted intensity of life force. They found themselves mesmerized by hearing a talk, by having a conversation, by merely making eye contact from far off. Some found this unpleasant and left; others were inspired to make a leap. K felt both things at once.

All who became followers thought their personal experiences with the Prince marked them out for a special fate, a life beyond the norms they'd known. Continuous and grotesque displays of naked, paranoid egomania ensued. Each persisted in clinging to the certainty that he or she alone was truly, secretly on the right track, that he or she alone was "getting it" or had "gotten it". The Prince might try to break through this outlook with harsh rebukes, to soften it with the most tender and thoughtful affection; he might orchestrate campaigns of gossip and arrange long series of painful practical jokes; he might encourage the man's mate to be unfaithful; he might ignore the person altogether and have others do likewise; he might see that all that person's needs were tended to, or all of the above. It seemed impossible for the Prince to convince his followers that in the infinite expanse of enlightenment, there were an infinite number of displays.

So the Prince created further manifestations and further contrasts. Those close to him did not meditate as much as the regular followers. They threw themselves into promulgating the Prince's teachings and expanding his organization. They freely hinted that their work replaced meditation. Most followers resented their blatant display of avoiding practice. K found later that the Prince had indeed requested them to make such a sacrifice.

8)

It was early spring. The air was still chilly, but the grasses were bright and the trees putting out tender green leaves. K found himself on the veranda by the Prince's lakeside cabin. He stood at the rear of a small crowd of the Prince's followers and could see him clearly without being particularly visible himself. The Prince was drinking tea with two of the closest disciples. He held up a pale blue porcelain cup that seemed to glow with light.

"Look. And when you hold it, think of whoever made this incredible thing. What skill he had, and that skill, he learned from someone else, and that teacher learned in turn from another. Back and back to the first person who thought of a cup altogether.

"And everything we have: cloth and clothing, houses, boats, wagons, everything; and every idea, philosophy, spiritual teaching, practical teaching, locution, all of language even, it was all created and nurtured by someone else.

"So in this moment, we should take our time and recognize that we are living in the outstretched hands of millions of men and women who have reached out from the past to touch us here and now."

9)

Beneath a flood of milky light from the full moon, a slender woman led K up through banks of snow to her tent deep in the woods. The sparkling snow crunched under their feet, and laughing they sometimes slid off the path. He felt as he followed her as if he had strayed into an ancient dream.

She was one of the Prince's closest consorts, a woman with flirtatious charm, slightly snobbish, but that evening eager, curious. K was surprised that he seemed to amuse her. In the morning she called out to him, using another man's name. They spent the next few weeks together. She ended their affair as she drifted off, but somehow she managed to transform his infatuation into friendship.

10)

"The world is not arranged for your benefit, you know. The world has continued this far and will continue without reference to you. You may wish to believe that your perceptions, feelings and all your responses are part of the world's consciousness of itself. You may wish to feel that your actions are part of the world's continuous evolving. Say what you like, but nothing is saved. Certainly not you, or me for that matter."

11)

"No matter what it looks like," an older student who was later the Prince's successor said to K, "He always strips away the layers we hide behind. He never doubts that every being is an actual living Buddha." The older student sighed, then laughed. "He's relentless. He makes ego unbearable."

12)

There was a game that was often played over dinner when K first tried to find a place in the Prince's world. Whoever had never played the game was told that the object of the game was for him or her to determine what the game was. He or she could ask any question to anyone, and the game did not end until the player figured it out. The game was that all questions were answered as if the answerer were the player him or herself.

As the game was played, usually over dinner, the answerer became more knowing and sadistic, and the questioner more frustrated. Generally the game ended when the questioner became flummoxed and the answerers became bored.

K decided to ignore the smirks and smiles. He realized that if he did not ask questions, the others could not speak. He restricted himself to asking for food to be passed to him or offering it to others. Since the others were obliged to respond as if they were him, questions like "Could you pass the salt?" or "Would you like some tea?" produced a situation in which the structure of what was happening soon became apparent.

This game fell into disuse when there were few who did not know its object. Nonetheless, the atmosphere of knowing insiders putting on the spot those less in the know, competition and general one-upmanship remained a feature of the community until its effective collapse.

13)

The Prince made many of his new students teach almost immediately. One of the earliest whom he encouraged in this direction said:

"But sir, I have no idea what to teach." The Prince replied:

"Whatever you hear asserted in the Buddhist teachings, say the truth of suffering or the origin of suffering or cessation, karma, relative truth, absolute truth, whatever, first look in you own mind, your own experience to find it, to find if it really lives in you. Then, if so, look and see where and how it lives or functions in you. It's not a question of hearing something like "non-duality" and trying to make your mind stretch into the concept of an experience. It's really about finding, uncovering what is naturally there already, primordially.

"Discover the passion that inspires you and others will ride this passion onto the path of dharma. You listen to the students. You listen to them. Like listening to the space of a valley or a stream, you hear the invitation to speak and what to speak"

When the Prince asked K to be his assistant, K asked him how he wanted things presented:

"No party line." Was the Prince's swift reply.

14)

K heard that his martial arts teacher had died suddenly. He asked the Prince what he could do to help his former teacher.

"You should guide his soul," said the Prince.

"And what is the best way to do that?"

"Just talk to him."

15)

The Prince passed K who was standing alone in a hallway. He whispered: "Perpetuating the love affair with our own loneliness, are we?"

16)

K's affair with the Princess' sister, Lady T, was almost an accident. They talked at a party, drank too much, ended up in bed together. K was moved by her tenderness; she perhaps found his self-proclaimed lack of ambition a relief from other suitors. Soon they were taking horseback rides in the woods and became inseparable.

Often, when they slept in the Prince's house, waked in the night by the shouts, the thunder of footsteps, more shouts, the crash of dishes as the

Prince and Princess careened through the house fighting. At breakfast, they would try to act as if nothing had happened, but the Princess or the Prince would turn to each in turn: "You heard what I said. Tell her I'm right." As the Princess said: "You know what I mean. Tell him." K would raise his hands in surrender and remain silent.

17)

K was not naturally given to being a devotee, and he couldn't resist occasionally making that plain. He'd been living with the Princess' sister for half a year when the Prince called him aside. "I think you should get married."

"To whom?" K replied.

"My sister-in-law, of course," he replied with exasperation.

Even if the prospect of such commitment was daunting, K and Lady T actually enjoyed each other. At the wedding ceremony, the Prince said: "Being married will bring you two to earth." Afterwards the Prince sent K a calligraphy with the note: "A gentleman always has time for confidence."

XII. CONTINUITY

1)

Edward is alone in Tokyo. His time there will soon come to an end; his friends have vanished; his current occupation and future prospects are uncertain. Depression shadows him. He spends his remaining days in his tiny dim apartment and stares at the manuscript.

He glances out the window across the narrow airshaft where occasionally in the evening he sees a stout, middle-aged woman in a faded housecoat moving back and forth, cleaning, putting away clothes, heating water for tea. These tasks seem to give her solitary life purpose. She is utterly unaware Edward is watching.

He has no particular reason to look at her. Light from the small square of lavender sky filters down between the buildings and is, at this level, charcoal colored. The dim yellowish light from the old woman's window draws his attention. It seems that his focus, his entire existence hovers disembodied in the filtered light. The simple tasks of daily life attract him, but he is living in the interstices like a ghost.

2)

Among Professor Akiyama's papers, this note is attached to the beginning of this section.

"All memories that ever were are still here, embedded in soil, trees, laughter, roadways, lakes, skies, starlight, rain, sorrow and wind. Even if the language of these memories is no longer intelligible, even if there is no one who can hear or see or understand or interpret these memory traces, even if these memories are glimpsed only as they disappear from our consciousness, they are still here as each patch of ground still holds the faint warmth of whoever has moved across the earth."

3)

The second and third sections of this Annal are devoted to the evolution of the Prince's court. The second focuses on the visit of the Supreme Abbot of Mount Koya and the third on the inspiration of establishing a kingdom. It appears that somehow the Abbot's grandeur and the elaborateness of the preparations play some part in this development. Nonetheless, these two sections are, for Edward, the most imaginative and seductive parts of the text. Even though the social evolution the text describes is not entirely attractive, there is an enthusiasm and hopefulness as if the writer, as well as those he describes, truly believe that they are part of a movement capable of changing the world for the better.

THE SECRET ANNALS: ANNAL 4 - Concerning K - part 2

1)

Shortly after his marriage, K and his wife were invited to a dinner that the Prince gave for the Princess' new riding instructor. The Princess had only recently met this equestrian master and both she and the Prince were determined to hold a most imposing banquet in his honor. Accordingly, all the Prince's closest followers, those charged with running the organization that was growing rapidly around him, were invited. They were told to wear their most formal clothes.

When the riding instructor arrived, he proved to be a most outlandish person. He wore canary yellow robes and had painted his face so heavily he almost appeared to be a female impersonator. His manner was more queenly than kingly. Though others were laughing in their sleeves, the Prince showed only the greatest pleasure in being honored by the instructor's company. The dinner was lavish and lengthy. A great deal of alcohol was consumed.

As the dinner became more boisterous, the Prince's Successor tried to turn the subject to something more serious. He asked:

"Sir, if enlightenment is the natural state, why did all the great realized ones of the past take vows, sit in the full lotus posture, and wear robes?"

The Prince looked around the table without saying anything.

"Because of compassion," K was dining for the first time in this group and blurted. The Prince said:

"That's it." The Successor looked at him with new curiosity:

"How did you know?" The Successor had once propositioned K, but did not seem to mind when K refused. Now K didn't know what to say. Almost immediately, the Prince had a coughing fit. It seemed he had swallowed something that was obstructing his breathing and he heaved, falling out of his chair, trying to gasp for air. Attendants raced to him, and massaged his chest. The atmosphere was tense and still. It seemed that the Prince could easily die. After a while, he recovered, and resumed his place, smiling at the head of the table. However, he soon withdrew.

This was the first time K had seen the Prince in this condition. He was told it had happened before, and indeed, K saw him have such fits many times thereafter. It was always terrifying, even if, as he sometimes suspected, it was an act.

2)

The Prince went to visit a friend's wife while she was in labor. She had a very difficult time and was in a great deal of pain. Afterwards the Prince commented in some surprise:

"It was very hard for her, but at one point she was screaming: 'Oh God! Oh God!' But I couldn't understand: why did she want to make a god out of her non-existence pain?"

3)

The first task the Prince assigned K was to find halls where his calligraphies could be displayed and sold. K had never done any such thing before, but succeeded in making arrangements that satisfied the Prince.

During that time, K had his first dream of the Prince. He dreamed that he was accompanying the Prince to a large assembly. A guard eyed the two suspiciously as they looked at one after another of the small masterpieces, each sitting on its own pedestal. After a while the Prince whispered: "This one," pointing to a gilded image of the Buddha, "We have to take it." K knew the Prince would not be denied, but was horrified. He could see himself being arrested and dragged off to prison. The Prince saw K hesitate, grabbed the statue, put it into his robes, and began lumbering towards the door. Guards began to converge on them. K jolted awake, bathed in sweat.

4)

The Prince invited K to travel with him, and one evening they were dining amid a crowd of followers. K looked out the door onto an unfamiliar night landscape; he looked around the table at all these women and men trying to impress the Prince; he realized he had no real friends. The Prince said:

"You don't have to believe every thought," and suddenly K was panic-stricken.

5)

"Perhaps you think of your ego as a complex of desires and fears that impel you forward, that create and then distort your relationship with outer phenomena, that cause you inner confusion and pain. And all of these feelings and experiences swirl, augment and continually frustrate each other. You would like peace from all this, wouldn't you?

And Buddhism, renunciation, non-attachment seems to promise a final disentanglement from all this suffering. Yes?

"And yet, and yet...

"Taking refuge in that which shrinks from contact, which dwells in unending silence, which is not subject to change or pain, which does not engage the world of such things.

To seek refuge in the end of all experience, the emptiness of all purpose is also a purpose and also a goal. As such it is another mask of ego, but a crueler one for being cloaked in a kind of superiority over all living beings. It is just a version of ego pure and simple. It is the ego of death. It is the ego of dying.

"So that is why we must let go over and over. We let go again and again, sinking deeper and deeper, down into the fathomless depths of ordinary phenomena. And at the very bottom, the very source, what do we find? An unending flow of limitless compassion.

"Perhaps you have heard that the Buddhist teachings, or the development of the Buddhist teachings are like a lotus which, in spite of being anchored in the mud rises and blossoms. An expression of purity that transcends its origins. But the truth is: one sinks deeper into the darkness and mud; one rises; one opens to the sun in flower: all at the same time."

6)

K happened to be seated next to the Prince for several hours at an afternoon reception. An unbroken stream of people came up, knelt and spoke to him about projects old and new: curricula for teachings; business ventures; personnel problems; concerns for health and well-being of the followers, and so forth. After one of the final guests had presented some plan or other, the Prince turned to K inquiringly. K shrugged. Then the Prince glared, pushed his face into K's and poked him hard in the chest and hissed intently: "Never forget: the family business is people."

XIII CONTINUITY

1)

Late one night, Edward goes to a neighborhood noodle stall and sake bar where he eats a steaming bowl of udon, drinks sake and reads whatever newspapers others have left behind. There are grainy photos of huge protest marches in the US, race riots everywhere. Edward doesn't want to know.

He turns to the back pages. In the science section, he comes across an article that concerns a recent scientific discovery in Europe. A map illustrates the article. Entomologists have found an immense set of interlinked ant colonies. All the ants are shiny black and fairly large, their genetic make-up is identical, and their huge, elaborately interlinked hives and colonies stretch from southern Spain, across all of the French Riviera, extending on through Northern Italy and spreading down into Yugoslavia. Members of one colony can enter another without disturbance. Individual colonies seem to grow or decline in response to natural disasters or human intervention as their populations shift to avoid destruction. This process has been going for on for at least two millennia. Thus there is a secret empire of ants whose domain still underlies much of the ancient Roman Empire and dates at least from that time. Scientific teams from Spain, France and Italy expect that further investigation will lead to a deeper understanding of the methods the ants use to communicate and organize their activities. They expect that many more colonies even further afield, will soon be found.

Edward looks around him. 'Why just ants?' he thinks. The suggestion of unknown societies thriving beneath the surface of our own world makes him smile. It echoes Professor Akiyama's notion that the Annals are documents important to a cult long hidden within the conventional world. Edward feels he can continue. He begins cautiously.

2)

Progress is sometimes smooth, but often not. Eventually his solitary and per-haps pointless labor becomes an ongoing struggle. Edward develops an incurable ringing in the ears. Though there is a medical name, tinnitus, there is neither a clear etiology nor an effective cure. The continuous noise, wavelike like a plague of locusts moving ceaselessly in the air, is maddening. Painkillers reduce the intensity but produce an anguished detachment from the world that Edward can endure only by working with single-minded determination. He translates The Secret Annals as if his life depends on it. Indeed sometimes it seems that his sanity does. It seems that his inner life is just an agitated, incessant electrical buzzing, while his outer life is a void punctuated only by eating, excreting, sleeping. He often dreams of ants. The Annals fill his mind with imagery that enables him to survive. He forces himself to concentrate on translation.

3)

The following section is the longest sub-section in the Annals and contains a vivid, if slightly random, evocation of the Prince, now his Majesty, as he set out to establish the Kingdom of Shambhala, There are loosely four main topics: the first involves proclaiming the kingdom, the second, founding it; the third gives a detailed account of the government and the fourth, the court. Though the text might make it seem otherwise, it should be remembered that there is no evidence that such a kingdom ever came to be. Professor Akiyama and Edward as well concluded that what is described here represents, despite its grotesque aspects, the deepest longings of the Annals' author or authors.

THE SECRET ANNALS
ANNAL 4 - Concerning K. - part 3

1)

Song From the Red Garuda's Flight

Winds surveying mind and beyond mind;
Where the golden feather-tips
Of the Red Garuda's outstretched wing
Touch the crystal radiance of space,
The wind of truth expands all at once and in all directions.

Where the Red Garuda's hidden tympanum
Is touched by the cold pure air of emptiness,
The bliss of song enfolds the whole of space.

Where the Red Garuda's golden eye
Meets the fire of a rising sun,
The bright visions of the pure world of Shambhala arise
In the center of the human heart
And on the very face of this earth.

Where the Red Garuda's wild love
Draws near to the heart of all,
The unchanging mind of the Rigden fathers,
Clothed in all the richness of the world,
Emerges from the gold and crystal palace of Kalapa
And appears now, free from time.

2)

The Prince determined that the time had come for his students to be accepted into the lineage whose teachings he held.

"Teachings that do not proceed from the lineage forefathers and have not been tested and expanded by the intense sacrifices of generations of men and women are like weeds without roots. The continuous experience of compassion that arises from meditation practice is the lineage and the blessing of lineage."

Accordingly, he invited the Supreme Abbot of Koyasan to visit the center he had established. This was no small matter since the Supreme

Abbot was virtually a monarch in his own right, traveling in an elaborate caravan with a large contingent of monks, guards, porters and attendants. It took the Prince four years simply to raise the money needed to receive the Abbot properly and to provide the kind of donations and gifts that would be expected.

The Prince spared no effort or expense in building a new shrine room and residence for the Abbot and his party. He had his followers refurbish the buildings of the encampment. They built new shrines and thrones, carved new statues and used yards and yards of brocade to line the walls of the rooms which the Abbot would occupy.

When the Prince entered a room where dozens of people had been working, everyone would stop until he had given his approval to continue. Usually, he would indicate one small change: placing a statue more to the left, raising a screen a half an inch, and when that correction was made, all the other defects became immediately clear.

Even so, it seemed that the Prince did not have so much respect for the Abbot himself. As he said to his community a few days before the High Priest arrived: "The lineage head himself may or may not have much realization. Either way, he bears the responsibility and the power of the lineage itself. Look at him with open eyes." On another occasion, he referred to him as "an ill-educated aristocrat."

When the day finally came for the Supreme Abbot to arrive, the Prince looked out over the new buildings and pathways and at the long line of students, all dressed in formal clothes, as the Prince had requested. Though it was obvious that many of the garments had been borrowed or bought second-hand, the Prince wept at their great efforts. "Thank you so much," was all he could say.

K was standing near the Prince and saw him weep. He was overwhelmed as it became suddenly clear how deeply and completely the Prince's love embraced every one of his followers. At the same time, K realized that he himself was afraid of being swallowed in this love, of losing himself in it and with that all sense of direction. K was ashamed of how pinched and poverty-stricken he felt.

The Supreme Abbot, the High Priest of Mount Kyosan, arrived in the early afternoon. He was preceded by mounted trumpeters, outriders on horseback, porters carrying leopard-skin trunks, monks carrying sticks of burning incense, and followed by more porters and guards. The procession consisted of more than a hundred men. It stopped, and the ten bearers lowered the gilded palanquin. The Abbot, enormous, radiant and wearing yellow silk and red brocade, stepped out smiling. The Prince suddenly threw himself on the cold ground in a full prostration himself and began sobbing. Later he explained: "His Holiness has attained complete realization."

When the Prince's followers saw the Prince treat the Supreme Abbot with such formality and devotion, they began to treat him likewise.

3)

The Prince relied more and more on his principal followers. Without them, it would have been impossible to carry out the innumerable tasks of his organization to make the enormous efforts involved in preparing for the Supreme Abbot's visit. K did not fare well in this period. The Prince's officials made it clear that in spite of or perhaps because of his seeming status as brother-in-law, he was, as he was told on more than one occasion, "not needed". K and his wife felt ever more frustration in the isolation that grew around them.

In the course of a long evening of eating and drinking with His Majesty, K mentioned the ways in which he was being excluded from any meaningful contribution to the Prince's work. In exasperation he asked about the officials: "Sir, where did you get them?" The Prince stared back with a look of dawning amazement on his face: "They grew on me...like trees."

K laughed, but it dawned on him that these men and women had indeed put roots down deep into the Prince's existence and had staked their lives in a way that he dared not.

4)

The Supreme Abbot was bedecked in all manner of gold ornaments and gold brocade. "Sire," the Prince could not help himself from saying despite the flood of devotion that welled up in him, "such opulence is viewed here as ostentatious and may cause people to think less of you." The Supreme Abbot smiled and replied: "You know, I think I will have some gold shoes made for me." The Prince was delighted by this reply.

5)

Late one evening after dinner, the Supreme Abbot who was by then fully accustomed to his new surroundings and very pleased, told two of the Prince's close students about his lineage and how he saw his place in it.

"In these times, none who have held this title has been very strong. Six hundred years ago, the third Supreme Abbot built a life-sized statue of the Buddha all by himself in one day. Another could fly. Now no one can do anything like that. On the other hand, I have discovered and trained more great teachers than anyone else in the entire lineage.

"But then again, the problem with me is that I do not necessarily tell the truth. When I say: 'The rebirth of this teacher is to be found in a yellow tent with a door that faces west by a green lake at the foot of a dome-shaped mountain in the Northeast near such and such village, and the family name will be so and so'; well, what do I know.

"But then again, I am infallible because the faith and devotion of all people will not allow it to be otherwise."

Then, as he looked at the stunned and puzzled faces of his two listeners, he burst into a booming roar of laughter.

6)
The Supreme Abbot was invited to speak before a gathering of scholars in a nearby town, and it turned out that the gathering was a banquet. The room was filled with scholars who were seated around tables where all were eating and drinking and gossiping. The Supreme Abbot had been assigned a throne at the end of the room on a dais. He entered, looked around, and saw that no one noticed he had arrived. He mounted the throne and sat there. Conversation abated only slightly.

"IMPERMANENCE," he shouted, then leapt off the throne and streaked out of the room. It seemed he had suddenly disappeared. All the guests felt a shock, but did not know exactly what had happened.

7)
As the Supreme Abbot's visit wore on, the Prince's attendants became more and more exhausted, and particularly they became tired of the endless ceremonial demands made upon them. Late one night as the Prince slept, at the Successor's suggestion, they decided to sneak out to a nearby bar.

Just as they were about to leave, the Prince appeared: "Going somewhere?" And when they explained what they were up to, he said, much to their discomfort, that he would join them. They went to an inn patronized mainly by wealthy travelers expecting the best of service. There, as they drank, the Prince would surreptitiously pinch the outraged waitresses, but he always managed to have his companions blamed.

"Wasn't that a pleasant evening?" he smiled when they returned to their rooms.

8)

During the Supreme Abbot's visit, the Prince's widowed mother-in-law also came to visit. She had formerly been considered an enemy of the Prince, and only after K's prolonged negotiations did she agree to meet him and to dine in his house.

On her arrival, the Prince had whisked her into a side room, and ordered his guards to let no one come near. When the two emerged some five minutes later, they were wreathed in smiles. The Prince raised both his hands to show K that she had given him all her family rings and crests, and that he was now the head of their joint families. They remained friends thereafter. Lady T was not entirely happy to have her mother at such close quarters.

Later, although he had some misgivings about his mother-in-law's former hostility to Buddhism, the Prince asked K to bring her to visit the Supreme Abbot. With the Prince himself serving as translator, the two chatted politely, until the mother-in-law stared intently at the Supreme Abbot, looked carefully at his monk's robes and blurted: "You know, if you were the marrying kind, you're just the man I would want to marry."

This was one of the few times when anyone saw the Prince caught completely off-guard, but the Supreme Abbot beamed at her and laughed.

9)

The long and impressive ceremony in which the Supreme Abbot enthroned the Prince's Successor was the high point of the visit. It took place in the main shrine hall and in full view of all the Prince's followers and an assemblage of local and foreign dignitaries. Long liturgies were intoned as offering upon offering; all kinds of grain, fruit, gems and auspicious symbols were heaped up on the shrine. The Successor wore a saffron brocade silk robe. The Prince extolled his Successor's great devotion and great gifts and emphasized that finding a successor was essential both to his own life work and to the lineage of awakened practitioners as a whole. The Successor, on his part, pledged his heart, tongue, hands and eyes to fulfilling the Prince's intentions.

K was following the Prince as he left the hall at the ceremony's end. Near the doorway, the Prince spotted a man who had until recently been one of his closest students but who had come to believe that he was so absolutely attuned to the Prince he had no further need to listen to him. The man was smirking. The Prince snarled:

"It could have been you."

Throughout the next week there were feasts and celebrations, and the Prince was insistent that the Successor's way of life now be in accord with his new station. He sent F, his trusted steward, to establish and run the Successor's household. But the Successor's faults as well as his virtues were well known, so many were puzzled and some unhappy with this new state of affairs. At the same time, the Prince installed many spies in his entourage.

10)

Before he left, the Supreme Abbot issued proclamations validating the Prince's work and his person. He also wrote a long elaborate document proclaiming the Prince's Successor as an authentic lineage holder.

As the Supreme Abbot worked carefully to write the proclamation, the Prince repeated the old joke that the splendor of the Supreme Abbot was so great that he was always surrounded by thieves.

"If you don't stop telling jokes like that," the Supreme Abbot said. "I'm going to make a big mistake on your Successor's document here."

11)

The final celebration in the Supreme Abbot's honor was a celebration of the summer solstice. This event took place in a broad dusty valley to the south of the Prince's encampment. Under the broiling sun in a cloudless sky, a large white embroidered tent in which the Prince and the Abbot sat was flanked on either side by rows of smaller tents to shelter the participants, followers and many guests. The tents were adorned with pennants and banners that snapped in the wind. At the entrance to this long open-air courtyard stood large paintings on cloth of the protector kings of the four directions.

The Prince entered wearing yellow silk robes, a gold breastplate, and a golden helmet surmounted by fluttering white pennants. He rode on a pure white stallion and was followed by his administrators, guards and attendants, all of whom were dressed in elaborate brocades. This procession, though very splendid, had its comic element: many of the administrators were poor riders and rocked precariously in their saddles. The Abbot laughed and was clearly delighted by the spectacle.

The Prince then dismounted, and in a huge bronze cauldron incised with tiger, lion, garuda and dragon, made an offering of juniper smoke. Clouds of fragrant incense billowed and filled all the surrounding tents as the Prince took his seat.

After this, processions of followers, organized by occupation, guild, schools and philanthropic societies, each under its own banner, trooped before him. Following that, plays and musical numbers were performed. Archery contests, wrestling matches and horse races followed, and after that, as the night deepened, recitations of poetry, songs and dances. A great amount of food and drink was consumed throughout. Love affairs were begun and ended, rivalries renewed, enmities dissolved, friendships sworn. The Abbot smiled but watched everything carefully.

At the end of the evening as attendants were helping him to mount his horse, the Prince turned to one of the local dignitaries, waved his arm slowly through the air and said:

"All, all of this is mine." His attendants cringed.

"I wish he wouldn't do that," said the Prince's Successor. An elderly poet, a guest of the Abbot, observed:

"This Prince was raised to be a king, and he is becoming one again."

12)

Soon after the Abbot's departure, the Prince began to teach about the Kingdom of Shambhala.

"The Kingdom of Shambhala exists inseparably in three ways: in the human heart, on the actual face of this earth, and as a pure realm pervading all of space. It exists in the human heart as the enlightened essence of human communion. It exists on the face of the earth in time. It appears and disappears, is seen and not seen, rises and falls. And finally it exists indestructibly in the infinite expanse of luminous space as a pure realm.

"It is pure in the same way that the pure realm of Amitabha or Ratnasambhava are pure because in the Kingdom of Shambhala, there is no obstacle to being completely awake, to perfecting and expanding that completely. However, unlike the situation in the awakened pure realms, in Shambhala, everyone is a human. The Rigdens are human. They all live, age, get sick, and they die. And there is pain.

"Human beings in this world here have become degraded. People have lost contact with the immediacy of the senses. People do not celebrate the brilliance of touch, smell, taste, sight, sound and consciousness. The senses have become the mere instruments of desires and ambitions. They are not recognized as the unceasing, multiform, direct display of awake. The awakened state lives in every instant as sight and smell, thought, taste and touch and sound. The awakened state is cultivated in music, food, perfume, caresses, language, calligraphy. The senses lock us in the magical world of mountains, seas, plains and sky, the world of time and seasons. The senses are the messengers of enlightenment in the world of ceaseless change.

"Thus the senses are the ever open gateways to the Kingdom of Shambhala. Thus, in this kingdom, change and the bardos are known completely as momentary shapes of wakefulness. All the uncertainty, groundlessness and all the arisings there are seen in their true nature as complete wakefulness. As Shambhala people, we do not cling to the ego fixation of being poor or unworthy. We are not trying to escape our situation or distract ourselves from it with material goodies. As Shambhala people, we practice with our lives. Or live our lives as enlightenment, which is more to the point."

13)

"What does this mean?" asked the Prince's Successor.

"The sanity of the Buddha's teaching cannot benefit people unless it is sustained in a social world and culture. We are going to have the real kingdom of Shambhala," the Prince explained.

"In a real place?"

"Definitely."

"And you will be king?"

"So it seems." The Successor was speechless, and after a long pause, the Prince continued: "You could smile, you know. Actually it's good news. We don't have to be so impoverished."

14)

One night, as they were drinking in the Prince's office, the Prince told K of his plans to found a kingdom in which all the teachings could be put into actual practice. K paled and felt nauseous. "So you mean we are not going to hide behind being a religion. We will actually do it."

"That's it exactly," the Prince replied as he looked out into the night. "The idea of kingdom will solve everything,"

Just the thought that they would follow the Prince in founding a real kingdom made K feel that all conventional realities were now translucent and faintly hallucinatory. He had a similar experience when a friend told him that the Prince had said that he loved him.

15)

    Invoking the primordial King, Indrabhuti, in words from the Sun of Sovereignty, it was proclaimed:

I, Indrabhuti, the primordial sovereign
Proclaim that enlightenment is not beyond the world.
It is the ground of the world.

Unoriginated, it is the source.
Unceasing, it is extinction.
Without location, it is like space.

Its radiance is the pulse of all thoughts and concepts.
Its glamour is the power of all attachments.
Its energy is the life force of all illusory lives.
Its stability is the foundation of all realms.
Its freedom is the pure play of all phenomena.

Because it is empty, it is the feeling of unreality.
Because it is the ground, it is the feeling of reality.
Because it is subtle, there is the experience of confusion.
Because it is unceasing, there is the experience of meaning.
Because it is non-duality, it is complete compassion.
Because it is compassion, it is the truth and the innate law.

Logic does not capture or penetrate it.
Renunciation does not purify it.
Meditation does not stabilize it.
Behavior does not expand or diminish it.
It is not an attainment of any kind.

Therefore my path, the path of Indrabhuti, is the path of King.
It is the display of liberation
Throughout myriad worlds.
It moves in those worlds,
And is inseparable from them.

My path is the display of liberation
Which is this world.

Moves in this world,
And is inseparable from it.

Looking on the vast array of space,
See the mandala of this world:

When you hear the cries and songs of countless beings here,
Smell their tired sweat and sweet perfumes,
Sense their terror, lust and longing,
That seeing, hearing, smelling, touching, tasting,
That knowing
Makes those worlds, makes this world
Inseparably yours.
This world is the co-emergent form
Of absolute enlightenment.

Moving from realm to realm
By awareness, by vision, by living,
By caring for the well-being of every living being,
By loving them;
All this is the same as the light of the sun passing through clouds.

XIV CONTINUITY

1)

Edward feels increasingly groundless. He clings to his work on the translation, but his stipend, his visa, and the lease on his apartment end all at once. He has to stop work on the Annals. Edward has sent his resume to a dozen universities, but has received no offers. He has a return ticket to Pennsylvania, but no desire to be there.

3)

Just before Edward leaves for the US, his father dies. He is too late for the funeral. He stays with his mother for six weeks. His sisters are both married, live in different parts of the country, and have returned to their homes. He's a stranger now in his hometown. His mother soon resumes her routine: lunch with friends, bridge club, volunteering at the hospital, church choir. She's always been self-contained. They have dinner together every night. They don't talk much.

4)

Edward is lying in the bedroom where he grew up. The decor is still that of a high school boy. He cannot sleep. As he did when he was a child, he holds himself rigid and waits. He imagines that light and sound pass through him, from air to sheet. He does not move. He holds himself motionless in the hope that still as a corpse, he will harmonize with the barren silent immobility around him and sleep will come.

5)

A chain store has made an offer on his father's business. The lawyers tell Edward what papers need to be assembled: years of check books, tax returns. He finds six letters, all in the same feminine hand stuffed in a ledger. They are love letters, unskilled but passionate. Edward is stunned. It never occurred to him. He reads the letters over and over to try and understand what this woman found so attractive in his father. He can't imagine. He wonders if his whole sense of growing up in a fairly happy family is based on not seeing what was happening. He looks at his mother's cool independence. Was it something she developed because his father was unfaithful? Or was it what caused his father to look elsewhere for love? There's no way to know. He decides not to tell his mother and burns the letters. Why keep them, he thinks, they could only cause harm.

6)

He is embarrassed, but finally calls his cousin in New York. She wrote occasionally and always seemed to be interested in him. He tell her he has nowhere to go. She doesn't hesitate and invites him to stay in her apartment. When he leaves, his mother gives him a concise little kiss on the cheek. "Take care of yourself," she says. It sounds like she doesn't expect to see him again.

THE SECRET ANNALS
ANNAL 4 - Concerning K.- part 4

1)

The Prince decided to establish the Kingdom of Shambhala on the face of this earth. Late one autumn, he took a small group of attendants on a long retreat in a hunting lodge deep in the northern forests. After a few days he sent for one of his most beloved consorts. When she arrived, the Prince presented her with new clothes of silver brocade and new shoes of turquoise silk, and when she had bathed and dressed, she entered his room and sat on a chair next to him.

The two of them sat, almost immobile for the next day and a half. The Prince had the shutters pulled back despite the cold, and they looked across a wooded valley. Food was brought in at the regular hours, and then the Prince would point out to her various details of the decoration on the porcelain, but otherwise they sat and watched the sunset and the moon rise and the moon set and the sunrise. The consort later said laughingly that it was almost as if she could see the planets and the stars actually move.

"There will be jackals, and there will be snakes, but we may continue," said the Prince.

2)

Daring, imaginative, tender, humorous and utterly devoted, the Prince's steward, F, and the Prince had a unique relationship of great intimacy and trust. The Prince later wrote: "When I met F, I met basic goodness in person." The Prince relied on F for all his domestic arrangements and once mentioned to his Successor: "Do you notice, F only speaks to me when I'm not thinking." It was very early one morning during this retreat when the Prince called his steward, F.

"It is time on this earth for Shambhala to exist. This requires someone other than a Buddhist Guru or religious figure. This is beyond spirituality altogether. So, there must be a King to join Heaven and Earth. I would be willing to do so, if it were requested."

"Sir, I request that you become King," F responded immediately. So, in concert with his cook, they planned very carefully for a small ceremony for the following day.

All the department heads who lived nearby were summoned, as well as some close friends. The day began with a ceremonial breakfast and was followed by readings of various kinds. The flag of the new Kingdom was proclaimed and its anthem sung for the first time. A smoke offering of the twenty-one kinds of precious substances was made. A feast followed during which poems and discourses were improvised by all present.

Then the Prince showed those present the flags, medals and uniforms that he had designed, and he revealed the way in which his personal attendants and guards would be re-organized as a genuine military organization.

"Thank you, your Majesty,' F said as he bowed.

"Perhaps it is not yet time to use that title publicly,"

"Soon?"

"Oh yes."

When the absent directors and other department heads were duly notified that evening, they reacted in claustrophobic horror. This man whom they had accepted as their absolute spiritual lord would now be their temporal leader as well. And this organization, for whose stability and legitimacy they had long labored, would now be deemed a seditious band of crackpots.

"We must," announced the Prince, "transcend our personal history. In fact, we must transcend history altogether."

3)

During this retreat, K happened to visit the Prince shortly after the ceremony requesting the Prince to become King. Though he had certainly heard rumors, K had no knowledge of what had transpired. The Prince was pleased to see him, and, without any explanation, immediately summoned musicians and singers who immediately performed a new Shambhala anthem.

"What do you think?" asked the Prince eagerly.

"It sounds like one of those dirges which priests play before they are going to ask for money." was K's reply. The Prince was not happy with this and never asked K's opinion on such matters again.

4)

"How shall we begin?" F asked the Prince.

"First, we should establish a court."

"Shall we start fresh with a new house?"

"No, that will be later. For now, we will change my old house."

"Shall it be formal or comfortable?"

"It should be absolutely as formal as possible. Even if we have to improvise somewhat, I do not wish to have any unconscious arrangements or unconscious activities. Everything should have its own place, and everything should happen according to schedule.

"Our court should be somewhat intimidating. It should wake people up and show them how to act as real human beings."

"Then we will need many servants."

"Yes, and guards as well."

"And uniforms."

"Absolutely," the Prince agreed happily.

5)

For the remainder of this retreat, the Prince was busy designing new flags, banners, seals, medals, emblems and uniforms. Artisans of all kinds came to visit him to assist him in these tasks. Assisted by various administrators, he also re-formed his organization and arranged new titles for those who worked in it. The Successor was appointed Prime Minister. Department heads became Ministers, emissaries became Ambassadors, and lesser functionaries also had a range of titles. Consorts became Ladies to the Court.

Many felt embarrassed, knowing full well that in the world at large, these titles would appear made-up, laughable and insanely pretentious. But each felt secretly transformed as if his or her title brought to life some specific and thus far hidden inner potential, even as the titles exacerbated the split between the ordinary world and the one that His Majesty was creating. Thus all felt squeezed as they became further enmeshed in His Majesty's existence. The atmosphere trembled with anxiety, fear, excitement and unimaginable possibility.

"The insignia of Shambhala will wake them up. The titles will give them new pride, but will also make them embarrassed and ashamed of themselves," the Prince said gleefully.

6)

K visited the Prince on retreat. The new direction of things made him visibly ill at ease.

He alternated between silence and sarcasm. The Prince was annoyed:

"You know, inspiration is an accident, a cosmic accident. We might like to create a logic for that. We would like to control the outcome of accidents.

"But you should have more confidence. The world of inspiration has its own continuity."

7)

Before he had left retreat, the Prince's house was redecorated according to his designs. Outside, the house was painted white, the eaves, door and window frames black and across the lintels five crimson circles. Gold finials were placed at the roof ends, and flagpoles were installed at the four corners of the house and in front of it. The rear of the house was fenced in and a large embroidered tent erected there. Housing for staff and guards was also built. Guard posts were constructed in front of the house.

Inside, the living room was arranged as a formal reception hall with a gold throne at the far end and rows of small golden chairs along the walls. Also on the main floor was a small study in which the Prince could receive personal visitors, a shrine room and a formal dining room. The kitchen was in a small separate building in the rear. Upstairs the Prince had a small suite for himself, and there were rooms for his family, guests, the Successor (now the Prime Minister) and his family.

When the Prince returned from retreat, a great smoke offering was made in every room and corner of the house and all the new out-buildings so that everything smelled of burning juniper and incense. The Prince's personal flag was raised, and he took up residence in the Shambhala court.

Unfortunately despite the efforts of the most talented craftsmen, the main reception room with its gilded moldings, gilded furniture and pale blue carpets was somehow vulgar and insipid. M, a very gifted painter, asked the Prince how he liked it.

"Oh, it's like a boring corner of the sky."

8)

During his first meeting with all the people who were to serve him on his return home, the Prince said:

"Clean everything and keep it completely clean. The spirit of the sky, the mountains, the valleys and the rivers are the perceptions themselves. When everything sparkles, it draws the drala and werma, the living presence of nature and the power of our ancestors. They will then come to dwell among us."

9)

From that time on, every hour of the Prince's day and night was run on schedule. Every moment, from when he first woke, when he bathed and got dressed, when he ate, when he met with his administrators or had interviews with new and old students, when he rested, painted and wrote, and when he entertained for dinner became as regular as the movement of the sun.

10)
   The Prince stepped onto this path carefully and presented his plans for the Kingdom bit by bit to slowly increasing numbers of followers. Not merely did he teach and introduce new practices, he made the kingdom a physical reality every day by acting as if it were already real.

11)
   The Prince went to great lengths and used innumerable methods to train his ministers and other followers to fulfill their responsibilities in a larger world. One favored training ground was the dinner table. The Prince gave an endless number of formal dinners. Although occasionally interesting, mostly these were events of considerable tension and tedium.
   Prior to sitting down, the guests were notified that they were expected to eat with elegant table manners and were then instructed in these alien forms. This meant that food was consumed with great awkwardness. Vegetables frequently flew off plates, and large hunks of meat dangled helplessly off chopsticks beneath the withering gaze of the Prince and his servants. Conversation was constricted as each guest looked furtively to his neighbor for guidance in how to proceed.
   The Prince himself rarely said very much, and the guests either sat in terrified silence or produced forced, brittle and always stupid conversation. These meals, one knew, could last anywhere from forty-five minutes to ten hours. Many felt that they were going to expire from boredom alone. And at the very same time, all knew that the Prince was capable without a moment's notice of the most complete displays of rage, passion, scorn, tenderness, detached rationality or inconceivable strangeness. Thus all sat there hopelessly bored and totally alert. The claustrophobia was intense. It was many years before the guests realized that at those dinners, the Prince had shown them directly in the context of secular social life the true mind of meditation.

12)
   Late one cool autumn night, the Prince was sitting alone in the tent at some distance from his house.

"Would you like company for the night?" asked M who was serving that evening as his personal attendant. The Prince shrugged and then nodded.

"Who would you like to be with?"

The Prince stared at his attendant and replied: "Someone who truly loves me."

"And who would that be, Sir?"

The Prince began to cry. He wept for hours, the tears virtually squirting out of his eyes. His shirt and robe were soaked and there was a great puddle of tears on the table before him. His attendants also cried with him for hours and hours.

13)

One of the Prince's ministers was invited to speak before a gathering of local notables to explain what was going on in the Prince's residence. The minister was extremely nervous and told the Prince that he didn't have the confidence to do the job well.

"Use my confidence then," said the Prince. And with that he blew on the minister. The Minister all of a sudden felt filled with power and energy and was able to do what was necessary. It disappeared when his task was complete. He contemplated this for a long time.

14)

The Prince enjoined his ministers with the most bloodcurdling and solemn oaths never to reveal any of his plans and deliberations. Unbeknownst to them, he consulted on everything with the guards, particularly the women who saw to the security of his personal quarters during the night. He would wake in the darkest hours and go to the kitchen where he would personally make snacks for them and ask their opinion of the kingdom, its location, his policies and appointments. They too, of course, were sworn to secrecy.

15)

Despite the many considerations shown to him, K was unable to find much enthusiasm for the project of the Shambhala Kingdom. He was most outspoken about his doubts until the Prince arranged for the Duke to make the long trip to meet with the Supreme Abbot of Mount Koyosan.

K was shocked to find the Abbot mortally ill. The Hierarch however still conducted himself with great grandeur and smiled and laughed as the morning sun fell on his golden robes.

"You must not discriminate," he told K, "When your teacher rises into the sky on a lotus, and when your teacher sits in an alley eating rotten fish, you must not discriminate between those two things."

K did not find this talk itself very inspiring, but at the same time, it was as if his original mind, completely awake suddenly dawned as a brilliant, spring-like, completely clear noon-day sky whose radiance and unobstructed openness pervaded everything. He felt he was returning home.

Much later, K realized that in cherishing this experience while belittling what the Abbot had said, he was doing exactly what the Abbot had warned him against. Nonetheless, K's doubts, at least as regards practice, were resolved.

He sped back to notify the Prince of the Abbot's deteriorating condition.

16)

When told that the Supreme Abbot was dying, the Prince set out immediately. On arriving at the Abbot's deathbed, the Prince, already exhausted, was overcome and began sobbing uncontrollably. All his devotion and all his loss poured through him.

Suddenly in the midst of his wracking tears, he turned to one of his attendants and said: "How am I doing?"

When he left the room, the Prince encountered the Supreme Abbot's regents in the hallway. They were young men and looked to the Prince for confirmation of their fears and counsel as to how to continue. Looking into their expectant faces, the Prince made a fist with his thumb in the air, wiggled it, smiled broadly and said: "It's a boy."

Later as he and his entourage left in a carriage, the Prince explained: "You have to cry; it's traditional, you know." Even so, no one doubted the Prince's deep sorrow, as it was now clear the Abbot would not live for very long. K realized that the Prince did not perpetuate any mood or feeling no matter how deep.

17)

When the Prince returned from visiting the Supreme Abbot, he asked an attendant how everyone in the Shambhala Court got on in his absence. The attendant said he really couldn't say since he had barely seen most of his co-workers.

"You mean you haven't even sat down to dinner together once while I was away?" The Prince was utterly shocked when he found out that this was indeed the case. So he called a meeting of all who lived in his residence and all who served and attended him in any way.

"You are my family and my blood itself. You must celebrate together even in my absence," he told them. One of his courtiers whispered out of earshot:

"This organization is being run by two kinds of people: those who hate others and those who won't acknowledge they exist."

18)

For a time, the Prince was taken with the notion that he had, in K and Lady T, an extended family. He took pleasure in dropping by their house, sitting in the kitchen and chatting about family matters. On one such visit he discussed his sons:

"The two younger sons have been recognized as incarnations of famous teachers, so in that way, they're taken care of. The eldest, I'm going to make him my Successor as ruler of Shambhala. He's not an incarnation... well a monk maybe, but nothing special. But I think he will be a good leader of men."

19)

"You shouldn't have told that story," one of the eldest son's followers said to K. "Even if it's true, it undermines people's faith."

"Then why do you think the Prince said it to me?" asked K. "Maybe his sense of the world is more complex than having faith in one version of things, no?"

20)

A follower of the Prince who had been the Supreme Abbot's beloved carriage driver came to visit him. The Abbot beamed and sat up very straight as the driver entered. "Ahhh," he said. And then turning to his other attendants and smiling happily, the Abbot remarked:

"Why is it that whenever I see this man, I think he is going to tell me a lie?"

The driver was abashed, but when the Prince's Successor heard of this, he laughed.

"If he understood that, he would realize the Mahamudra on the spot."

21)

When news finally came of the Supreme Abbot's death, the Prince organized a long traditional ceremony lasting for days on end. And while the participants chanted and sang the ancient texts, the Prince beat drums, crashed on cymbals, sang and cried.

He beat his head against the throne on which the Supreme Abbot had sat, calling out again and again: "Come back. Come back." And he called on everyone in the vast shrine hall to write poems to the Supreme Abbot. Then, as he left, he insisted that all sing the anthem of Shambhala, over and over for many hours.

22)

> In continuous yearning for you,
> The unborn mind of this
> Merges in the ceaseless mind of that:
>
> The Dawn of Vajrasattva.
>
> "About time," I hear you say.
>
> Joy without tongue,
> Sadness without voice
>
> Burning where inseparable
> On the glowing ember point.
>
> The dust flies off the mirror.
>
> I promise to fulfill
> What you promised to me
> And gave.

23)

Despite the objections of all his court, the Prince determined to bestow exalted titles on his sister-in-law and K. All the courtiers were opposed.

"We must give people a chance," the Prince insisted.

Slitting a vein in his own wrist and then slitting the wrists of Lady T and K, pressing in turn their wrists to his so their blood would mingle, he made himself the blood brother of each. Punching a needle almost through their thumbs he drew blood for their signed oaths. But later just before the investiture, he told K: "I've told my son, my ministers, my Successor about this. Every single one of them is against you. What will you do about that?"

"I'll outlast them all," was K's sudden reply. It was clear he did not mean he'd outlive them.

Then the Prince asked: "So then, what will you do with this title?"

K hesitated and replied: "I will be kind and be a good example to people."

"That's pathetic," the Prince snarled.

Later, the Prince asked K to take some followers into his house to train them as servants, but K perhaps out of modesty, but certainly to the Prince's disappointment, refused.

"Someday, you will understand what we are doing, and then you will be proud of what you are," the Prince told him.

Whether rightly or wrongly, what K came to understand many years later was that his title became real only when he simply became it. The title was him, and he was on his own.

XV. CONTINUITY

1)

Edward flies to New York and arrives in mid-winter. His cousin, Margaret, lives by herself in a large older apartment on Park Avenue. She's tall and thin, has a long oval face, pale skin, chestnut hair; she's good looking in a cool, carefully turned out way. She is obviously making a lot of money. She gives Edward a room and leaves an envelope with $1,500 on the bureau. He thanks her awkwardly. She tells him not to worry and seems patiently amused. The situation is embarrassing. He writes more letters to colleagues asking for leads and sends out more resumes.

2)

While he waits, he goes back to translating the Annals. Absorption in language, sentence structure, turns of phrase, word choices carry him into a world whose unfolding is more steady, more promising even as it becomes stranger and somehow more threatening.. Working carefully on translation is a rejection of chaos, a rejection of failure, of uncertainty, and, at the end of day, leaves him feeling like a merchant returning from a strange but prosperous voyage. It may be an illusion.

3)

Margaret is friendly enough but usually comes home very late, sometimes not at all. She does not tell him about her life nor encourage him to ask. The envelopes of money appear on the bureau unasked from time to time. Edward assumes she is keeping her distance as a way of letting him find his way on his own. He is lonely. One night, Margaret comes home early. They have a glass of red wine together. He tells her about the love letters to his father.

"Not possible!" She shakes her head.

"But true."

"He wasn't the type, Edward. He just wasn't." She asks to see the letters. He tells her he destroyed them; she shrugs. "Do you remember who wrote them?"

"Sure. A Mary Bryant."

"The mousy one at the store? Husband got killed in Korea?"

"I guess."

"Hunh." She shrugs. "Who would've thought?" She sips her wine, reflects. "Such a hard ass, straight arrow, your dad." Edward waits until she's put her lips to the glass again.

"I think my mother knew." She raises an eyebrow, gives Edward an appraising gaze.

"Growing up between those two, you can see why you might have gotten a little...mmm... otherworldly." Edward looks away and blushes. He's never really thought of himself that way. "You know, Edward, you really ought to get out and look around more. I wish I had the time..." Edward realizes she actually likes him. It's like having a sibling. He'd like to ask her why she couldn't join him for a walk some evening, but knows better. He begins to explore the city on his own.

4)

That night Edward dreams of Professor Akiyama. He sees the old man's face, bloodless and taut, mouth half open as if about to say something. His eyes stare upward, empty. It is clear that the old man has died tormented by something left incomplete.

THE SECRET ANNALS : ANNAL IV - Concerning K. - part 5

1)

 His Majesty had not yet found a proper location for his future kingdom, so he transformed the encampment into a training ground for Shambhala. At that time, he devoted a great deal of energy to strengthening his military organization. Many who had previous military experience had already been charged with guarding His Majesty and ensuring public order when he or any of his distinguished guests appeared in public. Now they were divided into four 'banners'. These banners, called Tiger, Lion, Garuda and Dragon were to be stationed at each of the four directions and each had a single general. Each banner consisted of five smaller battalions called 'arrows' of which one was a cavalry division, two were infantry, one was for transportation, and the last was for "unconventional weapons" and was, in effect, made up of rangers and scouts.

 Those who were His Majesty's personal attendants constituted a fifth banner called Sun. This was the only banner whose entire membership had no other employment. Except for their officers, all the other banners consisted of men and women who had other livelihoods.

 Each banner had its own color of helmet and pennant; white for Lion, orange for Tiger, red for Garuda and blue for Dragon. Their armor was of polished steel, and they were armed with bows and arrows, swords and lances.

 Secretly, His Majesty imported weapons-instructors mainly from Korea, and each of his troops embarked on a private regimen of martial arts. Thus when all joined together for the month-long training exercises which His Majesty instituted, it was a vivid and imposing sight. Drawn perhaps by the splendid equipage of these soldiers, many new followers came to join the military.

 Earlier, when unarmed guards had first been provided for His Majesty, many of his followers who had been attracted to the pacifism of the Buddhist path were disconcerted. But now, as a full-fledged military began to form, there was considerable outcry. Many were frightened at what they saw as the trappings of a military dictatorship, and quite a few former followers left and wrote broadsides which they posted decrying the change of events.

 Some of this fear was the result of the fierce and single-minded dedication of the military members themselves. His female warriors and in particular his two great women generals were amongst the most intimidating. These two generals, one tall and fair, the other small and dark, both beautiful, radiated an invincible willingness to undergo any hardship and risk any threat to fulfill His Majesty's wishes. As someone remarked, it was really the extent of their love for him that frightened people because it went beyond any conventional boundary or qualm. They stood on either side of His Majesty as he wore a steel gray wool robe and a polished iron breastplate and stood on a platform in the autumn wind, watching his guards train. At the conclusion of the exercises, he proclaimed:

"Wearing our uniforms, being skilled in martial arts and being exact in our drill formation, we will use the symbols of aggression to overcome aggression. We will paralyze aggression itself. We are not afraid to do this. It is necessary to use these symbols and shapes and convert to aggression for the purposes of non-aggression. Otherwise there is no possibility of final victory over war, either in us or in the world at large.

"We are not doing this just to make our own little projects safe. We must do this for the future of the world."

Accordingly, His Majesty had all his military, from the highest to the lowest, take a public oath in the presence of his ministers and all the citizens in which they vowed to serve the people and to postpone any enlightenment which they might realize until all those present and all those who would follow His Majesty in the future would themselves be completely liberated.

Most, even if they did not care to be involved in the military, were deeply moved and so understood His Majesty's thinking, but those who had left saw all this as mere trickery, and continued to denounce His Majesty and his actions.

2)

The Minister of Security became one of the very most important people in His Majesty's entourage. Small, scholarly, shy and fastidious, this Minister was born of a genteel and cultured family. He had some distinction as a scholar, but in the chaos of the times found no outlet for his talents.

When His Majesty met him, he was severely depressed, and His Majesty swiftly made him his personal secretary. In this capacity, he served His Majesty purely and well. He was peerless in conveying His Majesty's words and intentions to others and in communicating the concerns of everyone to His Majesty. When His Majesty established his Kingdom, this Minister was made the Protector of His Majesty's written utterance and the Field Marshall of His Army. He found the former task gratifying, but the latter one burdensome.

"Our task is to proclaim the real possibilities and the reality of enlightened society. This display might embarrass you, but we are not just philosophers hoping for someone else to do the work," His Majesty told him.

3)

THE REALITY OF KALAPA

The Kingdom of Shambhala is real:
It is alive as a place on this earth;
It is alive as a realm of pure inspiration;
It is alive in the human heart.

Shambhala is primordial heart,
The heartbeat that lifts our body,
The flow that quickens our mind.
It is the reality of inspiration itself.

All that gives a man or woman reason to live,
All that is harbored in isolation or in concert:
Whether as ink, as weapon, as faith, as sun, as wisdom,
As courage, as love, as daring, as delicacy,
As fear, as regret, as longing,
As certainty, as uncertainty,
As pure gold
Flows in the primordial meeting place
Of all who yearn and fight darkness and despair.
Of all who are gallant and who fight madness.

Shambhala, inspiration, heart:
These are the same.
It is real, undying, present, now.

To say the name of the self-arisen kingdom,
To call out its name: Shambhala
Draws humankind together,
Uplifts all hearts,
Shines, and shows the path in darkness.

Shambhala is the heart of inspiration.
It exists because of the power of inspiration.

It is inspiration itself.

4)

In the first year following His Majesty's proclaiming the Kingdom, there was a great ball in honor of his birthday. This took place in early spring and was celebrated in the encampment's public square. At one end, on a high dais before an immense Shambhala flag, His Majesty, in his most formal civilian garb, sat on a high golden throne. A broad carpeted aisle whose entrance was marked by four great sculptures made of ice led up to the throne. On either side were tables filled with all manner of food and drink.

At a trumpet signal, a grand march of all the subjects in order of precedence began. All were dressed as elaborately as their circumstances permitted. First two by two, later four by four and eight by eight, the subjects would be presented, bow, and stand aside. During this procession, there was only surreptitious eating and drinking. Formal dining followed, during which time those who wished to speak personally to His Majesty did so. Following this, ceremonial gifts were presented to His Majesty, and long encomia and toasts were made. When this section of the celebration ended, His Majesty himself gave a short speech of thanks.

Then followed the grand ball itself. All the ministers and close followers had been obliged to learn an archaic and rather difficult dance for this occasion, and generally, they were clumsy and hated it. The Successor, now called Prime Minister, had made sure he excelled at this dance, and when he swirled His Majesty's wife around the floor, they were very much admired. Late in the evening, His Majesty directed the mass of dancers in complex patterns resembling cavalry formations. This resulted in frequent collisions and occasional spills.

Then His Majesty stood, the anthem was sung, and he marched down the central aisle with his attendants. The celebration was over, leaving a mass of tired and slightly stupefied people in its wake to look for clothes that had been mislaid and carriages that waited far off in the night.

His Majesty however was exhilarated. He rode through the encampment all night long, pausing to sing the anthem outside the windows of his ministers, family and consorts. He did not sleep until the sun had risen.

5)

During this period, K's marriage dissolved.

His Majesty had become quite attached to his mother-in-law, the Grand Duchess, and was increasingly insistent that his family now take part in all court events. Lady T, now Duchess of K, and K, now Duke of K, were increasingly the object of His Majesty's anger for their half-hearted participation. He began attacking them. Neither K nor Lady T could understand. Lady T felt responsible for having placed her husband in a position where he was becoming estranged from his teacher. K didn't want to increase his wife's doubts about His Majesty. They avoided talking to each other about what distressed them most.

K confided his anguish to one friend only. That friend proved false, used the information to his advantage and became Lady T's lover. "Our relationship is just too claustrophobic," she said to K when she left.

6)

The divorce between the Duke and Duchess of K happened quickly and without much note.

Soon after, the Duke of K found that his seat at formal receptions was being moved from its former exalted place at the front, back amid the mid-level functionaries. Though indifferent to this kind of status, he resented being moved like a chess piece. "No," he said, "At the front or at the back," and left before the ceremony began.

Soon His Majesty sent a courtier to speak with the Duke of K.

"We are doing research into the histories to determine what the proper protocol is for dealing with someone in your situation."

"Oh," quipped the Duke, "I think you'll find that usually the inconvenient marital connections of rising dynasties are simply killed off." When His Majesty heard of this remark, he laughed and retained the Duke in his former position.

7)

One evening, His Majesty's mother-in law, now called the Grand Duchess, was invited by His Majesty to a formal dinner. The invitation required that all awards and medals, which His Majesty had designed and begun to distribute, were to be worn. She asked the Duke of K to escort her, but when he arrived wearing no medals or any other insignia, she asked him:

"Where are your medals?"

"I don't have any medals." he replied.

"Well then wear your sash."

"I don't have a sash."

"I'll make you a sash."

"Thank you, but I don't need a sash."

"Listen to me, if you wear a sash, he'll give you the medals."

8)

Her Majesty was His Majesty's only wife at that time. She did not care for life at Court and preferred to live in the country at her horse farm. Many people came to study riding with her, and His Majesty was very proud of her discipline and her accomplishments, and he was hurt by the many complaints made on her account.

Her Majesty was punctilious in attending all public receptions and made considerable efforts to represent His Majesty impeccably. Her addresses were formal, slightly fierce and not devoid of humor. She was, despite her deeper insecurities, a woman of powerful will. Regardless of her violent and unpredictable temper, she was always able to attract a loyal group of followers and attendants. She was less loyal to them, however, and never forgave any slight or insult, even if it were later proved to be imaginary.

Her attendants nonetheless followed her everywhere, as her passion for horsemanship and horses took her on many journeys to distant lands. Her passion for horses was almost to the exclusion of all others, and some said it surpassed her concern even for her children, especially as they became older. Despite his other involvements, His Majesty always missed her.

9)

G was a very young woman with pale skin, lustrous hair, and shining green eyes. She was quite small but moved quickly. His Majesty met her on his travels, fell in love with her and brought her back with him. Much to the annoyance of his other consorts, he treated her extravagantly, buying her clothes and treating her with deference and every honor.

G treated these displays casually as if they were embarrassing. She found the atmosphere of the court tedious, and indeed His Majesty's attentions claustrophobic. The Ministers and attendants disliked her because she was clearly ambivalent about an honor they would have coveted. When she ran off for a time or generally when she was not with him, His Majesty sat and stared despondently. His moods, at that time, altered entirely according to her treatment of him. He wrote poems constantly.

10)
> The sudden heat
> Of an unsuspected skin
> Pressed against me
>
> Unravels the past
> With a wish
> To lick the line
> Along your hip.

*

> The colors of the columbine
> On our incandescent lips
> In the silence of sunrise
> Which calls our bodies
> Thick as clouds
> From the dark bed.
>
> Dawn from your breath
> Reveals an earth
> Showered in sparks.
>
> Light flows like lava
> Across my face and tongue
> As my carriage drives eastward home.

*

> In secret
> Essential to the word's work,
>
> I wait for your return
> And wander in thought:
>
> A desolate journey
> Of clear definitions,
> Of mountains and cold nights.

*

On a broad slate sea,
You think an undertow
May carry you
To a point of land.

The desperate lover
Pursues uncertain love.

The unanswered message
Pulls him out to sea.

*

Stinging like smoke
And delightful
Alcohol compels
The memory of flesh.

*

The gifts of love
Like a small black hair
Are too prodigal to number,
Too elusive, too complete
But endlessly encompassed
In that tight sticky curl.

11)
    One evening, His Majesty summoned one of his Ministers. His Majesty and G were seated opposite each other, and it was obviously her intention to leave once again. His Majesty suddenly threw a vase across the room, and shouted at the girl to leave him. Then he turned to the minister and said: "No one, no one undermines my confidence."
    That was the end of the affair.

12)
    After careful divination and many consultations with travelers, cartographers and geomancers, His Majesty determined that the kingdom should be founded on a large peninsula on the banks of the vast deep waters

of the northern Sea of Japan. This choice was determined by such practical considerations as the peninsula's natural boundaries, the narrowness of the isthmus that was its gateway, the paucity of inhabitants and so forth. Less practically, it was also important that the body of land itself suggested the profile of a goddess in whose palm lay the future administrative capital which was, at that time a fishing village and minor trading center called Shan.

This area was legendary for its remoteness, its harsh, cold, damp climate, its backward and tradition-bound populace and its poor food, consisting almost exclusively of millet and dried fish. So at first, His Majesty told only Her Majesty, the Prime Minister and a few others of his decision.

But word spread. No one could keep a secret. Many of those who heard were sickened by the idea of living in such a place and were equally frightened by the prospect that they would no longer be able to escape His Majesty at all. In this atmosphere of doubt and claustrophobia, His Majesty was relentless, scorning in every way he could the ingrained disposition to comfort seeking. At the same time, His Majesty went out of his way to encourage, cajole, comfort, tease the many who were filled with doubts into staying with him.

"If you will only cut your subconscious gossip, the Kingdom will become reality," he said.

XVI. CONTINUITY

1)

Edward begins exploring the neighborhood. The imposing buildings with polished brass doors and cold-eyed doormen speak of a world where he is not invited, but the tree- lined side streets promise settled happy lives. It's a wealthy part of the world. Walking past the well-kept town houses, a faint whiff of Chanel Number Five seemed to linger in the stillness. He takes his washing to a laundry where a Hungarian man must first evict his ancient overweight hound from the scales before weighing the laundry to be washed and dried. He buys three apples at the dark grocery store. The clerk, a Jamaican, holds the apples: "A pound and a quarter ... Trust me?" Edward is a little ashamed that he wants to see them weighed. The clerk is right. "It's all I do, man," he smiles forgivingly. In a cafe nearby where wealthy young women treat their children to hot chocolate, he reads an article about Martin Luther King's assassin. He overhears one woman tell another: "He just doesn't understand. You can't live on $35,000 a month." It is for him an unknown world made of many worlds. An extraordinarily beautiful woman, splendidly dressed and *made up, sweeps from her front door into a limousine. Unseen in the shadows, a bum is staring at her, masturbating. At a bakery run by two old German women, a line of working men wait for coffee and cinnamon rolls. Two stout men in suits stride down Lexington Ave. "But Harry, I tell you. An exclusive business is a lonely business." A drug dealer, a handsome, slender black man in black leather, whispers: "Something for the head?" He eats rice and black beans in a Dominican restaurant with a glow in the dark sputnik decor. Four children are sleeping in the booths. A woman on the piss-smelling subway steps, thin and dirty, leers at him. "Gimme a quarter. OK. Gimme a kiss. You're going up. When you're on your way down, you fly down those stairs like a bird." A young woman looks over her shoulder at him frightened and hurries her children into the apartment building. Two large black women, laughing and joking walk side by side, push wheel chairs with wizened, silent, white women swaddled in blankets. He looks through a door into a restaurant kitchen. Inside there are shouts and crashing pots, clattering dishware. A Chinese chef, a cigarette in his mouth, stares moodily as he shakes a frying pan.*

2)

Edward expands his wandering. One day it's the German section in Yorkville: bakeries with baroque cakes, immaculate butcher shops, chrome Konditorei, unsmiling occupants. He waits in an empty butcher shop. The butcher insists he take a ticket. Edward shrugs. "Order must be," the man states solemnly. In a Hungarian restaurant further downtown, the owner leans on the back of his chair gasping asthmatically, serving delicious roast duck. Further downtown, Little Italy: olive oil, garlic and cheese, and children's voices from the street: "Ma, it's me". A key wadded in a sock sails down to the waiting child. Edward is moving almost invisibly in the teeming welter of human life. The sweaty crush of Chinatown. Restaurants full of Chinese farmers eating early morning congee, fortune tellers, men butchering chickens, cobblers, and dumpling makers all working on the street. Edward thinks he sees Harumi turning a corner ahead. He runs, but she has disappeared in the crowds.

In the Ukrainian neighborhood on Second Avenue, storefronts filled with Russian orthodox icons and sour nostalgia. Edward is sure he sees Mrs. Akiyama striding purposefully into a dry-cleaning store. He follows her. The bell mounted on the door tinkles, it's sound muffled by racks of clothes. There is no one there. The dusty muslin curtain behind the counter parts and an old man with thick glasses looks out. Edward rushes out the door.

3)

It's a world of fragments: florist shop filled with orchids, a house where Marcel Duchamp once lived, a window with prosthetic limbs, hand-made lingerie, the bar where Dylan Thomas drank himself to death, another where Jackson Pollock drank, a window of gilded furniture, Japanese fans, second-hand shoes, Isaac Bashevis Singer's apartment, a locksmith shop. He sees Charlie Mingus raving on a bus, Phillip Roth buying a tie, Vladimir Horowitz entering an apartment house. Moments hint at totalities that do not arrive. Space itself seems utterly porous.

How long, he wonders, has he been searching for some...completeness?

4)

He reads ads and the backs of others' newspapers in the subway. Students are being shot to death. Bright red lips whisper promises from pages, screens, billboards, Headlines announce killings, beatings, tortures, bombs and lies. Walking down the dark humid street, TV's and radios blare. Everyone hears words emerging from the mouths of images. Edward feels himself coming adrift. Perhaps it is a kind of freedom, he thinks.

Words popping out into the air, surfacing in his mind open slight shifts. Reality moves. He feels a little ahead of things. Sometimes a little behind. Sometimes Edward can only cling to passing sensations, thoughts, phrases.

"I that am severed like a reed root cut
Should a stream entice
Would go.
I think.

He repeats this over and over.

THE SECRET ANNALS : ANNAL IV - Concerning K- part 6

1)

His Majesty estimated that it would take three or four years for his followers to prepare themselves mentally and tactically to make the move to the true Kingdom of Shambhala. Aside from expeditions to the peninsula itself, the most important preparations had to begin before the move. He intensified training his administrators so that they could function as ministers in an actual government; he drilled his attendants and guards so that they could act as civil police and soldiers. His business friends were pressed to become financiers, and his doctors to be public health officials.

As he planned the move to Shan, post riders and couriers streamed in and out of His Majesty's residence bringing messages and information from the provinces and from distant nations. The hoof-beats of their sweating horses resounded through the day and night. And after reporting to the minister to whom they were attached or directly to His Majesty, they assembled in an inn near the gate to the court. There by mingling with these far-riding men, one could learn all the news and gossip of the kingdom and its environs.

Late one night in the middle of a hailstorm, a messenger from the southeast arrived at court. His Majesty was awakened and received him at once. It seems that two weeks earlier, some unknown person had thrown a rock through one of the monastery windows, and attached to that rock was a message saying that Ikkyu, the reclusive teacher whom His Majesty had revered above all others was alive, would soon be visiting.

His Majesty felt that this news, coinciding as it did with his decision about Shan, was highly auspicious. He immediately began preparing a suite of apartments. No matter how high or low, all his followers assisted in covering walls with silk, painting the center inside and out, making new banners and refurbishing all the brocades on the shrines.

Then nothing happened for two weeks. Every day His Majesty asked many times if Ikkyu had arrived, and his disappointment was always evident. Finally, he was told that a lone small man, with long black hair and quite handsome but of no great bearing calling himself Ikkyu had arrived, and was at the door asking for him.

"Ask him in, offer him tea, and I'll be along in a minute," His Majesty said casually. But when he entered the room where his teacher sat quietly sipping tea, he wept and prostrated himself on the ground, while Ikkyu watched with an embarrassed smile. His Majesty had the doors closed, and spent the next three days alone with his teacher.

2)

Subsequently, it was announced that Ikkyu would formally enthrone and empower His Majesty as an Earth-Protector monarch. The ceremony was swiftly arranged, but as many as could came from all directions to attend.

There was great expectation that the ceremony itself would be lavish and fascinating, but in fact, it was long and rather dull. The only point of interest came when His Majesty removed all his clothes except his under-wear and changed into one of his more elaborate uniforms. This was mod-erately comic. When Her Majesty did likewise, more decorously, she dis-robed behind a screen. Otherwise, the ceremony consisted of Ikkyu chant-ing in a rather flat voice for ten hours. At the conclusion, His Majesty had been enthroned as a monarch. Henceforth all the followers, and not just the courtiers, referred to the Prince as His Majesty.

3)

As the students came to take more teachings from Ikkyu they became accustomed to his style, which was unadorned but gave the feeling of great clarity and immense space without any entertaining aspects whatsoever.

His Majesty said of Ikkyu: "He is the only one who knows my mind."

Ikkyu said of His Majesty: "In the ordinary way, if you wish to follow the path of enlightenment, you must go to someplace very quiet, and first calm your mind, and then continue your practices in solitude. However, with this extraordinary teacher, you can experience naked mind directly."

One day, as Ikkyu was doing his practice, sitting serenely on his throne, His Majesty entered the shrine room with one of his ministers.

"He's absolutely extraordinary," whispered the minister.

"Yes," replied His Majesty, "But we don't want to be like him, now, do we?"

Later, at a meeting with all his officials, Ikkyu asked His Majesty: "How far apart in levels of realization are your best students from your worst ones?" His Majesty didn't hesitate:

"As far apart as the thickness of one sheet of paper." The older stu-dents and particularly the Prime Minister looked extremely unhappy.

4)

When His Majesty announced to his ministers and his military commanders that the time had come for him to visit his future capital, Shan, and to survey the future kingdom, all assumed that this expedition would take place in stealth and secrecy. His Majesty however proceeded very differently.

He had his armorers make two elaborate suits of armor: one of black lacquer with gold lacing, another of white lacquer with silver lacing. He also had armor made in gold, silver, bronze and iron, and helmets adorned with all manner of pennants and peacock feathers. He acquired an ancient Han sword of steel with a handle of ghzi, and he even had new boots made from leopard, snow-lion, tiger and lion skin. His tailors made new formal robes: one of heavy orange silk with a turquoise sash, another of red brocade with a yellow sash, a third in navy blue brocade with a gold sash. Most astonishing of all was a robe of incomparable splendor made entirely of spun gold brocade brought to His Majesty from Mongolia.

Ornate saddles and bridles adorned with all kinds of semi-precious stones and engraved with an array of fanciful designs were also commissioned. In fact there was no aspect of his wardrobe and his possessions that was not newly made and whose manufacture he did not supervise down to the last detail.

His Majesty also saw to it that all his entourage, from ministers and generals down to maids and messengers would each be appropriately garbed in new military and formal clothing. There were new saddles, saddle cloths and bridles for the horses and shiny new weapons, and a vast array of flags and banners bearing the Tiger, Lion, Garuda and Dragon insignias, as well as his own royal standard.

New tents, including an embroidered royal yellow and black tent, complete with Persian carpets, furniture, porcelain dishes, copper cook-stoves, were provided for the expedition. The Prime Minister had a yellow and violet tent, and all the ministers and generals also had theirs.

"I thought we would be traveling quite discreetly," said the Prime Minister dubiously.

"Oh, I think they will like the idea of a king once they see one," His Majesty replied airily.

So, despite the misgivings of almost everyone except His Majesty, the expedition with eighty cavalry horses and the same number of pack horses set off like a great royal progress, with banners flying and harness bells jingling.

5)

During their two-month journey through the mountains and across the desert, they encountered no bandits and only occasional hardship. And when they arrived first in Shan, the entire populace turned out to gape at the unimaginable splendor of their unexpected visitors.

After the great encampment was set up on the outskirts of Shan, His Majesty sent written invitations to the headman and all the notables of the town to come for dinner. Many of these worthies could not read, and so the messengers were obliged to read them their invitation.

Early in the evening, they duly arrived, dressed in their seal-skin robes trimmed with mangy fox-fur, sporting long hoarded decorations from long departed Han emissaries and bearing ancient rusted swords. As they waited in His Majesty's tent, furtively eyeing the carpets, the inlaid furniture, the brocade wall hangings, stiff and suspicious, they were determined not to be impressed by the splendor of His Majesty's array. Their resentment was fueled by His Majesty's unaccountable delay in greeting them, but they were served tumblers of rice wine which first they sniffed, and later, as time passed, they swilled down.

Wearing his black and gold uniform, His Majesty entered suddenly followed by a large entourage. Slowly they marched up to greet him on his throne; he smiled and exerted his considerable charm. He asked them each about their families, their business, their hardships and their accomplishments. So, by the time the meal was served outside under the glittering stars, amid a ring of blazing torches, all were experiencing a sense of profound happiness and well-being. The suspicious guests were utterly won over.

For the next few weeks it did not stop raining. His Majesty and his party visited every home in the town, drank at every little wine-shop, visited every store, inspected every fishing boat and ate at every inn. Children and later young adults, then old people, and then everyone came to visit the camp. They gaped at the horses, weapons, tents and other fine accoutrements. They were given meat dumplings soup, sweets and tea. Everyone in the village experienced an unimagined level of excitement and glamour and prosperity. Their happiness and amazement was such that it only occurred to those entrenched in their own power to ask what His Majesty was doing there in the first place.

When it came time to leave, the people of Shan gave a great feast for His Majesty and his entourage. The food consisted of many kinds of fish, principally salmon, cod and eel cooked in many ways. There were also many kinds of bland edible tubers, scant bitter greens and a cloudy rather sour tasting strong drink.

As the evening progressed, various villagers who were renowned for their abilities as dancers and singers entertained the party. Though many of his ministers and entourage found the food depressing, the drink quite nauseating, and the entertainment rustic and tedious in the extreme, His Majesty seemed blissfully content, and even the most bold did not dare to indicate his views. At the end of the evening, His Majesty gave out gold and silver coins with his profile embossed on them.

In the morning, the village turned out to see His Majesty off, and, except for a dozen or so hide-bound notables afraid of losing their sway over the others, they all begged him to return. Thus His Majesty, without ever making his plans known, began the conquest of his new Kingdom.

Then setting out from Shan, moving in a clockwise direction, His Majesty and his party circumambulated the broad peninsula and marked the borders of the Kingdom.

In each village, no matter how small, His Majesty stopped for a week, and at each inn, no matter how primitive, His Majesty and his retinue, dressed in their most formal garb, dined, made toasts and made long semi-spontaneous speeches on the glory of the Shambhala Kingdom. In each of the four cardinal directions, they erected gates, and in each of the interme-diary directions they erected columns with tridents at the top.

The endless fish, the rain, the droning, nasal, tuneless singing recit-als, the cold, the constant smell of smoke and marine life and wet fur, the endless dressing up, and speechifying soon reduced all but His Majesty to a kind of slightly nightmarish stupefaction. Behind His Majesty's back there were many complaints and a general amazement at how one could come to be in this strange inhospitable place, dressed like gods and eating smelly food, and altogether being so utterly uncomfortable.

6)

At night after dinner, His Majesty would assemble his entourage and have them sit in rigid lines to the right and left of an improvised shrine. Dressed entirely in white, His Majesty would kneel on the floor before the shrine, light lamps and incense, offer water, perfume, food and musical instruments. Then he would speak for a long time. He praised the beauty of the land and wept at the horrors that men had inflicted on one another to possess it. He invoked the deities of earth, water and sky. He praised and made offerings to the nature deities, the kami who are the forces of life pervading the physical world. He called on the ancestral sovereigns who brought peace and order to the world. He wept and cried as he begged for them to take their place in the human realm. He offered them his existence and his life.

Then, after hours of tearful supplication, His Majesty would call for a short sword. Slowly, he would open his robes, take a deep breath, unsheathe the blade and deliberately draw it across his bare abdomen.

Sometimes he would touch the skin leaving a thin red mark, sometimes he would cut deeper and there would be blood. No one knew if, one evening, he would actually plunge the sword into himself.

On other occasions, His Majesty would pretend to take poison. He would thrash and writhe on the floor for hours. Though everyone knew that the drink had merely been strong alcohol, the protracted feigned death was somehow no less horrifying.

The Successor remembered these evenings with dread. No matter how formulaic they became, no one knew if one night, His Majesty might not actually kill himself.

7)

Another ceremony that His Majesty improvised at that time involved repeatedly enthroning the Successor. Again, the courtiers would sit in rows on ether side of the shrine. The Successor, dressed in his finest black robes, would be seated in a high-backed chair in front of the shrine table.

His Majesty would supplicate, make offerings and weep for several hours. He would offer the Successor to the ancestral spirits. Then attendants would bring a small black lacquer box that His Majesty would tie on top of the Successor's head.

The courtiers would then sing Shambhala songs and the anthem over and over for several hours.

"That little box really hurt," the Successor said later. "But when I mentioned it to His Majesty, he snarled: 'Do you think being a ruler is in any way comfortable?'"

8)

A month into the circumambulation of the Kingdom, when they had reached about the halfway point, His Majesty had the first of a series of "attacks". He would suddenly become violently ill with stomach pains and headaches and blood would pour from his nose. Whether it was day or night, in rain or sun or fog or gale, he insisted on sitting on his throne in the center of his encampment with his ministers, generals and consorts arrayed in rows before him. He likewise insisted that his soldiers redouble their guard and stand at full combat readiness. But when his doctor sought to treat him, he sent them away. The local demons and protectors were coming against him, and he was, one by one subjugating them. He offered himself in this battle with the most primal energies of place and mind without any consideration for his own comfort or happiness.

Thus His Majesty sat without moving for hours, only pausing to take a sip of rice wine, sometimes uttering a violent, piercing cry. However on four occasions, he called for paper and ink, drew a great circle and slashed through that with the primordial stroke.

Once having made a complete journey around the perimeter, they struck out to cross the country, which they did four times, thereby indicating the division of the land into eight principal regions. And in the center of the kingdom, on an almost circular plateau which had a deep blue lake on its eastern edge, His Majesty proclaimed the future magical capital of Kalapa, and this they circumambulated sixteen times.

As they crossed and circled the land, the hooves of the horses in the cavalcade cut a circle around the kingdom's perimeter and around its central spiritual capital. This trail also described the eight counties that were arrayed in the form of an eight-petalled lotus. Thus the land was marked with the form of Shambhala itself.

Through all of this, the psychic attacks on His Majesty continued unabated so that when they finally left, he was so weak that he could no longer ride horseback and had to be carried on a camel in a palanquin. In fact, the entire expeditionary force returned somewhat bedraggled and worse for wear.

When he returned south to his home, His Majesty went to bed for five weeks, after which he returned to public life as strong as ever. However it was widely remarked that his complexion and his mien had changed. He was no longer so ruddy and dark and his face had the color and sheen of white jade, and was as immobile as if carved from stone.

9)

POEM
Traveling on the glowing path of love,
Rise through the light and dark of the sky
Past conception of the stars.

The pure heart of the human realm opens
As an egg of silver light,
As a circular sea of gold light,

And shows within itself a vast lotus,
A realm, a kingdom
With ranges of misty snow mountains,
Fragrant dark forests, grassy pastures,
Turquoise lakes and flickering streams.

Here at the center, on the highest point,
Vast, golden and serene is the Palace of Kalapa.

From here emerge the Rigdens, one by one,
In armor and brocade with golden crowns.
The face of each is different
Each displays to you his attributes,
The secret emblem to counter the evils of the age
In which he rules.

The lightning flashes
Reflecting from their helmets, their armor
Their jewels, and their swords
Are songs of spontaneous insight.

They appear one by one,
Each in a blaze of multi-colored light,
Rulers of the past present and future
Dancing slowly in a circle.

As their eyes meet yours,
You feel you are drowning in a fathomless lake
Where fear, excitement, hope, self-doubt
Are washed from you,
Even as you drift into a world you have not quite known.

In the immense courtyard of the palace,
Surrounded by crimson colonnades with gilded capitols,
They sway in stately dance.

Then emerge the Queens of the Mother lineage,
With soft smiles and imperial poise,
Followed by Ministers, Generals, Warriors,
Horses, elephants,

It is as if all the mountains, seas,
Animals, plains, sounds and scents, tastes
Are massed around them as cloudbanks in the sky.

From a smile,
A jade cup of amrita is offered to you,
And you drink.

Empty awareness radiating the light of great compassion
Without limit.
All expansion.

The form of the body
Is inseparable from love and prayer,
Conquers
The wounds and fragmentation
Of individual history.
Emanates, from the heart
The true Shambhala.

XVII. CONTINUITY

1)

   Why, he wonders, do some streets seem to promise quiet happiness; others speak of glamorous worldliness, secret sexuality, desolation, energetic activity, serious thought, craziness, lyrical partings and new friends? Edward walks through the night and hears these whisperings about people he could become, friends he could have, times in which he could have lived. It is a kind of intimacy that grows as he walks through the city by night.

2)

   Edward sits in a chair by the window reading. Outside, suddenly he hears a growing roar like a forest fire. He opens the window, down the block a huge crowd has assembled in front of a glass-walled apartment building. An apartment is on fire. Smoke is pouring from a shattered window. A mob is shouting.

Edward does not stop work on the translation. He finds the sheer arbitrariness of the structures that the Prince creates both repellent and comforting.

3)

Edward is wandering along a mid-town side street with many famous restaurants. Discrete neon signs, brass plaques, the dim warmth glowing through the doors and the opulence of their glimpsed interiors are tantalizing on the cold wet street. He imagines the world of the occupants as one of constant friendship, parties, conversation, beautiful rooms, beautiful intelligent women. He sees Lauren Bacall sitting at a table. She looks up. Their eyes meet. Cold winds and sudden sadness enfold him. He goes to a bar.

4)

Edward's loneliness intensifies as he walks through the door. Recessed lights punctuate the trails of smoke drifting through the bar. Light shines only in the eyes of waiting men and women. Eyes thirsting for a face, a glance, a gesture. They are looking to find a body to inhabit, like ghosts hungering for birth. They desire to fall in love and be loved. Edward feels that he is living on the edge of the world in a crush of thoughts too crowded to articulate. He leaves. Young boys, lynx-eyed hookers, wait at the door.

5)

Edward is slightly drunk. It is just after mid-night, and he is walking uptown along Fifth Avenue from a bar where he has become something of a regular. A block ahead, he sees a couple and a woman friend, American, but all are dressed in traditional Japanese clothes. The women are dancing on the pavement and laughing as the man tries to wave down a cab. Edward thinks they are probably leaving a costume party. They are young. Edward cannot escape the impression that Lady M and her two artist friends have come to life. Before he can reach them, a cab pulls to the curb and sweeps them away. It is difficult to acknowledge such an experience.

THE SECRET ANNALS : ANNAL IV - Concerning K- part 7

1)

"Our Kingdom is realized by true command. True command rises from truth itself, non-deception. And it is made manifest by immaculate clarity, precise articulation and timing."

So saying, that autumn His Majesty moved his entire government and his court. Three months later after they were all ensconced, he arrived in Shan surrounded by his personal attendants and his full military entourage. Unaccountably, no suitable residence had been arranged for him, so he went to the Prime Minister's mansion and moved in with his wife, consorts and staff.

The Prime Minister had expected that his Majesty was going to live in an encampment with his soldiers, but it soon became clear that His Majesty had no intention of leaving, and that, in fact, he was making the Prime Minister's house his own. The Prime Minister took this development very poorly, and with considerable bitterness and recrimination soon moved out and built himself a smaller but by no means modest residence.

This taken care of, His Majesty set about turning the Prime Minister's lavish residence into the seat of the Shambhala Court itself. Some of those charged with this alteration came to His Majesty to complain of the lack of various luxurious timbers and other goods.

"We make do with what we have!" His Majesty thundered. This was one of His Majesty's principles, in people as well as things.

In this way, the Shambhala Court, with its complex of public spaces, government offices, temples and private quarters for His Majesty and including gardens and a tea pavilion, was completed in the next eighteen months. Large tents were set up and used to fulfill these functions until the buildings themselves were finished.

2)

His Majesty insisted that the first great public room to be completed be the throne room in the Shambhala Court. The throne room was a wide hall with a raised platform across one of the longer walls. Light filtered in through parchment screens on both the shorter walls. In style the room was extremely austere. There were no furnishings on the black highly polished lower floor, while only plain woven rush mats covered the platform. On that platform was a golden two-paneled screen. In front of it were two gold brocade bolsters on which His Majesty would sit, to the right of which was a small black lacquer table adorned with turquoise.

Those having an audience sat in warrior posture directly on the floor, and only those of higher rank or those being singled out for some especial honor were provided with a small hard pillow covered in black cotton.

When His Majesty was to enter the shrine room, those waiting would first hear the sound of a bass drum beating regularly from somewhere far off in the palace. This was followed by the sound of a bell. As the sound of the bell came closer and closer, the level of tension in those present rose. And when His Majesty was about to enter the room, there would be a crash of cymbals. All put their heads to the floor and waited without looking up, often for some time. When the bell was sounded again, all sat erect.

His Majesty would then be seated on his cushions, a silver fan and glass of clear liquid to his right. Further to his right, seated attendants held his sword, his bow and arrow and his scepter. To his left were female guards and consorts, and behind them all were a row of guards holding his personal ensign, the flag of Shambhala and various other battle standards.

Even though there had been no specific discussions with the local people on the subject, His Majesty had always acted as an earth protector sovereign. He invited all the inhabitants to be received in the throne room, and one by one they were formally presented to him. The suddenness and completeness of this apparition before them gave all in attendance, whether old followers or new citizens, a sudden shock. As they sat there, they felt engulfed in a golden lake of honey where they could neither move nor breathe. He announced his intention to continue in his patronage of all local workers. No doubt the overwhelming presence of the military, and the complete absence of any countervailing force played some part in the ease of this governmental transition.

His Majesty then gave titles, honors and gold medals to all the local dignitaries. Some were made advisors to the new government and some were invited to accept appointments as purveyors to the royal household. He announced his intention to continue in his patronage of all local workers.

3)

Despite the fervor of all around him, the Duke of K found the atmosphere at court unbearably claustrophobic and did everything he could to avoid all but the most important events. His Majesty was annoyed that one whom he had so loved and honored continually held himself aloof. K felt continually squeezed into some way of being that felt out of control.

"You're missing so much," a minister who had once been a friend but now generally avoided him said.

One evening the Duke of K was at a dinner party seated next to His Majesty's attendant, D. D was speaking ardently of his devotion to His Majesty. The Duke of K remarked: "That's all very well for you. But I'm afraid that even if I were the student of the world-honored Tilopa and Tilopa said to me: 'If I had a worthy student, he would jump in the fire right now.' I would say to Tilopa: ' Well I hope you find such a student.'"

"Then that would be your story," D replied. This made a lasting impression on K.

4)

Early the following spring, His Majesty took his army out into the mountain forests north of Shan for an encampment that would last two months. The encampment began while the cold winds and snow still filled the high terrain, but within weeks, warm winds crossing the lake from the west brought the beginnings of spring and with it mud. By the end of the encampment, summer had begun, and the broad high plain on which the encampment took place was filled with lush grasses and wildflowers. One of the strangest aspects of the encampment was the freedom and ease with which all the wild animals: deer, elk, groundhogs, badgers, foxes, squirrels and all manner of birds moved through the rows of tents and the formations of soldiers.

The encampment itself was a great circle of tents around a central parade ground. His Majesty's tent, larger than the others but otherwise the same, was surrounded by those of his senior officers and ministerial guests and was placed at the point where the circle backed up against a steep granite escarpment. Beyond the circle and guarding it were the formations of other infantry and cavalry divisions. All tents were marked by the appropriate banners and pennants which, as they fluttered in the breeze and snapped in the winds, gave this otherwise serious enterprise a brilliant and joyful look.

During the period of the encampment, His Majesty's government continued uninterrupted, sustained by a continuous flow of mounted messengers and by long visits from all the ministers. But the main work of the camp was training new troops and keeping the veterans in battle readiness. During the day, there were martial arts training, practice in hand-to-hand combat, horsemanship, archery, scouting and tracking and marching drill. At night, His Majesty would address the troops. Here he taught the profound and subtle methods for the fundamental conquest of aggression in the individual and in the world at large, and here he proclaimed the brilliant expanse of non-aggression itself. Indeed the encampment never slept, as troops practiced maneuvers in the dark and guard shifts protected every access.

The culmination of the encampment was a series of skirmishes in which all would put into practice what they had learned. Command of the contesting divisions was given to senior military officers and to ministers as a way of testing their leadership, ingenuity and general understanding of His Majesty's unique approach to warfare.

On one such occasion, the commands were given to the Minister of Security and to the Prime Minister. In the battle that ensued, the Minister of Security established a camp in the center of a nearby field, surrounded it with guard posts and kept his men in perfect and impeccable formation. The Prime Minister took to the woods and adopted a freewheeling guerrilla strategy. By picking off guard after guard, and later by rushing the Minister of Security's diminished, exposed and rigidly deployed forces, he succeeded in killing off the entirety of his opponent's army. Killing here meant striking an opponent with a bag of dye, and one so marked had to withdraw from combat.

When the two generals returned to His Majesty's tent to report on their strategies and the outcome, His Majesty was utterly enraged. His fury pervaded the very air and caused both men to quake. He found it disgusting that the Minister of Security had thought only of his own perfection and nothing of the protection of his men; and he thought it even more vile that the Prime Minister only thought of killing rather than entrapment. And he ordered that the two should try again the next day.

During the night, the Prime Minister came to His Majesty. For the first time in his life, he could not imagine how he was to carry on and he felt that he really could not fulfill His Majesty's commands. He asked His Majesty to be relieved of his command the next day.

His Majesty took his hand and spoke to him softly and urgently.

"You don't understand. The dark ages are coming towards us ever more swiftly. The cruelties, hardships, and barbarism of the present are nothing compared to what time is going to bring. The suffering for all beings will be inconceivable and, utterly caught in pain, their ability to find any enlightenment shall be ever less.

"The radiance of goodness shines in the senses. Brilliance stops subconscious gossip. The power of goodness draws the elements towards whatever or whoever displays courage, bravery, mercy and elegance. These powers will move towards whoever behaves this way, regardless of his or her ultimate purpose. They are impersonal. For the benefit of the future, we must capture them."

The Prime Minister was shaken, but fulfilled His Majesty's wishes.

5)

His Majesty sensed that the Prime Minister's loneliness was weakening him. He advised the Prime Minister: "Get a lover. Whether it is a man or a woman, it doesn't matter. But it must be someone you can trust completely. Tell that person everything and don't hold back."

When the lover whom the Prime Minister chose was a man, when the Prime Minister made that man his secretary, factotum and heir and isolated him thereby from all other contact, His Majesty made no objection.

"You know," His Majesty told the Duke of K, "He is always much better at choosing women than men."

Soon after, His Majesty requested the Duke to establish a bureau of spies. The Duke declined.

"You'll report only to me," promised His Majesty.

"I'm afraid we have a hard enough time getting along as it is," said the Duke as he refused.

6)

A woman friend of the Duke of K found the protocol of the Kingdom unbearably pretentious and missed bitterly the easy informality of earlier times. She railed against all the pomp and corruption to any who would listen. She wanted to talk to His Majesty about her misgivings and grievances but found it impossible to get an appointment to see him. The Duke intervened and, despite His Majesty's exasperated reluctance, secured an audience for her.

Afterwards he asked the woman what he had said.

"He said that he deeply appreciated my intelligence and honesty, but he wanted me to understand that by speaking as negatively as I do, I cause others to experience the doubts they are concealing from themselves. He thanked me for this, he said it is a service to the kingdom even if he thought it might cause me to lose friends."

7).

His Majesty sent the Prime Minister and his wife on a long diplomatic mission to all of the surrounding lands with a view to the future annexation of the adjoining states. The problem was extremely intricate and every possible decision seemed to lead to a stalemate on another front.

"So how shall I proceed?" asked the Prime Minister.

"More over it." His majesty thundered.

"But how, how could I be more overt?" the Prime Minister replied in dismayed incomprehension.

"No. MORE OVER IT. MORE OVER IT."

This was one of his Majesty's great proclamations of method. His Majesty then instructed the Prime Minister in great detail on his deportment, emphasizing the kind of clothing he should wear and paid special attention to the formal clothing to be worn at evening dinners.

The Prime Minister was duly obedient and wore the prescribed garments. But he found that every single time he wore such clothes, sometime, in the course of the evening, he was mistaken for a steward or some other kind of high-level slave. He endured this humiliation with a mixture of bitterness and humor.

During this mission, the Prime Minister found himself plagued by many doubts concerning His Majesty's intentions in creating a secular society and about his abilities to realize the Kingdom of Shambhala on this earth. In the middle of the night, as the Prime Minister sat disconsolately looking out of the upper window in an inn, staring at the empty desert that stretched out beyond him, a messenger arrived, bearing a message from His Majesty.

"Are you having doubts? Don't worry, Sweetheart. It will work out."

Late one night, as the Prime Minister was telling K this story and about the comic humiliations that preceded His Majesty's message, he stopped and eyed K's robes carefully.

"That's really beautiful silk. Where do you get it?"

"Some place that was going out of business." The Prime Minster smiled and sighed.

"That's just it, you know. You actually have good taste. I don't, so I have to buy things only at really expensive places." He shrugged.

8)

His Majesty's schedule, by this time, was almost invariant. He would rise quite early. An attendant would enter, bow, and offer him tea. He would tell his dreams as another attendant wrote these down in a note-book. He would be escorted to the bath where he would perform his ablu-tions, one attendant handing him his tooth stick, another his washcloth, another his razor, another his bath towel, and another his hairbrush. This was always done in the same order and the various implements were always put back in the same arrangement, regardless of the large variety of people who attended him.

Despite the routine nature of these tasks and whether he spoke or not, the attendants always felt that on each occasion they had experienced something very personal with His Majesty.

He then put on an informal robe and returned to his room where he had his breakfast. The master of the household would enter, and the names of the day's attendants, the meals to be served and the guests who were expected would be discussed.

Then he would get dressed more formally, either in military or civil-ian garb. The Minister who was to supervise his schedule would then arrive, and they would discuss what needed to be done that day. If there was very little, and His Majesty had arranged his government so that many people were capable of seeing to the day-to-day affairs of the realm, then he and the minister would simply sit in his study until it was necessary for him to see someone.

Then there was a light lunch, and then a nap or a journey through the city and into the countryside. In the late afternoon, there might be more meetings or audiences in the throne room, but this time was also spent writing edicts, poetry or making calligraphies.

His Majesty would then dress for dinner and would stay with the guests until he was tired. At that point the whole morning ritual would be performed in reverse, except for the shaving, which took place only in the morning. As he slept, guards lay in front of his doorway and stood guard throughout the court and at its gates.

XVIII. CONTINUITY

1)

Beneath everything he sees and smells and hears, it seems a wide terrain of feelings, images, intuitions is opening. The world's fluid and limitless display prom-ises a journey Edward fears, and longs for.

He is walking at sunset across Central Park. He hears hoof beats behind him. He turns. A small Asian woman in a black velvet military jacket sits erect in the saddle of a huge black horse. She emerges from the shadowed woods and charges straight at him. She gives a cold smile and doesn't slow down. Edward throws himself to the side just in time. She canters past, almost hitting him and doesn't look back. Edward is outraged, but feels an unaccountable pride at this small defiant figure. For a second, he has moved into another strand of time where he sees her flying across the steppes. He hears soldiers on horseback cantering behind her.

2)

The moon is hard and bright as new silver. A man is walking on the moon. In grainy black and white images, they show him pretending to play golf.

3)

Edward meets a woman at an art gallery opening. They have coffee a few times. She invites him for Sunday supper to meet her father. "Cut your hair," says the hard-mouthed flinty little man before they have even finished shaking hands. Edward is unnerved, but smiles politely. "You know what I've been doing this afternoon?" "No sir." "Watching war movies. World War Two. I missed that one." Edward gives a serious nod. The man stares at him as if boring a hole. "There's nothing that can quell the violence in my soul," he snarls." Edward thinks: even my father wouldn't have said that. After a silent meal he leaves. At the door, the girl smiles at Edward.

"Isn't he sweet?" Edward looks at her, sees no irony. If she has intended to get rid of him, she has succeeded.

4)

Edward has a rare dinner with his cousin Margaret in an expensive clubby restaurant. He tells her that no one has given a positive response to the resumes he sent out. She offers help, and he accepts.

"And I'd love to read the translation you're doing. Maybe you should send it out with your resume."

He stammers about needing to finish it all before showing parts of it. She nods understandingly, but Edward realizes that spending so much time translating a text universally regarded as a forgery may be perceived as a problem. He can't explain this to his cousin.

5)

Edward goes to a huge anti-war demonstration in Washington. He has never been in such an overwhelming throng. Everyone shares a desire for a new world. It seems that revolution actually could occur. The country is on the verge of a new order, a future that will sweep the past away.

He returns to New York. People do not know how to live in their skin. Poised on a cliff above a hot smoky abyss, all are aware of not knowing.

Edward sits at a bar next to a small handsome onyx-eyed Apache. The Indian tells him that there were all kinds of informers, all kinds of wiretaps. "Any one who talks on the phone about politics, drugs or anything even a little illegal is asking for it."

6)

Edward wants to fall in love. He wants the feeling of being a ghost to stop. He wants the feeling of skin on skin.

Edward consults an astrologer. The main result is a momentary relief in being told that he has some kind of fate, that his life has a shape.

He realizes every time he meets someone, he is trying to enter a new world.

7)

One evening, a friend of his cousin's invites him to an engagement party. He tries to speak to everyone, to make new friends. After an hour, he realizes that no one knows the couple whose engagement is being celebrated.

8)

Edward looks at random in the Annals. He reads:

"You have never chosen a single one of your thoughts. You have not invented their contents."

He is not comforted and flips to another page.

"A gentleman always has time for confidence."

THE SECRET ANNALS : ANNAL IV - Concerning K- part 8

1)

The outer purpose in the establishment of this kingdom was to make a place to which all people might look as a haven, a hope and a model. The inner purpose was to allow all the citizens to realize their innate enlightenment while living utterly ordinary lives. To that end, His Majesty trained his ministers and conducted his cabinet meetings.

His Majesty made his ministers responsible for information about the Kingdom, for ideas on how to improve its functioning, for punctiliousness in carrying out whatever was needed. At the same time, His Majesty wished for his ministers to be able to function as his personal representatives in counseling the many subjects whom he was unable to meet. For these reasons, the weekly cabinet meetings were not just administrative gatherings, but were part of His Majesty's method in training the ministers. They were the entire Buddhist and Shambhala teachings on the spot. They were "the practice of fruition".

For this reason, even years after his death, the ministers would come to regard these meetings as the paramount moments in their careers, and those sessions at which His Majesty was present were especially vivid in this regard. Each of the 12 or more ministers would bring with him a report on the results of his last week's labors, activities and problems within his domain and plans for the near and distant future. This would be subjected to the scrutiny of the entire cabinet, which was rife with differing points of views and personal rivalries, as well as to the concentrated attention of His Majesty.

The cabinet meetings were held in a large corner room on the second floor of the Shambhala Court. In the winter, light filtered in through the paper windows and filled the room with a bright even light, but in the summer, and sometimes even at His Majesty's command, when it was still very cold, the screens were drawn back, giving access to the surrounding balcony with its pine balustrades, and to a view of the entire city below and the great lake beyond. The room itself was large with a high coffered ceiling, a black polished floor and paneled in a honey-colored cedar that was both warm and faintly aromatic. On the longer wall was a large map of the kingdom. Beneath it was a large brazier for smoke offerings. On the narrower wall was a large painting of Suchandra, First King of Shambhala, that surmounted a small but elaborate shrine. On either side of each were the flags of Shambhala and His Majesty's personal standard. A long black lacquer table surrounded by red lacquer chairs in the Han style and his Majesty's gilded chair in a similar style at the far head of the table were the main furnishings.

The ministers, wearing formal dress, would meet in a small anteroom where they would encounter a compliment of guards and senior household attendants. They would be offered a small glass of strong alcohol and would then enter the cabinet room where the shrine was lit and a smoke offering filled the room with the heavy astringent scent of cedar and sage. Often, His Majesty himself would have placed a flower arrangement at the center of the table, and this arrangement, sometimes made of lovely spring flowers, sometimes of pine boughs, sometimes just of rocks with moss lying directly on the table was often taken to provide some hint to the tone of the meeting to come.

A great atmosphere of anticipation and anxiety prevailed which the Ministers would seek to overcome by shuffling papers, exchanging documents and examining the agenda. This document was drawn up by the court calligrapher days earlier. Each would find it at his place at the table, but none had ever seen it before. Often, citizens other than ministers were given seats at His Majesty's or the Prime Minister's invitation. The meaning of their presence was the subject of whispered speculation on the part of the regular cabinet members.

When the buzz and busywork subsided, the Prime Minister would enter and take his seat to the right of His Majesty's chair. Then the Minister of Security would leave the room, go to His Majesty's private office or his residential suite and request that he preside over the cabinet meeting.

As the procession of guards escorting His Majesty slowly through the hall was heard coming closer, the tension and general energy in the room rose. At His Majesty's entry, all stood and bowed until he was seated. His Majesty was seated with two guards at attention on either side; then the ministers sat and took their first full look at the sovereign.

His Majesty, though always meticulous in his manner of dress, gave particular attention to what he wore on these occasions. Usually he would wear the somewhat subdued but elegant robes such as a prosperous merchant might wear, but sometimes he came dressed as a native Shan chieftain. Later in his life, he usually wore a military uniform.

Before the formal meeting began, he always took time to acknowledge each of those present with a glance, a smile, a shrug, a small hand gesture, then he would look over the pile of papers which had been placed before him, sometimes noting the excessive amount of documents generated. Then he would sit at attention and all would bow to begin the meeting.

The minutes of the preceding meeting were then reviewed and follow-up questions asked before the business of the current session was undertaken. While this took place, no casualness of body, speech, or mind was allowed. Everyone focused completely on the matters at hand. It was unheard of for a minister to approve of something in simply a pro-forma way. Each was expected to present her or his insight to the fullest. This led to many heated debates in which His Majesty took great delight. Generally however, while His Majesty paid close attention to all that transpired, except for a whispered comment to the Prime Minister, he rarely said much.

These meetings lasted about three or four hours and were usually interrupted by an intermission in which tea and small but elaborate snacks were served in a very formal manner. When the food was cleared away, the meeting would resume. His Majesty often would conclude the proceedings by offering a general commentary on the needs of the kingdom and the conduct of government. He would then thank everyone for his or her work. All would then bow. His Majesty, as slowly as he had entered, would depart.

At the conclusion of such meetings, all the ministers and all those present were completely exhausted and drained by the sustained attention and the need to be continuously on the dot. Most went home to bed. His Majesty however was always energized by these sessions and usually entertained until all hours of the morning.

His Majesty insisted that his ministers not succumb to doubt and hesitation; he said:

"Because enlightenment is real, whether you feel it or not, whether you are overcome by depression or neurosis, you can always CRANK IT UP."

2)

From time to time following his cabinet meetings, much in the style of the Han Emperors, His Majesty would issue memorials.

MEMORIAL

We request the attention of our government, including the Prime Minister, Ministers, Generals and Members of Our Household:

I have given up personal security, reputation and comfort to establish the Kingdom of Shambhala.

You may feel you are protected by your connection to me. You may feel you are in danger because of your connection to me. But the questions of our future and our protection are in your hands. The questions of material well-being, the spiritual development of our subjects, the education of our children are in your hands. It may be tempting to think of our relationship as one between friends, lovers, between employer and employee or master and slave, for that matter. The point is: there is no individual project.

This is not the dedication which a religious conviction requires, nor is it the dedication which a social cause demands. This is our personal and interpersonal life. It is between me and you and is a fact. We do not hide from this nor do we hide it from others. There is no deception, absolutely none. You must expand this yourselves to our subjects and to our world entirely.

H M Earth Protector of Shambhala

PS.

You may feel that now we have established something, we must move forward or backward or sideways or up or down. Actually, we must deepen and expand together. More in and more out. If any of you are unclear about how to do this, you have my permission to consult any of my consorts. They will be able to give clear instructions on this approach.

3)

The social events at the court were similarly formulaic. Before dinner began, the guests would be asked to read a short poem. As each read the poem, His Majesty would correct their inflection, intonation and pronunciation. The guest would read the poem over and over, and correction would follow correction until His Majesty was either satisfied or did not feel anything more could be accomplished. Then the next guest would read the poem, be corrected, and so on, until all who were there had had their turn.

4)

One of His Majesty's translators could not bear the process of the endless readings and corrections of the poem and asked His Majesty why he insisted on doing it so often.

"If one speaks properly, with proper weight and intonation and stress given to the vowels and consonants, words will emerge in their own power. Sentences will have their own power. Phenomena can be transformed by that power."

Then His Majesty pointed to an ancient wooden statue that he always kept nearby. It depicted the great poet-yogi Milarepa, in which the yogi held his right hand cupped to his right ear.

"The traditional meaning of this posture is that Milarepa is listening to the dakinis' speech. "But," His Majesty continued: "really he holds his hand to his ear so he can hear himself think."

After these recitations, dinner would be served. Sometimes all the guests would be offered food, and sometimes only His Majesty. In either case, the guests were provided with whatever they wished to drink, be it tea or rice wine or water or all three.

Throughout the meal a certain game would be played. His Majesty would be a certain person or object. He would carefully write the name of that person or object on a piece of paper which he then folded and placed beneath the base of the candlestick nearest him. The guests would try to find out who or what His Majesty was by asking about it or his various qualities. Such questions as: "If you were a horse, what sort of horse would you be?" "If you were a color..." "If you were food..." "If you were a musical instrument..." Each guest was permitted three direct questions and when all the guests had asked questions, if they had not determined the answer, they would start over. His Majesty was often the moon, or a king of Shambhala or a victory banner. The questioning could take hours because His Majesty liked to cheat.

During one such evening, His Majesty interrupted the game to go to the bathroom. An attendant accompanied him out of the tent and as they walked towards the latrine said: "Sire, I think I know what you are."

"You should," replied His Majesty pleasantly. "We've been doing this fucking thing often enough."

Following several rounds of the game, His Majesty and his guests would sit outside around a campfire while one of His Majesty's secretaries would read in high stilted diction various episodes from the annals of the history of Shambhala. These evenings usually ended just before the sun rose.

Perhaps because he found them claustrophobic, K was not included in most government functions or court activities. He did however hear a great deal about them. Otherwise, he busied himself in commerce to support his mother-in-law, The Grand Duchess. When finally he was invited to court and witnessed this guessing game, he was impressed at how His Majesty had devised a mode of socializing that allowed him to observe his guests' minds while the guests could see how His Majesty's mind worked, all without any extraneous material.

5)

To serve at the court was a great discipline requiring concentration, tact and humor. Though sharp when their attention wandered, His Majesty treated all who served him with interest and courtesy. The same could not always be said for the guests, who sometimes made vulgar displays of ordering the servers about like slaves. The servers were trained to retaliate by serving the boor with inedible portions of food, putting salt in their wine or spilling gravy on them.

When their tasks were complete, there was often great merriment, drinking and card games. His Majesty's steward more than once found couples copulating in the linen closets.

"There is always a lot of passion around His Majesty," he said.

6)

Aside from the many other rigors pertaining to dining at the court, there was also the matter of the food. As time went by, the food at court became stranger and stranger. Guests were frequently offered boiled lambs' heads, served from iron cauldrons carried round the table. At each place setting, common hammers and chisels with which to split the skull were placed beside the silver chopsticks. His Majesty delighted in encouraging his guests to eat the eyeballs, which were considered a great delicacy in some culture or other.

Those who dined late at night with His Majesty had the opportunity to eat one of his favorite dishes; a stew made from frozen meat sliced thin, covered with fiery hot sauce, and then boiling water poured over the whole thing. Another late night favorite was beef preserved in tallow.

However, there was not a continuous flow of luxurious food at the court. Often there were times of hardship; then beans and rice were ladled out from the silver tureens onto the delicate porcelain. It also happened that due to some budgetary error, there was no food at all. Then His Majesty's Master of the Household was obliged to send out messengers to find people who would invite the King to dinner. His Majesty viewed all of this with great good humor since he genuinely enjoyed the society of his subjects.

7)

That winter, His Majesty began giving very formal dinners every night of the week. The guests at each of these dinners were, with few exceptions, the same and consisted of the cabinet, several nobles, and military dignitaries. Every night, each of these Lords and Ladies put on their finest clothes, went to the Court and sat with the very same people, gave virtually identical toasts and spoke utterly stilted spontaneous discourses on the Kingdom of Shambhala.

The guests all felt the growing desire to have a drink, something to eat, a cigarette, a conversation, a break, and so felt the claustrophobia of her or his own existence. They could not imagine that His Majesty had gone to the trouble to make such a thing visible not to torture them but to allow them to discover a way to live within the embrace of their own phenomena.

K was seated at a long boring formal dinner between the Minister in charge of Religion and the Minister of Education. Neither was interested in conversation, but when someone began to give a long fulsome toast to the latter, he turned to K and said: "Why is it that whenever someone praises me, it's always someone I have no respect for?" K was astonished, as the minister continued: "I never like being in places where I am not acknowledged as the most important."

K was ill at ease trying to befriend people who would never like him and whom he would never really like. Under such circumstances, there was little he could contribute to the society His Majesty was shaping. But pretentious and weird as it all was, he couldn't help feeling some kind of deep, painful and strangely exuberant geological shift taking place. Like before an earthquake, everything around His Majesty seemed preternaturally still and wildly unstable. It was as if His Majesty were the pivot for a vast alteration in the relationships amongst men and gods and, in so doing, eliciting a new more naked kind of life for rocks and skies and humankind. Even in its utter pettiness, this was unbearable, inescapable, exhilarating to be near.

8)

In wealth, in exertion, in discipline
Our court is costly.

But our court creates and radiates
Discipline, exertion, wealth and humor
Through our entire kingdom.

It is a glorious light
Seen through the entire world.

This is what we make together.
Who cannot love this court?

All of us, throughout the entire world,
We cannot resist our own display of Awake.

XIX. CONTINUITY

1)

    Pain from the incessant ringing in his ears, discouragement from the lack of response in his search for work cannot be ignored. He is determined to keep working, but he is restless. Every evening, he leaves the apartment and walks for hours.

2)

    Late one night Edward walks home through a half-abandoned neighborhood. Two twelve- year-old Hispanic kids huddled in a doorway turn and call out. "Hey mister, got a dime?" He knows if he stops, they'll rob him, if he doesn't stop they'll feel justified in attacking since a dime, everyone has that. He keeps walking. "Stop or I'll kill you, man." He looks. One boy has a gun. Edward looks around. No one is on the street. The air looks hot in the orange streetlights, but it is cold. Edward turns and walks away. He thinks: "It's not my moment." He waits, but the bullet doesn't come.

3)

    One evening as he walks to dinner, Edward looks down to the light shining in a basement apartment. A slender young blond man, naked, is lying on a couch, stroking himself, staring out the window. He walks on.

4)

    Edward feels he is vanishing into the glut of images of men and women and lights.

    He dreams he is lying in bed in a hotel room. There is a knock on the door. It is Harumi and she sounds concerned. He realizes he cannot not speak or move. He is not breathing. He tries to call out for her help. He cannot.

5)

    Edward is coming home at about four in the morning. He sees a taxi stop in front of his cousin's apartment. She is in the back seat with another woman; they are kissing passionately. He is surprised for a second, then it all makes sense. He wants her to know he understands, so, a few days later he mentions what he saw.

    "I don't mind that you know, Edward, but if I'd wanted to tell you, I would have." She smiles. He feels close to her.

6)

    It begins to seem that some of the people he sees on the street resemble characters in the Annals. He becomes more and more certain that somehow the events he is translating are projecting themselves in the present.

    In Chelsea, he sees a couple who again completely resemble the artist and his dancer girl friend in Lady M's memoirs. He sees a pair of young men in suits walking into a jewelry store. Something in their cocky manner makes him sure they are two of the Prince's followers. He sees a woman in an art gallery; she reminds him of Lady . herself. Early one evening on Lafayette Street in lower Manhattan, he sees exiting a car a stocky oriental in a gray suit who looks like a Hawaiian businessman. A young blond man in a long dark overcoat and a theatrical black fedora accompanies him. A small crowd waits to greet the oriental. They smile as he hurries into the building. Edward can follow if he wants. He is suddenly frightened. He is certain if he does, he will cross into a parallel world from which he cannot return.

7)

    He wakes one morning in the dim light of a shabby loft. He doesn't recognize where he is. He is lying on the floor amid dust and peeling paint. He is in the arms of a woman he may have met at an opening the night before. He is not sure. She smells slightly of formaldehyde. Two couples he doesn't know are sleeping on either side of them.

    He leaves without waking anyone. The blue shadows of early dawn hover in the street. Pink light glows on the brickwork of the top stories. A pigeon flies through the brightness overhead, and Edward can discern the subtle shifts of tint and intensity as light touches the feathers on the bird's under-wings.

8)

    It is an evening in early fall, and Edward is leaning out the window of the apartment. The ledge is a deep marble slab, cool to the touch. A warm breeze rises in the dark air from the streets below, carrying the smell of traffic, of cooking, sweat and faint perfume, laughter, the blare of honking horns, shouts. The world is rushing onward in the air while Edward leans out, still and alone. As if being pulled, he feels how easy it would be to let go and fly out the window. There is nothing holding him back. He pulls back quickly.

He mentions this to his cousin. She becomes apprehensive. He tells her more of what he is experiencing and how it relates to translating the Annals. She's worried about Edward's growing obsession. She decides now to intervene. She insists he see a psychiatrist. Secondly, she decides to use her skills to find him a job. Edward knows that she is only concerned for his well-being, but he is on the verge of finishing his translation. He has too much invested in the project now and refuses to do anything else until it is complete. They strike a bargain. He promises to finish the Annals as soon as possible, but he will consult a psychiatrist in the meantime. Then he will accept whatever job she finds. Actually these plans are a relief. Edward does not like to admit it, but he has growing doubts about the accuracy of his sense of reality.

THE SECRET ANNALS: ANNAL IV - Concerning K - part 9

1)

For many years, His Majesty had yearned to see the Korean kingdom of Silla. He had made use of designs originating there for the construction of his palaces, government buildings and temples. His Majesty encouraged his subjects to learn the music of Silla, its martial arts, painting, methods of cooking, gardening and decorum and to make use of its furnishings, lacquer ware and clothing.

In the time before the plans for the visit to Silla had been completed, His Majesty began rising earlier than usual. He would wear the austere black silk robes favored by the nobles of Silla. He would sit before the warrior shrine and make huge arrangements of flowers in such profusion that the shrine itself could not be seen. Then he would place three rows of nine bowls each before the shrine and fill them with rice wine. He would drink the first row of bowls. Then he would pour the contents of the second row of bowls over his head. At that point, he would retire to his private quarters and change his clothes into bright red garments. He would return to the shrine room and, smiling, drink the rice wine from the remaining bowls.

None of the attendants could understand what all this was about, but they speculated amongst themselves:

"It's as if he's courting."

"But who?"

"Not a person, obviously."

2)

The planning for the visit took two years since there were so many things to see and so many places to visit. In the end, everything was arranged: the immense party of government officials, consorts, advisors and attendants were assembled, all wearing their finest traveling clothes and uniforms, and the enormous caravan of horses and wagons was packed and ready. Four divisions of mounted guards were at the ready. This entire panoply, as well as many of the citizens who came out simply to look, was waiting at the central gate of the Shambhala Court. Only His Majesty was missing.

His Majesty's attendant, Yoji, came to look for him without success, and so called for help. Several hours of futile search ensued. Finally this attendant happened to look in the toilet that was reserved for guests. There was His Majesty slowly and patiently cleaning the floor. "Sir," said the shocked attendant, "Would... would you like to visit Silla today?" "Not so much," His Majesty replied. Nonetheless His Majesty did leave for Silla that very day.

3)

The journey traversing land and sea was very long. When finally they reached the small Kingdom of Silla, they were greeted at the gates of the capital by the king, his cabinet and court. His Majesty and his party were housed in a palace, a sprawling complex of pavilions with white walls and vermilion columns set amid a vast park and formerly the home of the ruler's mother. Interpreters, guides, cooks and all manner of servants were assigned to the visitors from Shambhala. Each, according to his rank was also given bolts of silk and brocade, gold and silver coins, jade, tea, wine and porcelain bowl, ewers, dishes and urns.

Pleading fatigue and ill-health, his Majesty did not attend the lavish banquet offered on his arrival, nor later did he visit the many monuments, temples, gardens to which he and his party were invited. Despite many requests and invitations that came each day, he did not inspect the stables of Silla, nor its libraries, nor did he see its many ancient treasures, nor its renowned holy places. He saw only those art works that were brought to him. He met with none of the dignitaries from the government, the religious establishment or the scholarly world who, drawn by his great reputation, wished to meet him.

Despite persistent invitations, he met with the ruler of Silla only twice: once on the second day of his visit when they had tea together and again three months later just before His Majesty left. Young Koreans were fascinated by the men and women in his Majesty's entourage, and often came to drink with them. This and His Majesty's seclusion caused both consternation and outrage. Silla's courtiers and officials made it increasingly difficult for his Majesty's party to travel in the country, to visit temples or to explore any of the sacred sites. His Majesty's departure was not an occasion for sorrow.

For the entire time he stayed in Silla, His Majesty preferred to sleep during the day and eat and drink through the night with his current consort, a noblewoman named Ou Yan. They had been separated for many years and he had pined for her. They stayed in bed together, never wearing clothes even when the servants entered and even when the Head of His Majesty's Household visited each morning to read off the list of scheduled activities and invitations, which were inevitably declined. His Majesty met with his traveling companions only once. On that occasion he taught elocution. And he left his quarters only to visit one temple, the resting place of the scholar-poet-warrior sage who had founded the Kingdom of Silla. He sat there for a long time and wept.

On their return, when asked about His Majesty's unorthodox, even rude behavior, Ou Yan remarked:

"The Sovereign Earth Protector of Shambhala visited Silla, but did not find it necessary to alter his personal schedule in order to achieve his purposes there."

4)

His Majesty returned earlier than anticipated to the Shambhala Court from his long journey to Silla. The court staff had not been notified in time, and so his Majesty found everything quite dusty, overcoats left on chairs, hats on the floor, boot marks in the hall, rugs skewed, the kitchen full of unwashed pots and dishes, beds unmade, latrines unclean.

He was clearly angry, but said nothing and began at once to wash dishes himself. The court attendants, completely abashed, exerted themselves to restore everything to proper order.

"Sir, how could this have happened?" asked his steward F, who was furious and upset.

"They still live in their heads. They still think that their bodies, their world, this earth is lesser. There is still a lot of resentment. Being alive takes constant effort. Even enjoyment takes effort."

His Majesty then ordered an outdoor shrine to be constructed in the forest near the palace to house the Goddess of the Sun, the deity who had established the royal house of Silla.

"I have requested that she dwell amongst us and she has consented. I have brought her home with me. She is the life force of the sun. She dances the seasons across the sky and she keeps the lineage of true governance alive."

When asked how he brought the deity back from Silla, he replied:

"I brought her in my pocket." Later when the small rustic shrine was dedicated, in his high rough voice, His Majesty sang this song with great ardor:

"Golden, stately, radiant,

"Slowly, she places on clouds her bright petal steps.

"Lightly, she gilds the snow peaks.

"Sparkling, she dances across the sea.

"Shifting, she rests in the fragrant pine branch.

"Golden, stately, radiant,
"Splendor of all that is seen, felt, heard and known,
"Her passions light the high plains of the sky.

"She flies in the dawn breeze.
"And sails like the hunter's arrow.
"She quivers in the deer's startled cry.
"She curls in the white petals of new plum blossoms.
"She whispers in the cold waters of the melted snow.
"She opens in the green scent of sprouting grass.
"She glides in the clatter of the weaver's shuttle,
"And sighs in a lover's lament.
"She descends on banks of shining clouds,
"And flashes on the warrior's sword.
"She is the luster of a ruler's crown.

"She rests in stillness on the fragrant pine branch.
"And her hair is perfumed with galaxies of stars.

"If, in an instant,
"An ocean of sorrow parts,
"She appears.

"Amateratsu Omikami
"Goddess of the Sun,
"Splendor of all that is seen, felt, heard, known.

"Golden, stately, radiant,
"Slowly, she places her bright petal steps:
"Lightly, she touches the snow peaks,
"Sparkling, she dances across black tormented waves,
"Subtly, she rests for a moment in the fragrant cypress glade.

"You see her now
"In the primordial mirror,
"The great circle of the sky.
"She gives to you a man of happiness."

And with this, he prostrated to the sky and turning he prostrated to the entire court. His Majesty said:

"The Kingdom of Shambhala cannot end. It does become invisible. It becomes unavailable to the senses. It re-absorbs into the realm of pure aspiration. This happens when people can't relate to the senses of their bodies with interest and passion and daring and courage and love and vision. That is why the kingdom is said to exist at some times and not exist at others. And that is why the goddess of the sun, who always exists, brings it into being now and everywhere."

5)

Many of those who came to Shan experienced a much harsher life than they had expected. They had followed His Majesty to this distant place expecting to find some kind of perfect paradise and were disappointed and sometimes bitter when all the problems of ordinary life, material needs, emotional upheavals, thoughtless conduct still continued.

"It is the mind of the people which is decisive. We have not simply come here to make an ideal form of government. The meaning of being a citizen of Shambhala is that one is a warrior. The meaning of being a warrior is that over and over, again and again, one battles with inner and outer obstacles. One wins or one loses. One celebrates or laments. Then one undertakes the next battle. The warrior path may sound glamorous, but really it is more like being a professional soldier."

6)

His Majesty sent for the Duke of K. It was rare for him to do so and the Duke was surprised and a little apprehensive. They met in His Majesty's office; conversation meandered, and the Duke could not tell why he'd been summoned.

"I want you to remember me to your father." The Duke had almost forgotten, but indeed the two had met many years before.

"Of course," said the Duke, puzzled.

"I mean it," His Majesty insisted.

"I will," the Duke promised and indeed he was fastidious about keeping his word in such matters. He wrote his father sending His Majesty's best wishes. His father wrote back asking him to reciprocate. Two months later, the Duke heard that his father had suddenly died.

7)

The yearly ceremonial calendar of the Kingdom of Shambhala was established in that time. Summer was celebrated, on its first day, as the direct expression of the all-accomplishing wisdom; fall and harvest as the wisdom of equanimity; winter as mirror-like wisdom; and spring as discriminating-awareness wisdom. In between winter and spring came the most important of the yearly celebrations, Shambhala Day.

Shambhala Day was celebrated on the same day on which the Buddha's birth and death was celebrated. It was a day packed with public and private events. K called it: "ordeal by food and drink".

In general, for those in the court, the day began before first light. Those who were summoned to begin the celebrations with His Majesty began this day by toasting the New Year with a large glass of potato liquor that had been flavored with juniper. This was served at room temperature, and the result of drinking it was both slightly nauseating and entirely inebriating. This drink was followed by a long draught of icy cold mountain spring water. Time became slippery and it was impossible to get any traction as event followed event. The grueling celebrations produced an increasing sense of vivid unreality at whose center His Majesty floated and danced relentlessly.

Thus fortified, those fortunate to begin the day in this manner joined His Majesty in the Great Shrine Hall as the sun rose. He would address the subjects on the successes and failures of the past year and the challenges of the coming one. His Majesty then made the first donation, in gold it must be said, into the treasury of Shambhala. Then one by one, all would file by to receive His Majesty's blessing. In this convivial gathering, filled with old people, children and families of all kinds, the courtiers, being quite drunk, often felt oddly isolated and sad.

While the subjects left the Great Shrine Hall to join their friends and neighbors at large and opulent breakfasts, the courtiers returned to the Kalapa Court where they sat, men on one side, women on the other with His Majesty in the center, at long tables between two other guests who would be their company for many hours. The food consisted of the fieriest South Indian cuisine and vast quantities of rice wine. There were many toasts, though His Majesty generally said little. This meal lasted five hours after which the courtiers were encouraged to stay at the court and play board games together.

Only new participants generally took part, for all the more experienced people, knowing the rigors to come, went home to nap. His Majesty himself did this.

In the early evening, the courtiers returned to the court, wearing their most formal robes and all their decorations and medals. They were seated between the same people they had sat between before and were then treated to a heavy meal of roasted meats and boiled vegetables accompanied by vast quantities of grape wine. This event, also punctuated by toasts and speeches, lasted approximately three hours.

All departed swiftly from the table, raced for their carriages and arrived to attend, depending on the mood of His Majesty and on the year, either a gathering of the Shambhala subjects or a grand Shambhala Ball.

If the celebration was of the latter nature, the courtiers would be expected to: dance a very complicated dance, often to His Majesty's personal direction; listen attentively and politely to frequently incompetent performers who had come from many foreign lands; listen respectfully to many lengthy toasts and discourses; drink rice wine.

If the celebration was of the former nature, it would take place in the Great Shrine Hall, the obligations were the same except there was no dancing, men and women sat on separate sides of the hall, and often His Majesty would speak until the dawn of the next day's sun.

The Duke of K would remember until his dying day the great exertions he expended in the simple effort not to fall over in some combination of sleep and inebriation while all about him echoed the sounds of crashing glasses and thudding bodies. He, like all other participants, felt he had somehow gone beyond himself, and for a while, entered somewhere that, if occasionally absurd and not entirely pleasant, was so intensely alive.

8)

Despite all lofty aims, problems with ministers were continuous. Even those most devoted to His Majesty's vision could not surrender themselves so completely that the temptation to retain some personal advantage dissipated. The Foreign Minister was notorious for taking boys under his wing for more than training purposes and for traveling with them in the most expensive manner and billing these jaunts to the state. The Minister of Transport used state funds for home improvement. The Minister of Education fell in love with a woman who was insisting he leave his wife and left his duties unattended for months. Another Minister, when he traveled, insisted on being served as if he were himself a king. Another solicited gifts.

His Majesty did not fire these men, but rather used their misdeeds to train them. He said: "They are very ambitious and so they are capable of hard work. Some are dangerous. The most dangerous I keep very near to me."

Nonetheless, K began to see that these men and women, whatever their corruptions and misdeed, had thrown themselves into His Majesty's world more wholeheartedly than he could bear to.

9)

"Please do not forget: we are trying to make this Kingdom together from the unappeasable and unending human longing for goodness in this world. We are talking about the deepest and broadest kind of longing. We are talking about a longing very far beyond personal wants and desires.

"This is total longing, longing for the intrinsic goodness of everything to manifest here and now in every human heart and illuminate all the human behaviors of body, speech and mind.

"Now, ordinarily, we long for things like a good life, a better life for our children, a lover, friendship, joy. Sanity. We want to understand. We want to be understood. We want to sing. We long for whatever would finally make us whole.

"Longing pulls us further into the world. It is like riding in the maelstrom of phenomena. It arises because day is bright and night is dark, the earth is dense and fertile, touch is intimate, smells are subtle. Intelligence is sharp. There is strength, a power in our most basic human set-up. So longing here is an expression of confidence in basic goodness.

"This longing is bound together with a deep faith woven into the fabric of our being, a faith that fundamental goodness exists in or world and our being. That we can expand and we can affect the world.

"This is the endless longing of human mind itself. It's so intense that it's almost beyond duality. We share it deeply, but because of it we feel separate. It's as if all notions of subject and object are bound together in an unceasing wind of yearning and faith that scours the universe. And beyond. And this unceasing longing is the real energy that creates the Kingdom of Shambhala for all humanity."

10)

One year, His Majesty and the Prime Minister went on retreat together in the drafty stone castle of a borderland noble. It had been the Prime Minister's dream that he and his Majesty would spend the time devoting themselves to Buddhist Tantric practice, but His Majesty's intentions were otherwise.

His Majesty arrived with his translators and secretaries and declared that the time would be devoted to writing his memoirs. Thus, every day they all met in the study of the castle. His Majesty would dictate one sentence, and all were expected to criticize and make comments. The sentence would be changed, re-read aloud, and the process would resume until all the possibilities for improving that particular sentence had been exhausted. Then the next sentence would be dictated.

During the meal breaks, His Majesty would remark on ghosts he saw in the rooms and corridors of the castle: here a ghost cow and there a phantom couple having sex, and so on. Otherwise there was no time off from writing these fictional memoirs. The discipline was strict. If someone went to the bathroom and spent too long, His Majesty would send an attendant to retrieve him or her. The Prime Minister felt continuously ill. Even he was not allowed to withdraw.

Into this difficult atmosphere came a visitor, a minor functionary, who would later distinguish himself by his numerous desperate changes of loyalty after His Majesty's death. From the first, he was terrified and tried to avoid His Majesty. But on the afternoon of his arrival, he encountered His Majesty as the latter was returning to his work in the study. His Majesty, spotting the functionary, raced up to him, grabbed him by the lapels, and screamed into his face: "Never forget this." The functionary fled, and did, as far as anyone could tell, forget.

11)

During this time, His Majesty received a gift of a rare and powerful intoxicant. He decided to share it with his ministers and closest students. His Majesty explained to the courtiers present that the drug they were about to take was merely an artifice that increased the intensity of illusion. They swallowed the bitter substance, and His Majesty sent for the Prime Minister who sent a message that he had certain other social engagements, but promised to come as soon as he could. As the evening went on, the Prime Minister's absence became more and more evident. His Majesty sent messenger after messenger to summon him, but still he did not arrive.

When finally he appeared, he was quite drunk, swaggering, and inflated by the deference and flattery which those he had previously been with showered on him. He appeared with all the mannerisms of a bullying pimp and all the ministers were appalled and frightened.

"Ask him a question." His Majesty instructed one of the ministers: "Don't hold back. Say what you will."

"Why," asked that minister, "when the sovereign summons you, do you not come?"

The Prime Minister was suddenly terrified, and as he became more frightened, His Majesty became more wrathful and terrifying. He called for paper, ink and his brush. He marched down to the great hall of Shambhala with the ministers in a line behind him. The Prime Minister, quaking, carried His Majesty's brush; others carried water, the ink stick, the ink stone and paper.

When they arrived in the broad pristine ivory hall, His Majesty had the large blank sheet of paper unrolled in the center of the parquet floor. He plunged his brush into the ink and slashed violently at the paper. As ink flew everywhere, spattering the walls and floor, the ministers and attendants, all of whom were completely terrified, His Majesty screamed like thunder: "NO. NO TO EGO. NO."

All were thunderstruck. In this way His Majesty proclaimed the Great No.

Early next morning, the Prime Minister, pale, hung-over, full of fear and regret, came to beg His Majesty's forgiveness. When he arrived, he found the Great Hall in its accustomed pristine state. It was sparkling clean without a speck of ink or dust anywhere. It was as if nothing at all had happened, as if the night before had been completely effaced. The Prime Minster was terrified that all evidence of such a huge drama could be made to disappear. He trembled as he wondered if he had dreamed it all. He told K that nothing had scared him more deeply.

12)

Also the next day before first light, His Majesty summoned the Duke of K. Tea was served, but His Majesty sat silently by the window, leaning out with his chin in his hand, listening to a folk song sung by a woman far off. After some time, His Majesty put his head close to the Duke's and said.

"Last night I saw something that shook me badly. The Prime Minister is afraid. He may not be able to fulfill the mission I require him to fulfill, particularly after I am dead."

"Oh, I think he'll probably be all right." K said easily, trying to placate His Majesty's evident distress. But His Majesty slammed his fist down on the table, and one of the teacups fell over.

"You do not understand. I have a big investment in him. I cannot train another like him. He is crucial." Then His Majesty whispered his instructions to the Duke of K:

"There will come a time, you will know when it is, when I want you to go to the Prime Minister and help him fulfill my wishes." The Duke of K was unaccustomed to being trusted in any very great way. Nonetheless, when the time came, though he did not believe his abilities equal to the task, he did as he had been asked.

13)

It is not certain how this happened, but ten years after His Majesty began ruling the Kingdom of Shambhala from the capital, late one night as he ascended the stairs to go to bed surrounded by his attendants, guards and companion, he pitched over backwards and fell the entire length of the staircase. He landed heavily on the floor and struck his head. He was knocked unconscious and spent many days in bed before he could resume his work. Though he was able to continue as before, from that time onward, slowly but distinctly, his health began to fail.

Soon after, His Majesty said to his ministers and to his older followers:
"I have given you all you need to completely transform the world."

14)

THE WOUND OF KALAPA
The future Rigden steps from the perfumed shadows
Of the palace shrine,
Emerging on the cinnabar verandah.
As his robe of heavy purple brocade swirls past,
The subject who has come from far away,
Looks up at his face,
Youthful and golden behind the pearl strands
Hanging from his crown,

And suddenly sees a red wound
On his left cheek.
Spreading down from the outer edge of his left eye,
Searing his smooth skin.

Even as the subject recoils,
Attendants race forward.

*

Now the great lord lies in his bed.
A dark scar
Like a river of fire
Burning on his pale face.

The subject, dismayed and confused
Looks into the Rigden's obsidian eyes,
And knows he must reach out
And touch the burning wound.

His hand passes into the wound,
Into some other way of being.

*

Entering, swimming, swirling, utterly consumed
In the torrents of sensation,
Perception unfolds its innate purity
Beyond the concept of word or time.

In the passionate delirium of non-thought
The senses open
In their inner essence
As the gateways of Kalapa.

From here, the uninterrupted harmony,
The truth that is far beyond the limits of thought
Can be heard as clearly as a crystal chime:

A love which admits no obstacle or interruption
And binds, like a heartbeat, all duality
In the radiant pure heart of space.

XX. CONTINUITY

1)

Edward dutifully meets twice a week with the psychiatrist Margaret has found, a nice thoughtful man, Dr. A. G. Green. He works on the Annals. By night, he drifts through the city. For weeks on end, he won't see people who remind him of characters in the Annals. He will begin to think he is finally free of these 'sightings' as he calls them. Then, there they will be: some he has seen before and others who are new, sometimes in a trickle, sometimes in a big clump of women and men lounging outside a doorway talking, laughing, smoking. He doesn't see the oriental man again.

2)

He wonders if he is the focal point or just the background for the experiences around him. Is he the person who projects himself onto the screen of all these phenomena? Is he just the screen onto which these occurrences are being almost randomly projected? Does he shift between? And with these shifts, do the realities themselves change? These questions evoke a kind of tantalizingly fluid mind space that is slippery but not frightening. It's as if the Annals have become his inner refuge or vessel while he's floating in a strange and pleasant sea. This doesn't seem like the kind of thing a psychiatrist would be comfortable hearing about.

He tells Dr. Green about these sightings, even as he talks about his past, his failures, dreams, uncertainties, frustrations and longings. The doctor listens carefully, but asks only occasional questions.

3)

Edward is making steady progress on the Annals. Only one short section of the fourth Annal, and the brief fragmentary fifth Annals remain. They draw him steadily into the inevitable sadness of ending and an anxiety about what is to follow. Right at this time, his cousin unexpectedly finds a job for him. It's just a temporary appointment, filling in for a suddenly deceased associate in the Oriental Studies faculty at the University of Colorado in Boulder. But, as she says brightly, it's a start. Dr. Green advises him to take the job and complete the Annals there as quickly as possible. He suggests that Edward consider finding another therapist if finishing the text takes much longer. Edward agrees.

4)

Edward has a strange sensation. There is a wind at his back emerging from the distant past. Intent and pushing, pushing him westward.

THE SECRET ANNALS: ANNAL IV - Concerning K- Part 10

1)

When blackness pervades us utterly
Impenetrable by either sun or moon, and endless,
Then, O Rigden Fathers,
By your blessings,
We have entered into your heart's blood.

2)

In the eighteenth year of his reign, his body exhausted by unceasing toil, having abandoned forever the society of his homeland and the companions of his youth, and afterwards never having known a moment of private reflection, the King of Shambhala decided to depart from his capitol of Shan and retreat for a year.

Before leaving, His Majesty gave what would be the last of his annual three month-long teachings. An old student from one of the earliest such presentations happened to attend. Though devoted to His Majesty, this student had never had much interest in putting the teachings into practice, but he felt a desire to see His Majesty one more time.

The student was seated at the very rear of the tent, next to the door through which His Majesty made his entrance and exit. The talk went well, and the student was quite moved. But when His Majesty left, the student looked to his left and watched as he stepped through the tent door.

He saw His Majesty swing his foot out into the night air and swing his foot off the topmost step of the platform on which the tent was built. And as he watched, the student realized that the King had no idea where he was, where he was stepping and where his foot would land. The student was overwhelmed at His Majesty's fearlessness and complete confidence.

3)

"The Buddha uncovered the enlightenment that is the natural state.

"The Buddha showed the enlightenment that can be taught and he showed the enlightenment that cannot be taught.

"The Buddha taught the path that can be attained and he taught the path that cannot be attained.

"Enlightenment itself is not to be attained: it is received.

"It is received as the world. The totality of the world."

4)

Five days later, His Majesty broke off teaching and sped to his retreat place in his carriage, accompanied by a very small retinue. As he rode into view of the banners of the hastily constructed camp, His Majesty sighed. "I almost did not get here in time."

His Majesty returned to a place he had discovered on his first visit to Shan. It was a high round hill with streams on three sides amid surrounding foothills. A small military encampment was set up for the King, his attendants and the occasional visitors who would live there for a year through the long harsh winter, the brief spring, the brilliant summer, the poignant fall.

5)

His Majesty went immediately to bed and stayed there for a month. He ate little and became very thin. His head seemed enormous on his dwindling body, and his expression was wild and violent. His mustache, beard and hair grew long. Sometimes he slept for days on end, and then he would stay up for days. His speech became slow, his periods of silence long, his impatience with others' conversation great. His illnesses were more prolonged and more threatening.

Hearing of this, F, his former steward, returned. Four years earlier when it became clear that His Majesty needed to be sustained by a more rigid hierarchy, the two had parted company. Now, younger more ambitious people attended the King. F asked if he could once more be taken back into service.

"Of course," was his Majesty's reply, but when F came to his tent, he found himself assigned to serve as an absolute novice.

"I understand," he told the King, "It's over."

"Benefit your own people now. Found your own lineage." Groundless for many years thereafter, F found this mission, however impractical, was the only direction he had.

6)

The King then spent his days moving between this world and what is beyond it. Nakedly, he moved through realms of air, of water, of fire, of earth. In that year, the Queen of Space herself appeared to him and consorted with him. Later, warrior deities appeared and drank with him. He visited the Rigden kings in the pure realms of Shambhala and they counseled and corrected him. Demons made their incursions and he battled with them. The Goddess of the Sun appeared and smiled, but she was jealous of his consorts. All his bodily life was a support for these activities.

So, the King's adventures, alliances and battles to secure the future of the Shambhala Kingdom continued as ever, but the terrain on which these actions were played out was not evident to those who witnessed them. He spoke of his experiences as they happened, and dictated what he saw.

"You see, everything happens because we want it to stop."

"Where are you?"

"Right now?"

"Yes."

"In a world of blue."

"He is not holding back from showing us the world," said one exhausted attendant.

7)

During this period, His Majesty consorted day and night with the deity Vajra Yogini, the Great Dakini. She shared his bed and his meals and all his daily activities with him. He insisted that clothes be laid out for her and that a place be set for her at his side whenever he ate.

8)

As is said in The Blazing Mirror of Absolute Compassion:

Then Vajrayogini, in a voice
With the sound of an approaching summer thunder-storm,
Called to the Acarya:

"Here, now this very place is
The living reality of compassion.

"Here the six realms and the trikaya
Are simultaneous.
"This can only be seen in the light
Of all-inclusive Great Compassion,
Which is the Great Bliss.

"This world, exactly as it is,
The body, speech and mind of all the Buddhas,
Here, now and always reaches out to you.

"Now, in this very instant, here on this very spot,
The Dakini opens the unfabricated treasury of the innate,
The stainless great bliss, ever undispersed.

"Thus, from the universal heart of ceaseless compassion itself
Known only by direct experience
In the treasure-house of phenomenal existence,
The Four Abhishekas spontaneously arise."

9)

His Majesty would suddenly rise from his bed and announce his determination to travel with the Yogini and visit many lands to the East and West and South and North. One day it would be Silla, another time Rajagriha, then parts of Han, then Tuva, then Manchuria, Buryatsia, Nalanda and so on.

On each occasion, his attendants would pack as if for a long journey, have His Majesty's palanquin made ready, arrange a small caravan to accompany them and send messengers ahead.

Sometimes on reaching the door of his house, his Majesty would feel that these efforts had been enough and return to bed, but on other occasions, they would set forth. At various points, His Majesty would stop and describe the mountains, seas, forests and deserts they were traversing, and he would write poems on the beauties of these spectral landscapes.

At other points in the journey, guards, who had been sent ahead, would stop the caravan, ask for their passports and documents and would as well solicit bribes, as if they were indeed crossing a border to a foreign land. Then they would all visit the houses of various subjects who had been warned in advance. And there the hosts would pretend to be Korean people or Han or whoever, and they would wear odd clothing and speak in accents, and if they were pretending that their homes were inns, meals in some approximate style of that country would be served. His Majesty would then pay and return home. None of these voyages, and there were many of them, lasted more than half a day.

10)

When a consort asked what it was like to make love to a deity, the King replied:
"It makes human lovers seem like goats and chickens."
"But is she real?"

"Oh, at least as real as you."

11)

His Majesty would lie in bed for days and command huge towers of chairs, wastebaskets, lampshades, end tables and stools to be made around his bed. He would demand that offerings: flowers, candles, food, water and saffron water be removed from the shrine and held up, one by one, for his prolonged inspection. He gazed at them for hours. This was when the father lineages of warriors and the Rigden Kings came to him.

His Majesty asked whichever consort happened to be with him in bed to join him as he visited the pure realm Kingdom of Shambhala or paid a call on Gesar of Ling. He would ask her just to let go and come with him, but none were able to do so.

His Majesty was not disappointed, but said: "You only need confidence." Concerned for the effect this was having on his dwindling health, his attendants sent for a celebrated Buddhist doctor and priest. His majesty was excited about meeting him and awaited his visit anxiously. When finally the priest arrived, His Majesty refused to see him, and the ceremonies the priest performed had to be done in secret. Instead His Majesty now sent for various consorts, chosen simply because they were ticklish, and would laugh uncontrollably when he tickled them. This, he explained, was for the pleasure of the Rigdens.

12)

From the Feast of Kalapa:

Like the sun itself,
His outer and inner form change according to time.
But he is completely constant.

By a gesture of his mind,
The ayatanas shape themselves as realms,
By a gesture of his right hand,
The modes of human conduct are proclaimed.
By a gesture of his left hand,
All relative reality is resolved.

His fathomless mind with sovereign power
Enters unimpeded into the half-light

Of this corrupted realm of selfish delusions.
By his fearless compassion, by blood, and by ink,
By a leap and a single shout,
He directly enters into the hearts of living beings
In the stroke of the black Ashe.
He spontaneously dissolves all inverted hallucinations at the root,
And restores the pure light of true relative reality.

13)

As his attendants became increasingly worried and exasperated, the King shouted down an empty hall: "Don't blame me. Don't blame me. I'm just doing my job."

14)

Towards the end of His Majesty's retreat, word of his strange behavior had become well known among the ministers and the military. Alarmed at what sounded like a descent into utter madness, the Minister of Security and the Minister of Foreign Affairs went to visit him. They told the other ministers that they were going to evaluate His Majesty's mental condition.

"When could anyone ever do that?' said the Prime Minister.

When the Lord Protector reported his belief that His Majesty should not be allowed to appear freely in public, the Prime Minister lost faith in him.

"He always was too perfect a little gentleman," said the Prime Minister dismissively.

15)

When His retreat was almost ended, His Majesty told his attendants:

"I have transformed my existence at the molecular level," His Majesty confided just before he returned to Shan. There his schedule was much as before, but in fact, his attendance at all manner of events was either sporadic or brief.

His Majesty continued to meet frequently with his ministers, and, as always the well-being of the subjects, the economy, the condition of the various religious and teaching institutions and the security of the realm with respect to foreign influences were discussed, although he found it less and less necessary to contribute to such discussions.

Instead the project that most concerned him was the construction of various battle carts, battleships and engines of war, catapults, arrow throwing devices, cannons which shoot vajras and kilas, cannons which sprayed flaming grain-oil, immense wheeled fortresses, all of a type that had neither been seen nor heard of nor contemplated before.

In each meeting, His Majesty would ask how the plans and pragmatic aspects in creating such devices were progressing, and the ministers charged with realizing these projects would dutifully respond. A great deal of effort was expended on this.

"As is said in the Kalachakra Tantra itself, the time is not far off when these things will be sorely needed. But between combatants, victory and defeat arise from the vowels and consonants themselves. Their arising is the circle of eight victory banners, smoke, horses, elephants, lions, dogs, serpents, lions and rainbows of all colors. If aggression is to be overcome, blood must be shed."

The ministers, understandably, found this hard to comprehend.

16)

Later that year, saying privately that he was entirely disappointed with all his ministers, that they had no relationship to his subjects, he married ten new wives. Many of these women were very young and not familiar with the King's work or his teachings. Nonetheless, he made them cabinet members and gave them specific areas of responsibility. They also had the power to dismiss any and all members of His Majesty's government.

Many of the ladies of the court were enraged that His Majesty chose to marry relative outsiders and were even more furious that they themselves were excluded. The Ministers were worried about their loss of power. Even the Grand Duchess was apprehensive lest her own influence wane, and she found herself being urged by ministers, courtiers and servants to intercede with His Majesty. In consternation, she asked the Duke of K what she should do.

"Go see His Majesty," the Duke advised. "He is your son-in-law. He loves you, and he is by oath a teacher. So you must press him to help you understand his actions. Do not waver until you have received satisfaction."

The Grand Duchess liked the plan and said she would pursue it. When the Duke encountered her sometime later, he was quite curious as to the outcome and asked her about it.

"Oh," she answered gaily, "We had a very good talk. Everything is all worked out. He promised me that he would only marry two more."

17)

When the Prime Minister maneuvered to undermine these new Queens, sometime in the night his Shambhala shrine was destroyed. Ink was poured all over its white brocades; the offerings were all knocked over; the brush and arrows were strewn on the ground; and all across the shrine itself were the paw prints of a wildcat.

18)

Later when His Majesty again became very ill and confined to bed, one by one he had the Prime Minister, the Queen, his son His Majesty Regent, the head of the military and many close people come to him.

To each he would confide the machinations that later each of the others would use to take sole control of the kingdom and to undermine and exclude the one to whom he was speaking.

He urged each to retain and make use of the powers he had bestowed on her or him. "Never let go," he told each of them. But he instructed his military that, at some time in the near future, they should be prepared to take over the entire civilian government.

He made them each, privately and one by one, take blood oaths to uphold the Buddhist disciplines and to work all his or her life for the strength of the kingdom of Shambhala.

"Never forget this," he said, and he stared into each one's eyes with a gaze that was dark and fathomless.

19)

His Majesty said to the Duke of K:

"It hurt me that people were constantly telling me that you were crazy."

"But you listened to them," the Duke replied. His Majesty was seated in an arbor of the garden behind the court. He looked into the Duke's eyes for a long time. The Duke felt as if he were floating in fathomless space. Then His Majesty said:

"I will give you whatever you want."

"Thank you, sir. But you already have."

20)

The King then roused himself, and set out on an arduous tour of the kingdom and of all the lands and places where he had followers. This tour took nine months. The main activity of the tour was to provide public receptions in which His Majesty could meet with new students and see old ones once again. To many of his visitors it was clear that the King was bidding them farewell.

He was no longer able to walk and was often subject to strange dreams and unearthly inspirations, and he spoke only in the most cryptic utterances. Everywhere he went, people sensed that his end was not far off. They waited in long lines just to touch his hand and pay their respects. Many who came were old followers, but almost as many were those who had only heard of him and wanted to meet him, if only once.

21)

Many people came to ask for his advice. It was often the same. With great ferocity he would hiss:

"Just do it."

Alternatively, when consulted about problem of the state he would say:

"Couldn't care less."

He looked out over the crowds of apprehensive followers and said:

"Thank you. You are all so natural and…intrinsic."

Otherwise His Majesty lost interest in speaking and he insisted that those around him keep silent in his presence.

22)

On the few times in this period when His Majesty gave formal teachings to his followers, he would say:

"I know each and every one of you personally. I love all of you. You make me so proud, and you have prolonged my life. Please join us in the good, life-is-worth-living Shambhala. Life is worth living. Shambhala."

23)

After His Majesty returned to Shan for the last time, he had a stroke. And although he lived for many months, his body deteriorated shockingly, and he slowly lost all powers of speech.

Once, while speech was still available to His Majesty, the Prime Minister asked:

"Is dying so difficult?"

"No, not difficult. The only problem is it's so… fucking… painful."

"What should I do when I die?"

"See my face. No matter what."

24)

His Majesty's stroke made it ever more impossible for him to speak clearly. He made various noises, some quite undignified. Once a former consort came to him and knelt by his bed. He made a painful squawking noise as he looked at her.

"Oh," she told everyone afterwards, "He told me: 'Sweetie, you're the only one.'" No one heard this, but she was sure it was true. Subsequently the attendants were more cautious whom they let visit, but, as the Duke of K observed, who was to say that His Majesty did not mean what she thought.

25)

After a second stroke, it was evident that His Majesty would not live long. The Duke of K went directly from the stricken sovereign's bedside to the Prime Minister's house and told him of the conversation many years before in which His Majesty requested that he assist the Prime Minister. The Prime Minister dismissed the few guests, and the two talked through the night. Often the Prime Minister wept, recalling the many ways in which he had failed His Majesty. Thereafter he treated the Duke as a close friend, sharing his mind with him and at one point even empowering him as a Mahamudra lineage holder.

26)

The atmosphere of the court, once so busy now became glacial and tentative. Those who attended the King did not mingle with anyone else. Bulletins were issued regularly on His Majesty's condition, but they neglected to mention the almost daily crises to which the King was now subject. This was not done out of conspiratorial intent, but because these crises had become a matter of course. In fact, the attendants did not notice the King's inexorable decline, and many expected him to live and resume his duties. They could not imagine otherwise. Thus the same words: "His Majesty is responding well." originally used to denote His Majesty's efforts at speech, came, as he failed, to characterize his noticing a visitor, opening his eyes, eating.

This trick of language also had a blinding effect on the attendants and contributed to the strange immobility in the atmosphere of the court.

Those who came to visit His Majesty were shocked and horrified, and finally only those who did not weep and were not given to emotional excesses were permitted to see him. But those who did visit, after they had stilled their own distress, all noted a similar phenomenon.

The air and all the space in His Majesty's environment were suffused with a warm autumnal glow like a pale gold light: there was, despite the desperateness of His Majesty's condition, an atmosphere of profound peace at completion. Experiencing this, one could not believe that His Majesty's mind was not fully intact, only that the threads that bound His Majesty to this world were wearing out.

Later, just before he died, the atmosphere changed dramatically. One who saw him as he lay exhausted on his bed staring at his wife as if anchoring himself by her sight, described it as being melancholy, like a cool moonlit night, when the lover waits on the verandah, knowing his beloved will not come and has parted for good.

27)

As to the death of the King itself:

His Majesty lay virtually unmoving for some months. His attendants woke him each day, bathed him and dressed him in his military uniform. He was placed on his throne, to which he had to be tied to keep from slipping, and returned to his bed in the afternoon.

His expressions and abilities became ever more limited until on the last day, as he sat on his throne, he pushed himself up to a half standing position. He struggled for the last time to speak to his followers, but then he began vomiting enormous quantities of blood. As his attendants watched in paralyzed horror, blood sprayed from his mouth and sprayed over his uniform, the throne and the carpet on the stairs leading up to the throne. And as the blood poured out of him, he stared them all in the eye with an expression of absolute and all-consuming ferocity.

This continued for some time until there was no more blood in him, and he fell back, dead.

XXI. CONTINUITY

1)

Edward has a dream.

Professor Akiyama appears vividly before him, looking gaunt, just as he had in the year before he died, but now, though worn out, he is vibrant and full of life.

"But you're dead." Edward is seeking clarity.

The professor raised his eyebrows, shrugs. Isn't it obvious?

"How can this be?" Edward persists.
"It's a joke, " The professor explains.

2)

Edward likes Boulder. It is a mid-sized town with clear air, wide skies, nestled in the pine-covered foothills where the plains and the Rocky Mountains meet. The great ranges of snow capped peaks loom behind. Everything here is crisp, solid and bright. It is a place of daylight. There is almost no nightlife.

In the early 70's, it is also something of a hippie haven filled with a large contingent of colorful drug-experimenters, transient hirsute political activists, artists and a wide range of spiritual seekers. Cambodia is being bombed, but, as Washington assures the nation: "Peace is at hand." The Paris Peace Talks have diminished the confrontational fervor of the counter-culture.

Edward's colleagues at the university are pleasant. The students, for the most part, are reasonably intelligent. He works preparing his classes and makes a few casual friends among the junior faculty. They invite him on hikes in the mountains. Unexpectedly, he enjoys it. He is surprised at how much the simplicity and stability of his new life agrees with him. Over the next six months, he works only rarely on translating the Annals. Whenever guilt drives him to return to the text, he experiences a painful sense of claustrophobia. He wonders why Professor Akiyama and the Annals have had such a hold on him. His principal motive now in finishing the translation is to put it behind him. Life without the Annals seems both unimaginable and full of possibilities.

3)

One early summer afternoon, Edward is riding a bus down Broadway and notices an abandoned Public Service Building festooned with bright banners: red, blue, yellow and green satin printed in bold colors with Buddhist symbols: the dharmachakra, lions, tigers, garudas and dragons. They are exactly as described in the Annals. Hundreds of young men and eccentrically garbed young women mill in the parking lot. There is an atmosphere of cheerful excitement. A stocky oriental man with slicked-back hair is making his way through the crowd which parts before him.

In a panic, Edward turns his head away. He is overwhelmed by confusion as again the world of the Annals and the world of reality emerge one from the other and slide together. He closes his eyes, trying to pretend he hasn't seen them. He stays on campus for the next few months. He hurries to resume his work on this section, which describes the King of Shambhala's death, in the hope that completion and distance will weaken the text's influence on him.

THE SECRET ANNALS: ANNAL IV - Concerning K - part 11

1)

THE RED GARUDA'S SONG OF CONTINUING
On this great wind of sorrow and longing
We rise up.
On this great wind of love and longing,
The all-seeing Red Garuda spontaneously takes form
And carries us aloft.

SO
In the free radiance of space itself,
In the light of ceaseless love,
Our seeing takes shape.

SO
Winds surveying mind and beyond mind;
Where the golden feather-tips
Of the Red Garuda's outstretched wing
Touch the crystal radiance of space,
The wind of truth expands all at once and in all directions.

Where the Red Garuda's hidden tympanum
Is touched by the cold pure air of emptiness,
The bliss of song enfolds the whole of space.

Where the Red Garuda's golden eye
Meets the fire of a rising sun,
The bright visions of the pure world of Shambhala arise
In the center of the human heart
And on the very face of this earth.

Where the Red Garuda's wild love
Draws near to the heart of all,
The unchanging mind of the Rigden fathers,
Clothed in all the richness of the world,
Emerges from the gold and crystal palace of Kalapa
And appears now, free from time.

This is the love that cannot stop,
That is not conditioned according to its outcome,
That passes through the mirage of life and death,
That passes through world,
Through time and all concepts of reality,
That is radiant in whatever outer circumstance
That is the heart and heartbeat of all human life.

2)

As to the funeral of the King:

In order to enrich the land where he had so long labored and for which he had such hopes, His Majesty, dressed in his imperial robes, was buried in a deep pit just below the crest of Gold Dragon Mountain in a great ebony casket adorned in gold with the seal of the Kingdom of Shambhala.

His body had been embalmed with honey, juniper and myrrh to ensure that it would not deteriorate in the long period between his death and his burial. This long period was needed both to accord with the position of the stars and planets, to allow time for the arrival of the vast number of political and religious dignitaries who wished to attend and to make the elaborate preparations needed for them.

Preceded by pipers and doleful great horns, the body was transported on a golden palanquin carried by his soldiers over the long journey from the Kalapa Court to the high flank of Gold Dragon Mountain. Walking a slow march, this journey took twenty-eight days. At a stopping point each night, the dignitaries and priests who had preceded the body in carriages or on horseback came out from the houses which had just been built for this purpose, greeted the body of the Monarch and escorted it into the chapel which had been built for it. There, they would perform ceremonies and feasts long into the night. While all others slept, legions of carters moved food through the night to provision the stopping places. In the morning they would bid His Majesty farewell and hurriedly depart so as to be able to receive the monarch again at the next stop.

The funeral services themselves took fifteen days. Long offering ceremonies to the four elements were made in which vials of His Majesty's bodily fluids, his hair, fingernails, and so forth were offered to the earth, the waters, fire and air.

During this portion of the funeral, there were many rainbows, including a circular one that surrounded His Majesty's body.

Then one by one, each who had served His Majesty in any way what-soever came forward to the foot of the coffin. The Prime Minister, His Majesty Regent or the Queen recited a list of their deeds. Then each one read a four-line poem to the Monarch, bowed to him for the last time and stepped back. This took another fifteen days, and at its conclusion, all renewed their oaths to the Monarch. The anthem was then sung as the casket was lowered into the ground. All shouted the warrior cry for the fol-lowing six hours that it took to place an enormous obsidian boulder over the grave.

During this portion of the ceremony, the weather ranged from a bliz-zard to blazing heat, thunderstorms, hails, balmy breezes and violent winds that almost blew down the buildings.

When the funeral was finally complete, there was a great feast pro-vided for all by the government in which everyone ate and drank to excess and told and re-told the stories, often ones known only to him or herself, of the Monarch's many activities and deeds. Many of the religious leaders found this shocking and departed swiftly. But when the feasting was done, no one lingered and His Majesty was left alone.

During this time, there were no clouds whatsoever in the sky and the world seemed completely still.

3)

THE WAY OF KALAPA

Like a great city appearing out of the night,
The eight-petalled gold sun lotus of Shambhala,
Dwelling as the essence in the hearts of all
Suddenly unfolds with a burst of light and melodious sound.
The kingdom of Shambhala, complete and entire
With its snow mountains, verdant pastures,
Dense forests, and teeming cities,
With its great Capitol of Kalapa
Glowing like a crystal on the white anthers of a golden lotus
Displays itself in the heart of each and every living being.

In the center of the Kalapa Court sits the Rigden King.
He is the living essence of fearlessness,
And is unswayed by the uncertainties of life and death.
His deathless wisdom penetrates into all phenomena

And illuminates all questioning spontaneously and directly.
He is the essence of justice and power in the human heart,
And so possesses the six ways of ruling.
He spontaneously overcomes the poverty of ego-fixation
And so possesses the six treasures of a universal monarch.

The Kingdom of Shambhala, Kalapa, the Rigden King
Vibrantly alive in the hearts of all
Become ever clearer and more distinct
As they swell and expand, covering the entire earth.
They merge together as a single heart and single realm,
Pulsing, radiant with gold and rainbow light,
Filled with joy.

The glorious Shambhala dawns like the primordial sun
As a living reality in this very place and this very time.
No matter what arises or does not,
There is no need to depart from the joy of that.
It is so.

There are no regrets.

KI KI SO

*

CONCLUSION OF ANNAL IV

V. THE SECRET ANNALS: THE FIFTH ANNAL

"We, amnesiacs all, condemned to live in an eternally fleeting present, have created the most elaborate of human constructions, memory."

(Geoffrey Sonnabend: Obliscence, Theories of Forgetting and the Problem of Matter- An encapsulation by Valentine Worth — Society for the Diffusion of Useful Information, L.A. CA 1991- pp1-2)

XXII. CONTINUITY

1)

The world of the Annals again begins to engulf Edward.

Once in a small rag-tag Indian restaurant (a rarity at the time) run by a rather manic American and his long-suffering Indian wife, he encounters several self-important young men ordering large quantities of food to take out. The American owner is talking fast and sweating. He is nervous that his food will not please the person he refers to, in talking to the young men, as "Your master."

By accident, Edward overhears the owner refers to the teacher by name. He is startled and realizes that he has been so involved in thinking of this teacher as the Prince that he has never actually known the man's name. It is a strange assemblage of sounds. They are completely unfamiliar and evoke nothing.

2)

Another time, Edward is shopping in a large discount liquor store. A small powerfully built Tibetan man, stockier than the one he saw in N.Y. is limping through the aisles amid a large coterie of well-dressed men and women. Edward overhears him ask one of his attendants: "What do you think I look like to people here?"

The wily bald attendant hesitates: "A person afraid to be alone?" There is a pause while the others wait to see how the Tibetan man will react. Laughter breaks out only when he giggles.

3)

And yet another time, Edward is eating in a small booth at the back of a large restaurant. A large table has been put together in the center of the room to accommodate a banquet of some kind. Two gray-haired women in their late fifties, one quite heavy, are in charge of the arrangements. They direct a crowd of youngsters in decorating the table and making everything as they think it should be. It is clear that the two women are long-time rivals, dislike each other, but are accustomed to working together. Just as they finish, three younger men in suits arrive and make a great show of checking and correcting the seating cards, the flowers and generally demeaning the two older women. Then a crowd of pretty girls, more men in suits and a few in some kind of military uniform assemble. "He's coming," says one of the guards. Before he can see more, Edward leaves, throwing money on the table without even asking for the bill,

4)

Once, when Edward feels especially cooped up, he decides to go to the most expensive restaurant in town. It is perched up in the foothills and looks out over the flat tawny expanse of plains to the east. The service is horribly pretentious, and the food is overpriced. When Edward finishes his dinner, he realizes that the restaurant has filled with a contingent of the Tibetan teacher's students. He is seated amid them and seems both drunk and enraged. The atmosphere is thick and ugly as if a fight is about to break out. Edward does not stay to see more.

5)

One morning over coffee, a colleague tells of going to visit his dying mother. He says that his physician cautioned him: "Be sure you don't die with her." Edward wonders if something of the kind hasn't happened in his relationship with Professor Akiyama, if the world of the Annals is not somehow a world into which both have inadvertently surrendered some part of their lives irretrievably.

6)

Edward doesn't know whether he is projecting things from the Annals into his ordinary life, is living in echoes of text or has slipped into some reality that is neither the Annals nor his own life any more. Though he might once have found this state of mind almost exhilarating, he now finds it exhausting. He makes every effort to maintain the life of a normal academic, but is constantly afraid of losing his grip. The fact that his involvement with text will soon be over feels like an impending liberation.

He is more than relieved that the fifth and final Annal is so brief. It is written in a variety of hands, all evidently people of less educational distinction and culture. The kinds of paper in these sections date from the 16th century. It shows in an abrupt and truncated way the precipitous collapse of His Majesty's plans and way of teaching. It seems that the events referred to are so painful that the author cannot bear to give more than the most minimal and fragmentary recital.

THE SECRET ANNALS:: ANNAL V

1)

On the night His Majesty died, one of his ministers dreamed that His Majesty came into his room, shook him and woke him up.

"It's a bust," he said. And then he began to laugh wildly, shrieking like a wrathful deity. "But don't worry. I'll be around."

2)

A week after His Majesty died, the Prime Minister had a dream in which he and His Majesty were surveying a house that had been poorly restored. The Prime Minister was saying that new and better materials were needed, and His Majesty said:

"Stop. We make do with what we have."

The Prime Minister then asked where all the money was, and His Majesty just smiled. When the Prime Minister woke up, he laughed:

"He's leaving me an empty bag."

3)

A close woman disciple and occasional consort of His Majesty had the following dream two weeks after he died:

His Majesty was living on retreat in a small dark cave high in the mountains. As she approached him, she saw that he was gaunt and exhausted. A black tear was painted on the side of his pale face just below his right eye. She moved to help him, and he turned to her.

"The problem was…they all just wanted too much," he whispered.

4)

Just before His Majesty's funeral a former consort dreamed that she saw him once again, teaching in a large dirty yellow basement hall with a cracked brown linoleum floor and lit by flickering pale blue fluorescent tubes. His Majesty's speech was as sharp and buoyant as ever. Around him were followers arranged in the form of a rudimentary court and distinguished from the other listeners by wearing strangely shaped fancy shoes.

5)

Two nights after His Majesty's funeral, the Duke of K had a dream in which he saw His Majesty on a battlefield at dusk, wearing only a simple silk robe, which was torn and covered with blood. His Majesty slashed back and forth all around him in rage. He cut K on the right shoulder. Jolted awake, K realized that it was his own blood that had stained His Majesty's robe.

6)

Five years after His Majesty's death and after all the misfortunes and changes that ensued, the Duke of K dreamed that he was leaving the court, feeling rather bloated after a long and sumptuous meal. As he stepped onto the lawn, he saw all the old Ministers, attendants, former courtiers and old students of His Majesty, some now dead, standing there emaciated and weak. One cried out "We did not think that we were the ones who should give the dinner parties."

7)

Immediately after His Majesty's death, all looked to the Prime Minister to assume direction of the Kingdom until His Majesty's eldest son was trained. Even after that, the Prime Minister, as holder of His Majesty's teachings, would remain crucial to the governance of the Kingdom. The Prime Minister knew that there were many who doubted him and were lying in wait. He traveled extensively and taught.

"We don't have to hold to a small mind, a small heart. Second by second, over and over, we can be vast and genuine. We can care for our world, for everything in our world, with the same meticulousness, aspiration, effort, longing, devotion and humbleness that we bring to meditation practice. It could be painful, delightful terrifying. Who knows?

"Perhaps you've heard the slogan about practice that says: practice meditation as if every moment is the last moment of your life. I have a friend who says: live as if you will never, ever be able to practice again. Let's see..."

8)

Regrettably, the Prime Minister had contracted and seemingly communicated a lethal venereal disease. He secretly confided in the Duke of K about his condition. The Duke saw at once that the Prime Minister's promiscuity was completely entangled with his spirituality. He had plunged deep into the raging stream where torrents of spiritual yearning and the tides ordinary passion could not be separated.

The Duke thought for a long time before commenting. "It is so difficult, sir, to know when desire is the beckoning of a deity, isn't it?" The Prime Minister stared at him but said nothing.

Later the Duke thought that, though the Prime Minister had many flaws, his predicament had resulted as much from his daring and complete devotion as from his failings. This, of course, was the kind of irresolvable paradox, which His Majesty uncovered in the path of each of his students.

Nonetheless, when the situation became more widely known, it brought the Prime Minister into complete disrepute. Though some felt they must continue in their unquestioning loyalty to him, most of the Kingdom was in an absolute uproar. People who had managed to maintain friendships and working relationships for decades, now found themselves in mortal opposition to one another. Those loyal to the Prime Minister, those who now wanted to get rid of him, and those who sought some middle ground severed communication. Though the courtiers, namely His Majesty's wives and the chief of the military, had the power to dismiss the Prime Minister, they hesitated to do so. Ministers, whom the Prime Minister was accustomed to dominating, united to curtail his activities. The Prime Minister refused to step down, but abandoned Shan for a more salubrious climate. Wagonloads of his furniture and household goods spontaneously burst into flames. A few friends went with him into exile. Though His Majesty's eldest son became nominal ruler, there was no real governance. Many followers left.

9)

"You should quit," said the Duke of K to the Prime Minster, just before his departure. "You can't divide the community this way."

"I can't do that. I swore to his Majesty that I would never let go."

"Well then, you should do three things: acknowledge your errors; make clear that you were not relying on His Majesty's instructions in any error that you made; and renew your vows in front of everyone in the kingdom."

"I can't." Then these two who had become friends wept. They never saw each other or spoke again. Those loyal to the Prime Minister considered the Duke of K a traitor, and the Duke knew that they were right. On the other hand, he felt there was no choice.

10)

During the time that the Prime Minister was first stricken with the symptoms of the illness which would eventually kill him, and while he was making up his mind what his course of action would be, turquoise dragons filled the sky with thunder and sent bolts of lightening against purple clouds of infection. Many saw this.

11)

When the Prime Minister was about to fall into what was his final coma, he looked up and saw that he was surrounded by his doctors, friends and attendants, all looking very grave and some crying as well.

"Is this the sad part now?" he asked sweetly.

After their painful parting, the Duke of K could not bear to hear anything that showed the Prime Minister in a good light, but when he heard this, he wept.

12)

SONG OF PARTING AND RETURN
As your mind is parted from the dappled stream
Of karmic restriction,
You return to the primordial stainless flow
Of luminous empty Riga.

Your individuality, freed from the limits of duality,
Returns naturally to the vastness of boundless being.

As your emotionality departs
From the longed for solidity of subject and object,
You return to the shimmering rainbow-like array
Of intrinsic wisdom.

Your frustrated attachment to family and loved ones
Dissolves naturally into the deathless
Bright and pulsing sea of boundless love.

As you are parted from the harsh chaos of this world,
You return naturally in the heart of absolute and relative Ashe,
The life force and blood-flow of the innate Shambhala,
To your home.

Parting from all confusion, striving, love and fear,
Parting from all the flickering of outer and inner experience,
You return naturally into the heart of the only Father Guru
Whose hot and passionate embrace always has encompassed all
And draws you now.

13)

The Duke of K knew that he had betrayed the Prime Minister and he knew he could not have done otherwise. Many people had no doubt that the Prime Minister's actions had jeopardized His Majesty's teaching irreparably. The Duke saw that this might be so, but saw as well that among all of His Majesty's followers, none was as completely devoted, courageous and committed with all his heart as the Prime Minister. The Prime Minister had thrown himself into His Majesty's vision with all his virtues and faults, and he left himself no way out. He had exposed himself completely.

14)

After the Prime Minister's death, His Majesty's eldest son became the new leader of Shambhala. He changed the practices, teachings and organizational structure which his father had established. While many older students found these new teachings an extension of what they had learned before and followed them, others did not. Some continued with new teachers, a few practiced what they had learned alone.

15)

"What ends? What continues? His Majesty was not afraid of love. How can true love ever end? By what hidden pathways does love move through time?" said the Duke of K late one night.

16)

One of His Majesty's earliest followers, but one who had not remained close was utterly upset by his death. He did not stay for the funeral but went on a long pilgrimage to see Ikkyu and find out what he should do.

Ikkyu was staying in a monastery in the far north, and when the student arrived, the old priest received him happily, but grieved when he heard the news of His Majesty's death.

The student proceeded to ask where he should now go to find a new teacher. The old man did not move, but seemed to become the black embodiment of rage. In a terrifying hiss, he whispered:

"A new teacher? Have you put into practice what His Majesty gave his life to teach you? Get out."

17)

Almost immediately after His Majesty's death, those who had followed him and now still yearned for him found it irresistible to claim more and closer contact than they had experienced. They appropriated the experiences of others until they believed they truly had seen, heard, been there when... Many came to believe that they really had known His Majesty.

Often His Majesty's followers made a display of these memories to bolster their authority with new students, prospective followers or the merely curious. A few became well known by writing memoirs filled with borrowed recollections. And when His Majesty's teachings were altered by those who took his place, when the places he built were rebuilt, when his texts became supplanted by those of others, in short when the world he had created began to slip into shadow, all clung to their memories, real or borrowed, of the time when they had been once dazzled by intense sunlight. Memory became for them more compelling than the disappointing confusion of daily life.

18)

"I was never very close to His Majesty. I studied with him, but I think I missed the point. You know what I mean? I still just don't quite get it." The scholar shook his head.

"Yes. That torment, that's what he left with everyone. That's his gift to us. His legacy," replied the Duke of K.

19)

A quarter century after His Majesty's death, a yogi who had been a follower said to the aging Duke of K:

"Beings who dwell on the fringes of the mandala are too afraid to enter the mandala completely, but too smart to leave,"

"Oh," the Duke replied. "That explains it. That's me. That's what I am and always was."

20)

Thirty years after His Majesty's death, D happened to visit the hill of Kalapa where His Majesty had made his last retreat. The entire place was overgrown, full of brambles, and crows. There was no mark of what had taken place there. He wrote a famous elegy on this.

21)

    from THE RUBY OF KALAPA
    Ceaseless radiance without beginning,
    All-pervasive in the shimmering of all phenomena
    As liberation, as accumulation,
    As union and separation, as destruction,

    We receive the wordless bliss of luminosity.
    Light as sound, as color, as realm, as being.
    Light as inescapable mood and choiceless continuing experience:
    We receive the natural power of mind.

    So, immersed in the movement of a golden sea
    Of boundless light, pervading us utterly,
    We receive the radiant compassion of complete joy
    Which has no motive or end.

XXIII. CONTINUITY

1)

    Edward can no longer bear encountering hallucinatory echoes from the Annals in random moments of his daily life. Out of fear that he will come across these transtemporal doubles, he begins to confine his activities to as small an area as possible: his room, his class, his office and the library. For food, he orders out. He recognizes, however, that he cannot go on like this. He calls his former psychiatrist.

    Dr. Green sounds concerned. He suggests that Edward's intense work on the Annals has led him to project earlier obsessions onto situations that bear only a coincidental similarity. Edward finds comfort in the Doctor's confirmation fo his own suspicions. He wants to believe him, but cannot quite. Dr. Green then urges him to go to one of the public talks that this Tibetan teacher gives quite frequently. He is sure that by seeing the man and his followers face to face, Edward will see how his mind is playing tricks on him. Edward agrees. It takes a few weeks to work up the courage.

    It is a warm Sunday afternoon in early summer, and Edward walks stiffly up the long staircase amid an excited crowd of long-haired men, some in suits, and patchouli-scented women in outfits ranging from hippy to unconvincing matron. He is surprised how normal it all feels. It's an atmosphere of giddy anticipation reminiscent of the first days of school. The shrine room, by contrast, is still. Rays of golden light filter in through windows through which he can see the pine covered foothills nearby. A jarring orange and gold shrine covered with glass bowls stands between the windows. The air smells of incense. A too bright picture of three Buddhas hangs above the shrine.

Everyone sits on low cushions. Edward follows and finds a place as far at the back as possible. They all wait for more than three hours, and then, with a buzz, the Tibetan teacher enters. He wears a black suit. His attendants are dressed similarly. The scene is otherwise exactly as Edward has found it in the Annals. He watches with excruciating fascination. The teacher clears his throat loudly, smiles almost impudently and begins. The atmosphere becomes strangely intense as if all the boundaries that enable people and thoughts to keep their history or shape are being shifted. Edward is captivated, but all he remembers of the talk is the high voice saying:

"There is no goal. All notions of a goal are just concepts that we use to freeze the motion of reality.

"We have goals so that we can stop the movement of time.

"There is only path and the search for a path. We are seeking a path without a goal.

"There is a secret name for this path.

"It is called love.

"It is the path that we must discover and rediscover without end.

"Thank you."

At the end of the talk, Edward feels he absolutely must ask a question. Without hesitating, he stands and raises his hand. The teacher looks at him and nods. Edward begins to speak, but the teacher makes a gesture indicating he should wait for a young woman to bring him a microphone. While he waits, he looks up; the teacher is gazing at him. Edward feels completely alone. When he holds the microphone, his hand shakes. Someone giggles. He has no idea what he is going to say. His voice quivers, but he forces himself to start.

"What is enlightenment?" People laugh, but the teacher simply looks at him. Finally he answers.

"A word."

"And words change reality?" Edward asks as if just the two of them were having this conversation.

"Constantly."

"And memory?"

"What is memory? Is that what you're asking?" Edward nods. The teacher takes a long time to answer. Sun is streaming through the windows.

"Each instant is filled with echoes, isn't it?" He looks around. *"The past is always being... translated, making different links...new contexts. We can't grasp it. The past is...so unpredictable."* The teacher shrugs and smiles.

It is a very simple moment, not dramatic; Edward feels the contradictions that have tormented him momentarily dissolve. He smiles back. He feels that he has been in some impersonal but all-encompassing embrace. He feels at ease. Then others raise their hands. The teacher turns to them.

***

GLOSSARY

Abhisheka: (lit. sprinkling or anointing) Ceremony of empowerment enabling the recipient to do certain practices and reach certain kinds of attainment. There are four empowerments relating to body, speech, mind, and their essence.

Acarya: (lit. teacher) Title given to certain lineage holders.

Amrita: (lit: anti-death) That which sustains beyond life and death; that which intoxicates conventional views.

Ashe: (lit. primordial stroke) The stroke that cuts through doubt, and aggression towards self and other.

Bhagavan: blessed one

Bhumipala: Earth Protector

Bindu: (lit: dot or point) mind essence

Buddha: (lit. the awakened one)

Co-emergence: simultaneity of wisdom and ignorance

Dakini: (lit: sky-goer) wrathful or semi-wrathful female deity embodying co- emergent wisdom

Dharma: (lit. law or truth) usually here the Buddhist teachings, but may in other contexts refer to normative teachings of other kinds.

Dharmadhatu: (space of phenomena) all encompassing space

Drala: (lit. above enemy) The worldly and transcendent power inherent in direct perception of phenomena. The worldly dralas are the specific communicative nature of sky, mountains, earth, water and the underground.

EVAM: Union of prajna and upaya, wisdom and method.

Garuda: Mythical Indian Bird that is fully-grown on emerging from the egg, thus a symbol of the awakened mind.

Heruka: (lit. blood drinker) wrathful male embodiment of wisdom flourishing in whatever circumstances he finds himself.

Jnana: Wisdom, beyond concept; spontaneous presence

Kalachakra Tantra: lit. 'Wheel of Time'- the highest of the Yoga Tantras and a source for extensive lore relating to the Kingsom of Shambhala.

Kalapa: The capitol city of the Kingdom of Shambhala

Kapala: skull cup

Karma: (lit. action) the continuum of cause and effect, action and result

Kaya: (lit. body) form, as in the three bodies or forms of the Buddha: Dharmakaya (body or form of truth); Sambhogakaya (body or form of enjoyment); and Nirmanakaya (emanation body as manifest in physical form).

Ki and So: The syllables of the warrior cry bring down the power of Drala and Werma

Lungta: (lit. wind horse) The basic energy of wakefulness.

Mahamudra: (lit. Great Seal). A lineage of meditative traditions in which all experiences are realized in their essential nature as joining prajna and skillful means. Here the vividness of experience is spontaneously realized as the luminous display of the deity.

Mahasiddha: (lit great accomplished one) An accomplished lineage master.

Nadi: The inner pathways of the body through which the bindu moves.

Naga: Serpents, dragons and those treasure holders who dwell beneath the earth or sea.

Padma Sambhava: The great Indian teacher, regarded as the second Buddha, who brought Tantric Buddhism to the Himalayas

Phurba: three bladed dagger which penetrates passion, aggression and ignorance

Prajna: (lit. highest knowledge) the natural precision of awareness that penetrates all dualistic obstacles.

Prana: (lit. wind) inner energy by which the bindu moves through the nadis.

Rigden: The Title of the rulers of Shambhala

Rigpa: Ceaseless primordial awareness, the basic awareness that underlies and continues through all mental states, sleeping, wakefulness, life and death

Samadhi: (lit: absorption or concentration) sometimes a synonym for meditation.

Samsara: The endless cycle of painful illusion caused by ignorance, grasping and fixation.

Shambhala: An enlightened society in the human realm.

Shamatha: (lit. Taming or calming the mind) Letting the mind rest in the space in which thoughts arise, dwell, and decay.

Siddha: one who has siddhi

Siddhi: An aspect of realization in which the inseparability of relative and absolute reality manifest as power over apparent phenomena..

Sugatagharba: As in Tathagathagharba, innate enlightenment, but here the emphasis is on its experiential component.

Sunyata: (lit. emptiness) The realization that self and other are merely temporary and insubstantial constructs, and that reality itself is completely free from any kind of conceptual or emotional biases.

Tathaghatagharba: (lit. Buddha nature) Intrinsic complete natural wakefulness

Tilopa: The 10th Century Indian Mahasiddha who received the Mahamudra teachings directly from primordial awareness itself and passed them down in the lineages that became today the Kagyupa.

Upaya: (skillful means) The methods by which the inner realization of the lineage is conveyed.

Vajra: (lit. thunderbolt) a ritual object in the form of a five or none pointed thunderbolt that symbolizes the indestructible nature of wisdom and the awakened state.

Vajrayogini: The great dakini who is the essence of co-emergence and the principal of the natural transformation of ignorance and passion into wisdom and skillful means.

Vajrasattva: (lit. Vajra being) The principal of the innate purity if the awakened state.

Vipassana: (insight) That aspect of meditation that relates to mind as motion (as distinct from Shamatha which relates to the unmoving aspect); clear seeing into the patterns of mind and phenomena.

Werma: Lineage of ancestral protectors who particularly ensure prosperity.

Yidam: A deity through which the practitioner uncovers her or his own awakened nature.

Yogi: male practitioner

Yogini: female practitioner

ACKNOWLEDGEMENTS

This book would not have been possible without the help and support of many people. Foremost among them are:

The late Chogyam Trungpa, Rinpoche
The late Vajra Regent, Osel Tendzin
Joan Anderson
Zentatsu Richard Baker
Samuel Bercholz
Meg Federico
Phyllis Granoff
Kenneth Green
Gaetano Kazuo Maeda
Deborah Marshall
Caleb Mason
Susan Merwin
Hakubai Zenji Martin Mosko
Lady Diana Mukpo
William Osborne
The Ven. Sir John Perks O.L.K.
Chodzin Paden, Magyel Pomra Sayi Dakpo
The late Elizabeth C. Pybus
The late Tessa A. Pybus
Michael Root
Tami Simon
Kidder Smith
Robert Spellman
Randy Sunday
The Ven, Tulku Thondup
Robert Walker
David Warren
Jake Young
James Yensan

Many thanks to you and to all others whom I may have inadvertently omitted.

AUTHOR

Douglas Penick graduated from Princeton University, was a research associate at the Museum of Modern Art in New York and at The Institute for Architecture and Urban Studies as well as a chef at Gordon Matta Clark's Food. He studied and practiced Tibetan Buddhism under the Venerable Chogyam Trungpa Rinpoche for more than 30 years. He has written and taught on Tibetan, Chinese, Japanese, and Indian religion, history and culture. He wrote the National Film Board of Canada's prize winning two part series on the Tibetan Book of the Dead (Leonard Cohen, narrator) and the libretti for two operas: *King Gesar* (Sony CD w/ Ma, Serkin, Ax et. al.) and *Ashoka's Dream* (Santa Fe Opera) with composer, Peter Lieberson. He's also written pieces for choreographer Katsura Kan, and on commission from the New York Philharmonic, the Boulder Symphony, Denver Eclectic Concerts and others. He is the author of three books deriving from the epic cycle on the life of King Gesar of Ling: *Crossings on a Bridge of Light*, *Warrior Song of King Gesar* and *The Brilliance of Naked Mind.* His novel *A Journey of The North Star* was brought out by Publerati in June, 2012. Short fiction, essays and poetry have appeared in Bombay Gin, The Shambhala Sun, Parabola, Porte Des Singes, Cahiers de L'Herne, Publishers Weekly, Marco Polo, Embodied Effigies, Passionate Transitory, Agni. BODY, Corvus, Danse Macabre, Hyperallergic, Descant, Regnum Sacrum and elsewhere.